pm 16

BY THE
RIVER

A SUSPENSE NOVEL

JENNIE HANSEN

Covenant Communications, Inc.

Cover image: *Silhouettes of the Forest* © m-gucci

Cover design copyright © 2015 by Covenant Communications, Inc.

Published by Covenant Communications, Inc.
American Fork, Utah

Printed in the United States of America
First Printing: November 2015

20 19 18 17 16 15   10 9 8 7 6 5 4 3 2 1

ISBN 978-1-68047-659-0

BY THE
RIVER

As always, this book is dedicated to
my husband, Boyd K Hansen,
and to all of my family.

ACKNOWLEDGMENTS

THANKS TO ALL THOSE WHO encouraged me to write another book, especially the sisters I work with at the Oquirrh Mountain Temple and the people in my ward. Special thanks go to my children and grandchildren, who frequently checked on my progress and offered suggestions. When acknowledging those who made it possible for me to write this book, I particularly appreciate Mindi Huihui, Janice Sperry, and Lezlie Anderson, my beta readers. And of course, my thanks extends to the terrific staff at Covenant.

CHAPTER ONE

"Now what?" Kira watched in disgust as dirt flew in the air and Jasper's annoying bark changed to a triumphant howl. Her brother, Tracy, would be back in two days. She couldn't wait to give him back his stupid dog! Putting her fingers between her teeth, she gave a wobbly whistle. Of course, Jasper ignored her.

"Jasper! Come here!" Plunging off the trail into waist-high grass and weeds—still damp with early morning dew that chilled her bare legs—Kira struggled toward the large black lab frantically tearing at the riverbank while barking his head off.

That dog has been nothing but trouble since the first day Tracy showed up at my condo with him! She gritted her teeth and hurried toward Jasper. She wasn't a dog person, and Tracy knew it. Just because he and Dad were out of town on one of his frequent business trips was no reason for him to assume she'd watch his mutt while he was away. Just this morning the dumb beast had chewed up one of her shoes, spread the contents of every wastebasket in the house across the carpet, and spilled his water bowl over her clean kitchen floor. At the rate that dog was going, she wouldn't have a matched pair of shoes left in her closet by the time Tracy got back. Now he was defacing a public trail and making enough noise to scare away every hiker and runner within ten miles.

Kira burst through the tall grass and weeds before skidding to a stop on the sandy riverbank. "Jasper, stop that!" She reached for his trailing leash, but it slipped free of the dog's collar and lay useless in her hand. She reached for the collar, determined to reattach the leash. Jasper stiffened, and a low growl came from his black throat.

Startled, she backed up a step and stared at the dog, who wasn't behaving like his normal, friendly self. He stood stiff-legged with something dangling from his mouth—something that looked like a woman's shoe! Mere feet behind him, the river gurgled and flaunted its high spring runoff against a wedge of sand where the riverbank dipped low. Debris had collected against the bank.

"Jasper." She wasn't sure why she whispered or why she suddenly felt afraid. Jasper was a rambunctious pain, but he'd never growled at her before. Though the clearing felt secluded, it was part of a popular park trail used by runners, walkers, and nature lovers. The area was relatively crime free; a small number of attacks had occurred in secluded places along the trail, but they'd been late at night. In the early morning sunlight, it was a favorite running place for her and a few hundred other runners.

Then she saw it. A thin white hand protruded from the sand between Jasper's firmly planted front paws. A short distance away, a knee—a very human-looking knee—arched from the sand and jumble of twigs left behind by the receding spring runoff. Thick globs of sand were caked in a dripping pattern from the peak of the kneecap as though stuck to something thicker than mere river water. *Blood? Was she seeing a human body? A very dead one?*

* * *

A long, shrill scream shattered the peace as Ford loped along the trail, reveling in the burst of spring blossoming around him. He had a particular fondness for the long park and trail that followed the Jordan River the length of the Salt Lake valley. Its natural beauty was particularly inviting in the early spring. There it was again! Ripping his earbuds from his ears, he paused, searching for the source of the sound. Someone was in serious trouble.

The screams were close by, not far ahead of where he'd stopped to listen. Leaping into motion, he charged toward the sound. Just over the first rise, he spotted a figure off to the side of the trail and close to the water. The slight figure appeared to be a child. As he drew closer, he could see the screams were coming not from a child but from a petite woman. Something was frightening her. *A snake?*

Had someone fallen into the river? He increased his speed. Then he noticed her eyes were riveted on a large black animal. It took only a second to recognize that the dog wasn't threatening the woman but was focused on something on the ground. Probably just a garter snake, but he'd better make certain. His stride lengthened.

* * *

Kira closed her eyes and shuddered. Surely she'd only imagined— her hands went to her ears, and she wished the screaming would stop. On some level she knew she was the one screaming, but she couldn't seem to stop. Zigzag lines danced before her eyes, and she felt waves of blackness rushing ever closer. She fought to stay conscious, to stay in control. Her mind ordered her hand to reach for the phone clipped to the waistband of her running shorts. She had to call someone—the police! Her hand didn't move. Her mind couldn't grasp anything beyond the hand and the bloody knee.

The screaming stopped on a choked gasp of terror when hands gripped her shoulders, giving a little shake. Fear turned to panic, and she fought to free herself. The hands released her as quickly as they had surprised her. A voice came from far away, and after a few seconds, words began to register.

"What happened? Are you hurt?" The voice wasn't familiar, but somehow the deep timbre of the masculine voice felt like it was offering her a lifeline. She wanted to burrow into that voice as though it could protect her from something terrible. She stepped toward it. Her cheek brushed against a soft T-shirt stretched tight across a solid chest; warm, solid arms wrapped around her, warming her when she hadn't even known she was cold.

Someone screamed. It wasn't her this time. The scream was followed by a babble of voices. Slowly Kira attempted to straighten her slumped position. The abruptness of the arms releasing their grip on her shoulders caused her to stagger. After regaining her footing, she eased herself to a sitting position on a nearby clump of grass. She kept her head lowered, fighting waves of nausea. She tried to focus on the trees with their newly unfurled leaves, the hum of insects, and the rushing sound of water—but to no avail.

"Stay back!" the stranger's voice ordered. She glanced up to see a man she judged to be six feet tall, or perhaps a little more, with short dark hair and a solid build ushering a small crowd back toward the trail. "The police will want this area kept clear. We need to be careful not to trample on any evidence they might be able to use." The man—whom she was certain was the same man who had comforted her moments ago—and most of the gathering crowd were wearing running clothes, people like her out for a morning run.

As through a fog, Kira heard vague grumbling and a fresh outbreak of whispering. With her head beginning to clear, she considered double-checking to see if she'd really seen what she thought she had at the edge of the water. She was pretty sure she hadn't imagined the gruesome sight Jasper dug up. She winced, regretting the unintentional reference to the dog's activity and a reminder that she needed to take charge of him. She needed to be strong, but nothing in her life had prepared her for this.

Taking a deep breath she looked around—everywhere except where Jasper still stood as a self-proclaimed sentinel over his grisly discovery. She couldn't bring herself to look directly at the dog or the hand she knew still protruded from the sand at his feet. Almost a dozen people in various styles of running garb formed a semicircle at the edge of the trampled weeds that separated the trail from the river. Several held cell phones in their hands. None had moved back as far as the trail.

Between her and Jasper stood a single figure. She could see dark hair curling against his nape. He wore black shorts and a white T-shirt with a darker sweat-stained mark running down the middle of the broad, smooth back it covered. Well-muscled legs proclaimed their owner was no novice to running. Something about his stance made it clear he was accustomed to taking charge of whatever life threw his way. His presence seemed to lend her new life.

She should do something. Like it or not, Jasper was her responsibility. The sound of sirens drawing closer ended her attempt to rise to her feet. The man standing a few feet away seemed to have everything under control; maybe she wouldn't have to do anything. She cringed mentally from her own thoughts. What was the matter with her? She'd been trying for years to convince her dad and brother she was a strong, capable woman who could take care of herself and make her own decisions.

She'd caved in when it came to choosing a university in another state and had instead enrolled at Westminster College a few blocks from her father's home. He'd vehemently opposed her decision to buy her own home and move out of his large east bench home a year after graduating from college. Now faced with a real emergency, all she could do was huddle in the grass and act like some Victorian ninny! Where was the strong, take-charge woman she'd fancied herself to be all these years?

Swallowing the bile that rose in her throat, she forced herself to her feet and realized she still held Jasper's leash in one hand. With her other hand, she swept her tangled blonde curls straight back from her damp forehead. She could and would behave like an adult. She stood still, breathing deeply, as she watched a pickup truck with a police light bar across the top of its cab ease its way along a trail meant for hikers and bicycles. Following close behind it was a forensics van. Someone had made the call she'd tried and failed to make.

Two uniformed officers were charging through the trampled grass and weeds toward the group by the time she managed to take a tentative step toward Jasper. Keeping her eyes averted, she called, "Jasper!" She coughed and tried again. "Jasper, come here." She patted her leg as she'd seen Tracy do when he called the dog to his side.

Jasper didn't move but bared his teeth as one of the officers attempted to approach him.

"Your dog, ma'am?" She hadn't been aware of the other officer stopping beside her.

"My brother's, actually." She caught the officer's quick glance toward the man standing a few feet away. "N-no." She hurried to correct his false assumption. "Tracy—my brother—is in Bangkok." She stumbled over the words, unable to speak coherently.

"See if you can coax him away from the body." The officer spoke quietly as though he sensed the struggle she was having.

Body. She'd been trying so hard to shut out the harsh reality of that word.

"J-Jasper!" She tried to sound commanding. The animal showed no indication he'd heard her. "Jasper!" she tried again, raising her voice as best she could. The dog didn't even look her way; he continued to bare his teeth and snarl menacingly at the officer who was attempting to get closer.

A piercing whistle split the air, followed by a command to "come here!" The dog, who had ignored Kira, scooped up a bit of bright color that lay beside his feet and dashed toward the man who stood a few feet away. Dropping what appeared to be a shoe—the shoe she'd noticed earlier—Jasper eagerly leaped up to lick the man's face.

"Good boy." Large hands cradled the dog's head, whispering approving words.

Kira watched in disgust, remembering Tracy's insistence that the dog would be good company for her and protect her from strangers. Some protection!

CHAPTER TWO

SITTING SIDEWAYS ON THE EDGE of the seat in the police vehicle, Kira leaned her head against the cool glass of the open door. She was aware of a police officer talking to the man who had been the first to arrive after she lost her head and launched into a screaming frenzy. Her cheeks burned with embarrassment. Every runner on the path must think her a nutcase. Jasper lay at the man's feet, looking smug, though she held the end of his leash, which she'd had the presence of mind to snap onto his collar when the officer suggested they head to the parked truck to talk. She'd also managed to pull the bright tangerine and aqua-hued shoe from Jasper's clenched jaws. She'd caught the officer's slight frown when she handed him the wet, multicolored platform shoe with its five-inch spiky heel.

The officer had instructed her to stay where she was while he finished up. She wasn't certain whether he thought she was somehow involved in the grisly death or if he was trying to spare her the sight of the body being removed from its wet grave. She attempted to avert her eyes and her thoughts from the activity taking place a short distance away. Either way she was glad to be away from the gawking crowd that had gathered.

* * *

Ford answered the officer's questions, though his attention kept straying to the young woman who seemed to be still experiencing shock. Tousled blonde curls fluttered across her face as a gust of wind swept by. In addition to blonde curls, he'd noticed a pert little nose and deep blue eyes. At first glance she could be mistaken for a child, but the curves revealed by her running shorts and T-shirt said she was a woman. She appeared fragile and hurting, filling him with an almost irresistible urge to comfort her.

There wasn't much he could tell the officer. He lived in an apartment near Murray Park but preferred running on the Jordan River Parkway whenever he had time. He didn't know anything about the half-buried body or the woman and her dog who had discovered it. If he got a chance, he meant to change that. He'd like to get to know the woman. Something about her intrigued him, and he sensed she needed a friend.

* * *

She knew the tall man's name now. She'd heard him tell the officer. Rutherford Joseph Kettering. *Who on earth would name their kid Rutherford? Do his friends shorten it to Ruth?* She felt a giggle rising in her throat. Her attempt to cover it with a cough sounded more like a snort. Both men standing nearby gave her a questioning look, which she pretended not to see. She had a sneaking suspicion they already thought she was unbalanced or just plain crazy.

She wasn't certain she'd even made sense when she'd answered the officer's questions. She'd given him her name and address and told him she worked for a local credit union as a loan counselor; she also mentioned that though she ran three or four mornings each week, she only ran occasionally on the Parkway path even if it was her favorite place to run.

Most mornings she chose a path closer to her home. A small canal ran behind the development where she'd purchased her condo, and the dirt road that hugged its bank provided her usual route. Today was supposed to be her day off, so she'd elected to make the longer run and enjoy the birds and natural beauty of the scenic trail. She did recall telling the officer her car was parked at a nearby parking area, didn't she? She just wanted to go home, spend at least an hour in the shower, and put on clean clothes. She wasn't sure why, but she felt dirty, like she was the one who had been buried in sand.

She looked down at her bare legs, covered with bits of grass and smudges of dirt, and thought of the poor woman Jasper had found. She knew now that the body was female, though she'd guessed that due to the shoe Jasper had found. The woman wasn't a drowning victim; she'd been shot. Kira had been aware enough of conversations going on around her—including police officers, someone from forensics, and bystanders—to learn that much. There was so much more she wanted to know. Instinctively she knew that while the area was swarming with grim-faced investigators, curious onlookers, and even a television crew, her questions would be ignored.

Was it because Kira was the first person to discover the body that she felt some kind of connection to it? *Not it. Her.* The hand she'd viewed belonged to a woman who had hopes and dreams, most likely a family, a short time ago. Knowing her feelings made no sense didn't curb Kira's need to know whether the woman had been young or old, to wonder if she had been intentionally buried in the sand or had fallen in the water somewhere upstream and been washed up on that sandbar by the swift, high current, or to speculate on whether a threat lingered along the Parkway, endangering those who continued to walk or run there. She shied away from speculating about the pain and fear that must have preceded the woman's brutal death. A terrible sadness filled her with grief for a woman she hadn't even known.

The officer moved closer, leaning against the open door with one arm extended across the top of it. He spoke softly as though she were a child and he expected her to fall apart if he said the wrong thing. "I have your contact information," he told her. "If you'd like to go, you can. However I'll need to talk to you again as soon as possible. Take a couple of hours to clean up—yourself and your dog. Rest a little bit; then I'll see you at the precinct station." He handed her a small square of paper.

She nodded, unsure she could speak over the lump in her throat. The words on the paper blurred, and she had to blink several times before reading *Detective Bruce Daley, Homicide Division,* followed by a nearby address. Penciled in was the notation *11 a.m.*

Rising to her feet, Kira looked around, feeling a little uncertain. All she could see was the one word on the officer's card, *homicide*. She'd avoided thinking the woman had been murdered, but that one word screamed this wasn't a simple drowning.

Seeing what looked like a camera crew moving toward her, she gripped Jasper's leash tighter and moved toward the trail. Hoping to evade the reporters, she broke into a run. She was grateful and surprised Jasper didn't protest the use of the leash until she realized his willingness to trot beside her was likely linked to the fact that Mr. Kettering also loped along the trail beside them.

"You okay?" he asked.

"Yes," she mumbled. Feeling guilty for her less-than-sociable response, she added, "Thank you for . . ." She wasn't sure what she was thanking him for. He had tried to come to her aid, and she supposed he was the one who had called the police. He'd even controlled Jasper better than she'd been able to do.

"Do you live around here?" he asked after a few minutes.

"No. I live a few miles away, but I've always liked this trail, so I come here sometimes on weekends or holidays. How about you?" She was afraid he and all of the officers who had attempted to speak to her thought she was some kind of basket case. The more distance she put between herself and the scene they'd just left, the more normal she began to feel. The least she could do was carry on a simple conversation with the man who had attempted to help her. Besides, she had to admit, she was curious about Rutherford—or whatever name he went by. Certainly no one was called Rutherford in this century!

"I live in Murray and usually run on the high school track or in the park," he volunteered. "They're both close to my apartment. A friend wanted me to run with him here today, so I agreed. Then he didn't show up. When I called him, he said he overslept. It was such a great morning, I decided to run on my own anyway."

His movements were smooth and appeared effortless. She couldn't help admiring the play of muscles in his long legs. Snapping her attention back to the path where they ran side by side, she wondered aloud, "Do you think she was attacked by some psycho who was hanging out on this trail?" There was no need to explain who *she* referred to.

He hesitated before answering. "I'm no expert, but I don't think she was a runner. I saw enough to know she wasn't dressed for that."

"Or even walk." The implication of the shoe she'd removed from Jasper's mouth took shape in her mind. "Assuming the shoe Jasper found was hers, I don't see how she could walk in that thing. The heel was at least five inches and the sole an inch or more thick."

"Near as I can tell, that describes the current fashion trend. I teach high school students. You'd be surprised at the footwear some girls wear to class. Some of those poor kids hobble along on shoes that more closely resemble stilts. It makes no sense wearing shoes like that with jeans or shorts, but they do it." He stared straight ahead for several seconds before adding in a softer voice, "This woman wasn't wearing jeans. I caught just a glimpse of what appeared to be a short, frilly party dress."

"What I saw wasn't decayed . . ." On second thought, she didn't want to speculate how long the body had been in the water or thrust in the sand where the current made a sharp turn. She shuddered and wished they could talk about something else.

"I don't think she'd been there long . . ." His voice trailed off as though he too would prefer some other topic.

"Uh . . . There's my car." She pointed to a small red Jetta as they approached the parking area adjacent to a narrow strip of grass and a wooden structure she knew housed restrooms.

"Nice car. Probably gets good gas mileage." He gave the car an approving nod. "I don't know if we'll bump into each other again when we go down to the police station, but I'd like to see you again. How about lunch after we finish giving our statements?"

Kira hesitated. Even though he seemed nice, Rutherford Joseph Kettering was a stranger. He could even be a murderer. She didn't know where that thought came from, but he'd arrived awfully quickly after she discovered the body. She hoped it wasn't just because he was good-looking and he'd been nice to her that she felt she could trust him. "All right." She flashed a weak grin then added, "That's a first. I may sound old-fashioned and maybe I've read too many period novels, but I've never gone to lunch before with someone I haven't been introduced to. I don't even know what to call you. And by the way, my name is Kira. Kira Paxton."

Stopping beside a wooden picnic table, he pulled out his water bottle and took a long drink. With a self-deprecating smile he pointed to a black Ford 150 at the far end of the parking strip. "My parents named me after my great-grandfather then, thankfully, shortened Rutherford to Ford. It seemed like a good idea to shop for a Ford when I bought my first vehicle, and I guess Fords sort of became a habit. Rutherford Kettering, better known as Ford, at your service." He gave a mock bow, and they both chuckled then quickly sobered. It seemed wrong to laugh after what they'd just witnessed.

He walked her to her car and watched her coax Jasper into the backseat. The dog whined and protested but eventually made himself comfortable. When she was settled behind the steering wheel, she smiled up at him. "See you later, Ford."

He returned the smile. "Bye, Kira."

She shifted into reverse and carefully backed out of the parking spot. It was all she could do to keep a broad smile from spreading across her face until she remembered the partially buried body.

CHAPTER THREE

Kira raked her fingers through her hair as she looked down at the statement she'd just signed. Detective Daley hadn't pressured her, and she'd tried hard to remember if there was anything unusual that had happened before Jasper slipped his leash and took off running toward the river that morning. She couldn't think of anything, certainly not a gunshot. She hadn't even paid attention to whether there were two or twenty cars near where she'd parked. And, no, she didn't recall anything specific about any of the other runners she'd passed, or more likely, who passed her on the trail. She liked to run, but she knew she wasn't fast. Besides, her entire attention had been taken up with trying to control her brother's unruly dog.

"If you think of anything . . . you have my card?"

She nodded. She'd already tucked Detective Daley's card inside the zipper pocket of her purse.

"We'll find who did this." The detective seemed to want to reassure her. "The body hadn't been there long, so anything you can remember may help us find the killer."

"I'm sorry I wasn't more observant. The dog made a mess of my house this morning, and I thought if he went for a run, he might settle down . . ."

"No, don't feel bad. Your dog did us a favor. I just wish the area hadn't been so trampled by spectators." They sat in uncomfortable silence for what seemed a long time. The small office felt claustrophobic to Kira. It was only large enough for a desk, two chairs, and a battered metal filing cabinet. There wasn't even a window. A certificate of some sort hung on the wall, and she noted it was crooked.

"Uh, am I free to go now?" She felt like a schoolgirl asking permission to be excused. Because of her short stature, she was often mistaken for a child, so it was no surprise she felt like one at the moment.

"Oh, yes. Go ahead. That's probably all we'll need from you until the case goes to trial or you remember something you might have noticed this morning." He scraped his chair back and rose to his feet.

She awkwardly shook his hand, trying not to stumble over his reference to going to court. She hadn't thought that far ahead. Instead of putting the whole horrible experience behind her as she had hoped to do, she would be bombarded with gruesome memories for months, maybe years, and eventually she'd have to tell an entire courtroom full of people she'd reacted like a dithering idiot when her brother's dog dug up a body.

She hurried down the hall toward the lobby, trying to refocus her thoughts on her lunch date. Before her mother passed away when Kira was thirteen, she'd often reminded Kira and her brother that the best way to get rid of bad thoughts was to replace them with something good. Going to lunch with a good-looking man surely qualified.

Looking around the lobby, she stifled her disappointment. There was no sign of Ford. Two officers, deep in conversation, rushed past her, causing her to take a step backward. A commotion near a desk with a bank-teller-style partition between an officer and a woman who was either hysterical or drunk drew her attention for a moment. Then she turned her gaze toward a row of plastic chairs. Most were occupied, but none of the occupants were Ford. A female officer marched a large Polynesian teenager sporting nothing but sandals, a lava-lava, and dozens of tattoos toward the hallway she'd just left. A neatly dressed man in a three-piece suit brushed by her, and she moved farther back toward the wall, wondering if she should wait for Ford or just leave.

* * *

The officer across the desk from Ford was younger than Detective Daley, who had questioned Ford earlier. The younger detective's cocky attitude rubbed him the wrong way. Ford had shared the events of the morning, and he had nothing more to tell Detective Chetfield when the young detective was called out of the room. Ford was annoyed to be left stewing on an uncomfortable plastic chair. It wasn't the way he'd hoped to spend his day. When Chetfield returned he was strutting with self-importance.

"The victim has been identified," he announced. He peered closely at Ford as though expecting some kind of reaction and appeared disappointed when it didn't come. "The victim was a student of yours, I believe."

"A student!" The news was like a blow. Ford cared about his students and found it unthinkable that the life of one of the vibrant young people he saw each day at school had been cut short. "Who?" he asked, though he wasn't certain he wanted to hear the answer.

The detective moved a few items on his desk and placed his pen in perfect alignment with his notebook. Finally he looked directly at Ford as though trying to see right inside his head. "Marla Hayden. I believe you knew her *particularly* well."

Ford didn't like the insinuation behind Detective Chetfield's words. "I know her. Yes. She's in my fourth-period history class."

"Tell me about the little private meeting—" Chetfield's voice broke off as the door behind Ford opened.

"That will be all for today, Mr. Kettering. If we need anything further, we have your contact information." Detective Daley dismissed him. He sounded cold and stiff, but Ford noted he wasn't the recipient of Daley's glare. That was reserved for the cocky young officer whose face had turned a mottled red.

* * *

Kira's hand moved toward her mouth, and just in time she remembered she didn't bite her nails anymore. She'd paid forty bucks for the reward manicure she'd given herself for not chewing on her nails for three whole months. Actually she was amazed she hadn't chewed them down to the quick when she discovered what Jasper had dug up.

"Ready?"

She hadn't even noticed Ford's arrival. His smile seemed a little forced, and the way he took her arm and moved her a little too quickly toward the door told her his interview hadn't gone as smoothly as had hers.

Since they'd arrived in separate vehicles, they agreed to meet at a popular restaurant near the mall and were fortunate enough to find parking spaces near each other. Ford ushered her ahead of him into the restaurant, where a hostess seated them.

A few minutes later, Kira fiddled with her straw, glancing frequently at her silent companion's face. Several times she thought he was about to say something then changed his mind. He'd asked if Olive Garden was okay with her. It was nearby, and the food was good. She'd quickly agreed but had felt disappointed ever since she'd taken a seat across from him. He responded to her attempts at conversation with mumbled responses and sounded almost mechanical when he placed his order with their server. She felt herself shrink as she considered the odds Ford was merely being polite when he suggested lunch and that he hadn't expected her to accept. Or perhaps he'd had second thoughts about spending time with her. After a moment's reflection, intuition told her there was more to his withdrawal. She guessed something about his interview troubled him.

"Want to talk about it?" she mustered her courage to ask. It was ridiculous to sit there in silence. Besides, a listening ear might be what he needed. Clearly something had upset him, and she already knew he wasn't a man who got flustered easily. If it was just a matter of regretting being with her, it was better to know now.

He closed his eyes and pressed his lips together briefly before releasing a sigh. "I'm sorry. I'm not very good company. The officer who interviewed me received word during the interview about the identity of the body found this morning. She is, or rather was, one of my students. Her name was Marla Hayden, and she has been trouble since the first day school started last fall. Actually she's caused trouble since she was in elementary school."

"You know her? The dead woman . . . the body Jasper . . . ?" She wasn't making sense. It was bad enough discovering a dead woman but to actually know that person! Then it hit her. If she was in one of Ford's classes, she wasn't a woman but a child. No, not a child. A teenager. It had always seemed silly to her to refer to teenagers who were victimized in some way as children, but when they committed a crime, they were suddenly adults.

Ford went on, "She's just sixteen and in my sophomore world history class. She's smart enough to get good grades, but only works hard enough to maintain the necessary GPA to participate in extracurricular activities like dance club. I've suspected all year that her boyfriend was writing her papers and she was cheating on exams, but I couldn't prove it. Several of her friends transferred their daughters to different schools last semester because they'd been picked up with Marla for shoplifting and their parents didn't want their kids associating with her any longer. She's a rude, manipulative troublemaker."

Ford's words seemed like a terrible way to speak of someone dead, someone who apparently died tragically. She didn't know Ford well, but if he had negative feelings toward the girl, she suspected he had good reason. She mulled his statement over in her mind for several minutes, trying to come to terms with words that held a tinge of bitterness. She acknowledged that she'd painted a fantasy in her mind, picturing the dead girl as the innocent victim of some scurrilous stranger who preyed on unwary young women. Was it possible the girl was involved in something dangerous? At last she asked, "Do you think she was killed because she was doing something illegal?" She thought of drugs. Her own high school days were recent enough to know there were students who used and ones who sold. It wasn't unheard of for a high school student to be killed over a bad drug deal. News reports were full of stories about teenagers involved in drug trafficking.

"At this point I don't think the police know what the motive for her killing was. I got the feeling they were fishing for any information whatsoever about her and the people who might have a grudge against her. Unfortunately that includes me."

"You?" Surely they didn't suspect Ford of killing one of his students! Nothing she'd seen in Ford would cause her to think he was capable of harming someone.

"Yes. We had a difference of opinion just last week." She wished he would explain more fully, but he didn't go on. He placed a forkful of his entree in his mouth and chewed deliberately, a faraway look in his eyes; then he seemed to make up his mind to change the subject. "So how did you wind up with a dog you don't seem happy to own?"

"My brother, Tracy, and my father own an international company. Their work includes quite a bit of travel. Tracy usually leaves Jasper with Dad, but since Dad had to be out of town this week too, he assumed I would be happy to take the beast off his hands."

"Do I detect a bit of sarcasm?" Ford grinned.

Kira sighed. "I don't dislike dogs; I just have no desire to live with one or to have one dependent on me. Besides, Jasper is a big animal, and my house is small with a tiny unfenced yard. A big dog like Jasper should have room to run. Tracy had his own apartment for a while, but his work involves so much travel that he moved back home a couple years ago. Dad has a huge fenced yard, so Jasper doesn't get in so much trouble there. I've tried to convince Tracy that Jasper would be better off at home with a neighbor dropping in to feed him daily, but Tracy insists he needs to be with family and that he's used to spending most of his day inside, where he has the run of the house."

"I had a dog when I was a kid, but my family lived in a big old rambling farmhouse on nearly five acres. I don't think Rascal would have been happy as a house dog." Memories of his former pet were obviously pleasant ones.

"Speaking of an unhappy dog, I'd better be on my way. Jasper doesn't like being confined to my front room and will have found something to chew up by the time I get back." With a sigh, she gathered up her handbag and rose to her feet.

Ford rose to his feet too. He looked at her apologetically. "I'd like to see you again. I promise to be better company next time."

Warmth filled her. "I'd like that too." It was true. Even with Ford's distracted thoughts and the ordeal they'd faced earlier, she felt drawn to him and wanted a chance to get to know him better.

Kira's thoughts lingered on Ford as she drove. She didn't remember a time when she'd been so attracted to a man as she was to Ford. They'd spent little time together, yet she felt a connection as though they'd been friends for a long time. He was good-looking, but she'd dated other men who were attractive. She had never felt quite the same way about any of them. Could the emotionally charged discovery that morning and a trip to the police station somehow have affected her feelings, creating a bond between them that was only in her imagination? She tried to view her feelings realistically.

Her thoughts turned to the information she'd learned about the young girl whose body she'd found that morning. She would have liked to discuss with Ford more about what he knew, but she understood how difficult the topic had become for him. She sensed he was torn by guilt for disliking one of his students then discovering she'd died tragically.

Her phone rang as she pulled onto her street. A quick glance at the screen let her know the caller was Tracy.

She braked in her driveway and picked up her phone. "Hello! Tracy! Thank goodness! How soon will you be home?"

"You missed me that much?" her brother teased.

"No, I just want your dog out of here."

"Now, now. Don't tell me Jasper hasn't been on his best behavior."

"He . . . he . . . dug up . . ." She wiped furiously at her eyes. *Great! She was crying again, and Tracy would tease her about being a crybaby and tell Dad.* They'd be more convinced than ever that she was one of those incompetent females who shouldn't be living alone. They'd tried to talk her out of getting her own place two years ago, and when that failed, they'd tried every excuse they could find to persuade her to move back in with them.

"Hey! Surely it's not that bad." She could hear the laughter in his voice. "Whatever he dug up, I'll replace."

"You can't. She's dead!" She felt an urge to scream even as a voice in the back of her head reminded her to remain calm and explain that morning's events in a rational manner.

"Dead? He didn't kill Mrs. Gleason's cat, did he?" he asked in an incredulous voice.

"No. Jasper didn't kill anyone. He dug up Marla. She was only sixteen, and no one knows who killed her."

"Whoa! Wait a minute. You aren't suggesting Jasper dug up a real dead person, are you?"

"Yes, that's what I've been trying to tell you. I took Jasper running with me this morning. He escaped his leash and found a body partially buried in the sand along a bend in the Jordan River Parkway."

"Seriously?"

"Detective Daley seems to think it's serious." She couldn't resist the sarcasm.

"I'll be there in thirty minutes!" Tracy was the one shouting now. "My plane just landed, and it'll only take a few minutes to grab my luggage and pick up my car."

CHAPTER FOUR

"THAT'S IT; YOU BETTER GET packed. I'll follow you back to Dad's place."

"You've got to be kidding!" Kira set down the spoon she held with a clang against the countertop. "I'm in absolutely no danger here, and I was never in any danger this morning. I was upset but not in danger. Hundreds, maybe thousands, of people run on the Parkway trail every day. Moms push strollers there. It's overrun with kids on skateboards. Police officers on bicycles patrol it on a regular basis. Besides, that trail is two or three miles from here." She pushed Jasper out of the way so she could reach the refrigerator.

"Don't be difficult. You know there are long stretches of that trail where you never see another person. Besides, there's no reason for you to be alone clear out here when there's plenty of space at home, and you'd be safe and secure there."

Forgetting about the salad she was preparing for dinner, she stared in amazement at her brother. At least a hundred people lived in the condo complex that included her home, and the condos were surrounded by subdivisions of single-family homes. Two of her neighbors were highway patrolmen. There was even a house alarm on all of her windows and doors. What made him think she would be safer alone in her dad's house than alone in her own home?

"You and Dad never give up, do you? You're so sure I'm incompetent to take care of myself."

"Be reasonable, Kira. You're barely five feet tall, female, and skinn—delicate."

"Oh, and stupid! Don't forget to add that one." She glared at her brother. Taking a deep breath, she lowered her voice and attempted to reason with him. "I'm not a child; I may be small, but I'm all grown up, a college graduate with an MBA and a good job. My office is a few blocks from here. I like the neighborhood, and I'm perfectly capable of managing my own life."

"Dad offered you a better paying job, and it's just stubbornness that keeps you from working with us."

"He offered me a phony job sharpening pencils and running errands!" Even if he'd offered the kind of job she had trained for, she didn't want to work for her father. She wanted to be independent.

She'd been born premature and had suffered through complications requiring long periods of hospitalization followed by bouts of childhood illness. By her tenth birthday, her doctor had deemed her as strong and normal as any other ten-year-old, but her father and brother saw her diminutive stature as evidence that she needed to continue to be coddled and protected—as if size had anything to do with maturity. After her mother was diagnosed with breast cancer and passed away, her father and brother had become obsessive about protecting Kira. They'd opposed her interest in running or participating in any athletic endeavor, objected to her moving into her own condo, questioned whether she was strong enough to work full-time, and found fault with every man she dated. She took care not to mention to Tracy that she'd had lunch with Ford. She didn't want him to launch a background investigation and decide a teacher wasn't good enough for Garrett Paxton's daughter.

"At least come home until whoever killed that girl is caught."

She suspected he was attempting to manipulate her by making his demand sound like a reasonable request. She felt a sudden suspicion he was concerned about more than her safety. "When do you leave on your next trip?"

He grimaced and looked sheepish. "Thursday."

"Three days before Dad returns. Sorry, but you'll just have to leave Jasper with your girlfriend."

"Kaitlin can't keep him. Her apartment doesn't allow dogs."

"There are such things as kennels for dogs with absent owners."

"I'm not paying for a kennel when you could just go home where you belong and where you'd be safe. You know Jasper would be miserable in a kennel. Come on, Kira. It would just be until Dad gets home."

"No way." She'd given in too many times to Tracy's arguments, but no more. "Maybe Kaitlin will move into the house for a few days when you have to leave."

"Jasper!"

She jumped at Tracy's shout. She hadn't noticed the dog leave the kitchen, but there he was standing in the doorway with a mangled shape that looked suspiciously like one of her bedroom slippers in his mouth.

Tracy wrestled the slipper away from Jasper. Holding it between his thumb and forefinger, he dropped it into the trash. Before either could say anything, Kira heard her phone ring. Scooping it off of the counter, she placed it to her ear without checking the caller ID. "Hello," she said absently, her mind still on her mangled slipper.

"Kira, this is Ford. I called to apologize for my gloomy attitude at lunch and ask if you'd give me another chance. How about dinner tonight?"

"Just a moment." She turned to her brother. "Are you staying for dinner?"

He shook his head. "Kaitlin is expecting me." He gathered up the trash bag and stomped out the door with Jasper following on his heels, sniffing anxiously at the bag he carried. Tracy stopped on her front step. "I can't take Jasper to dinner with Kaitlin and me. It might be best to leave him here until morning."

She shook her head. She couldn't believe Tracy would try to convince her to keep Jasper overnight with a promise to pick up the dog in the morning. She shot down his argument by informing him she too had a date.

Looking unhappy he demanded to know all about Ford. "We could double date," he suggested, which she interpreted as, "I need to check him out."

She closed the door behind him, and he promptly reopened it.

"Size four?"

She nodded her head and grinned ruefully. It wasn't the first time Tracy had felt compelled to take responsibility for replacing a pair of shoes. She noticed he also didn't say anything further about leaving Jasper with her when he left on Thursday.

Turning her back to Tracy and Jasper, she accepted Ford's invitation. The salad she'd just made would keep and be a start on tomorrow's dinner.

* * *

Kira checked her appearance in the hall mirror for the umpteenth time while she waited for Ford to arrive. It had been a long time since she'd been this anxious for the arrival of a date. Actually she couldn't remember ever being so attracted to any of the men she'd dated.

"Slow down," she warned herself. "I've just met him and need to get to know him before I fall too hard."

In the mirror she caught sight of the toe of what looked like her other slipper peeking out from beneath the sofa. She snatched it up and frowned at it. It showed a few bite marks but was in better shape than its mate. She stared at it and shook her head. One slipper wouldn't be of much use to her. With a sigh, she dropped it in the trash just as her doorbell rang.

She'd seen Ford in running shorts and Adidas, and then in jeans and T-shirt, but oh my, what he did to Wranglers, a snap shirt, and leather boots. He was hot!

They seemed to share a tacit agreement not to speak of the morning's events. Over tender steaks at the Texas Roadhouse, she laughed over stories Ford told of the antics of his four younger brothers; she shared her frustration with her dad's and Tracy's determination to keep her a little girl. He related events that led to his love of teaching, and they shook their heads over how financially naive and unprepared some of her would-be clients proved to be.

A rowdy birthday celebration erupted at a nearby table. The wait staff clapped and stomped their boots in time to a rousing rendition of the birthday song. Kira could see Ford's mouth move but couldn't hear his words. She suspected he was singing along. He grinned. Reaching across the table, he took her hand, holding it until the noise subsided. The simple gesture filled her with a pleasant warmth spiced with a tingling awareness. An older woman decked out in a Western shirt and boots stood and gave a dramatic bow to those seated at her table, and the group broke out in applause. A glance at Ford told her he was enjoying the spectacle.

"Remind me to never tell you when my birthday is," Kira whispered.

Ford twirled an imaginary mustache. "We cowboys have our ways."

She laughed, enjoying the silliness.

They left the restaurant, and Ford drove slowly toward Kira's condo. When they crossed the river, Kira couldn't stop the shiver that ran down her spine.

"You're not going to let what happened this morning keep you from running, are you?" Ford asked in a soft voice. He seemed to read her thoughts.

"No." She hesitated. "I just won't run on the Parkway." Once her favorite running trail, now the Parkway was the last place she wanted to spend any time.

Ford seemed to be thinking. Then taking one hand from the steering wheel, he briefly touched her hand and said with a hint of a smile, "I think you should continue running on the Parkway. It's too good not to keep using. What if I pick you up tomorrow morning and we run together on a different stretch of the trail?"

CHAPTER FIVE

THEY HAD BEEN RUNNING ON various segments of the Parkway each morning for several weeks, and Kira was past feeling squeamish about the trail when Ford announced that he'd gotten a call from Detective Daley late the previous afternoon. "He wants to see me right after I finish classes today."

"Did he say whether they've learned anything more?" she asked. They'd avoided talking about the event that first brought them together, though she'd followed the news stories the first few days. She'd even admit to a morbid curiosity about the murder. The death of a young girl under suspicious circumstances had been the lead story on all of the local news outlets, but after several days she'd heard nothing more about the case. She was surprised Ford had been called back in to talk to the detective while she hadn't. Still, she was glad she didn't have to go back to the police station.

"Daley didn't say any more on the phone, but I heard on the radio this morning that the autopsy report has confirmed that Marla was shot in the chest at close range and there was no evidence of a struggle. The assumption is she was killed by someone she knew." His voice echoed as they passed through a tunnel that routed the trail under a street.

Kira found herself moving closer to Ford. Talk of the girl's death left her with mixed feelings, both a sort of fascination and a wish that she could never hear or think of it again. They ran for a quarter of a mile without saying anything more, closely matching their strides, though Kira knew that with Ford's long legs, he could easily outpace her. She paid little attention to the trees that were now fully leafed out and ignored the river where she usually watched for new duckling families. Instead her mind went back to that awful discovery. A month had passed, but the events of that morning were still sharp in her mind.

"I'm not sure why Daley wants to talk to me again," Ford mused out loud at last. "I already told Detective Chetfield everything I know, which isn't much."

"It's probably because you were one of her teachers. He might think you know who her friends were, if she got along with her parents, that kind of stuff. I think most crimes are solved by first finding out everything possible about the victim."

"I suppose, but in all honesty, there isn't much I can tell them other than the names of her boyfriend and two of the girls she hung out with. All three followed her around like sheep. I know I shouldn't speak ill of the dead, but she wasn't a girl I enjoyed having in my class. She was rude to other students, often tardy, and frequently belittled a kid who always had the answer for every question I asked. Her friends took their cues from her, treating the other kids like dirt." He seemed lost in thought for several minutes before continuing.

"I actually feel sorry for her boyfriend. He used to hang around the door waiting for her after class. I don't know his last name, but I heard some of the kids call him Aaron. I think he's a junior, and the few times I've seen him during the past few weeks, he looked like he's taking Marla's death pretty hard. I don't know why he put up with her insults and condescending attitude. He's a particularly bright, good-looking young man, and he adored her. I think half the girls in the school have a crush on him. I suspect Marla enjoyed flaunting him in front of the other girls, and it fed her ego to have him try so hard to please her. I suspect he did much of her homework too."

Kira had no sisters, but it hadn't been too long ago that she had been sixteen. There hadn't been a boyfriend in her life then. She'd had a couple of girlfriends, who were nothing like the girls Ford described; however, she'd known girls like that. Her brother had called them popularity princesses. They were all sweetness and charm while angling for attention from her handsome, athletic brother. Around those they considered inferiors, they were nasty and manipulative. She'd noticed that girls like that somehow always attracted a loyal fan club of insecure hangers-on who followed them about.

She sensed that Ford's appointment with the detective bothered him and that he didn't want to talk about it. She decided not to push the issue. They ran another half mile then walked the remaining distance to their vehicles. When Ford paused beside her before she climbed into her car, she turned her face up to wish him luck with his appointment. He surprised her with a quick kiss to her lips, one that left her longing for more. He'd ended their run with a brotherly hug before. She had to admit there was nothing siblinglike in her reaction to the way his lips felt against hers.

"How about stopping by my house after you see Detective Daley?" she asked, trying to appear calm and unfazed. "According to the weatherman, it's supposed to be perfect weather tonight, and I picked up some steaks we could grill."

"I'd like that." His smile did something to her insides she couldn't quite explain, but it filled her with warmth that lasted long after she got to work.

* * *

Throughout the day, though she had a steady string of appointments and several reports to prepare, Kira found her thoughts returning often to the quick kiss she'd shared with Ford that morning. Just thinking about it sent a flutter through her stomach. She found herself dreaming in anticipation of their date that evening. When she pulled into her driveway a little after five that afternoon, she was disappointed to see her brother's car already parked there.

Jasper ran to greet her when she stepped out of her car. He sniffed her shoes then sauntered back to Tracy's side. She noticed his girlfriend, Kaitlin, was with him, and they both wore huge smiles. Without saying a word, Kaitlin held out her left hand, displaying a diamond-and-sapphire engagement ring.

Giving a little squeal, Kira threw her arms around her soon-to-be sister-in-law. "I've always wanted a sister," she whispered in Kaitlin's ear.

Inside, Tracy handed Kira a high-end shoe box. Setting the box on the coffee table, Kira invited her brother and his fiancée to join her and Ford for dinner. It took little persuasion to convince them to stay for the cookout. Ford arrived within minutes and joined the celebration.

A short time later, Jasper's head lay in Kaitlin's lap, and he seemed to sigh with contentment as the young woman stroked his glossy head. His shiny coat was almost an exact match to Kaitlin's sleek dark coif. Kira couldn't help a flicker of chagrin. Jasper never looked that benign and content with her. There always seemed to be a war of wills going on between her and the furry beast. She did notice, however, that the immaculate Kaitlin's right sandal seemed to be somewhat ragged and damp, as though it had suffered a slight encounter with the shoe-crazy mutt.

"Have you set a date?" Kira asked as she arranged a veggie platter for their cookout.

"Probably October, though we haven't picked an exact date yet. Tracy has most of that month off, and I won't have any problem getting vacation time then." Kaitlin stood, rinsed her hands at the sink, then picked up one of the bowls Kira had removed from the refrigerator.

The men had taken over the grill while she and Kaitlin added the finishing touches to the salads. All they had to do now would be to carry the food outside. A nervous glance through the patio doors assured Kira the two men were getting along fine. Tracy had sabotaged enough of her dates over the years that she knew she had cause for concern. No doubt Tracy was giving Ford a more thorough grilling than Detective Daley had. She saw Tracy throw back his head in laughter. *That was a good sign.* Ford seemed a little more subdued, and she wished they'd had a chance to talk before Tracy and Kaitlin joined them for the evening. She was anxious to learn how Ford's appointment with Detective Daley had gone.

Following Kaitlin out the door, Kira carried a platter of sliced melon and pineapple. Taking care to avoid dripping any juice on her pants, she envied Kaitlin's ability to look perfectly groomed at all times. Even after she'd cuddled with Jasper, there wasn't a black hair or wrinkle in the other woman's pale lavender skirt.

Kira welcomed the slight breeze as they stepped outside. The day had been unseasonably warm for late May, but now the sky was overcast and a breeze stirred the tablecloth on the patio table.

"Look at that sky!" Tracy waved a spatula toward the north, and it became clear the day's heat was a precursor to a rapidly approaching storm. So much for last evening's weather forecast!

"I left my apartment windows open!" Kaitlin looked alarmed.

"It's still at least an hour away," Tracy assured her. "There's plenty of time to eat, and the steaks are done to perfection! We can eat and get back to your apartment before the rain starts."

Laughter rang out as they ate and got to know each other better. Kira found herself hoping the evening was just the beginning of a close friendship between the two couples. She'd met Kaitlin several times before and liked her. She was a couple years older than Kira, but they were comfortable together. Tracy seemed to like Ford. She hoped they'd be friends and he wouldn't try to break up the relationship as he had with every other man she'd gone out with more than twice. Kaitlin's presence may have put him on his best behavior. Perhaps she shouldn't be thinking of herself and Ford as a couple, but she'd never before had a relationship with a man that felt so right. Actually she'd never dated one man long enough to consider whatever they had between them a relationship.

They were just finishing their meal when the first fat droplet of rain splashed against the patio.

Kaitlin jumped to her feet. "We'd better go." She grabbed her plate and Tracy's before rushing inside, nearly tripping over Jasper on her way.

"I hate to leave you with the clean-up." Tracy looked apologetically at Kira as he snapped Jasper's leash to his collar.

"It's all right; I'll help." Ford matched action to his words by scooping up a couple of bowls and starting toward the kitchen. Kira followed with an armful of condiments, which she set on the kitchen counter. Together she and Ford stood at the front door to wave Tracy and Kaitlin off before returning to the patio to gather up the last of the items from their meal.

Once the leftover food was stored in the refrigerator and the outside table cleared, Ford settled on the sofa, and Kira seated herself beside him. He placed an arm around her shoulders, and she found herself snuggling closer. After a moment she glanced up at his face.

"Okay," she prompted. "What did Detective Daley have to say?"

Ford took so long responding, she wasn't sure he would answer her question. Finally he said, "He wanted to talk about Marla. Some of her friends reported that she didn't like me and that there had been some kind of trouble between us."

"You said before that she wasn't your favorite student. I don't see how that has anything to do with finding who killed her." She leaned back to more comfortably watch his face. Sitting curled against his side with his arm around her had become one of her favorite places to be.

"There's more to my dislike of her than just her being a difficult student. Daley heard some lies Marla made up and wanted to hear my side. She made some serious charges to the school administration concerning my conduct toward her. Her midterm grade wasn't as high as she thought it should be, and she was worried she might be dropped from dance club. She asked to see me after class just a few days before she was killed. She hinted pretty broadly that if I didn't give her a better grade, she'd end my teaching career. Her friends knew we were alone, and she said that if I didn't change her grade, she'd tell the administration I'd made inappropriate advances toward her and her friends would back up her story."

Kira couldn't believe what she was hearing. "Surely no one would take her accusations seriously!" She'd only known Ford a few weeks, but she couldn't imagine anyone taking such a ridiculous charge seriously.

"That's what I thought, but now I'm not so sure. She pointed out that the courts and public opinion nearly always believe the child when a minor claims abuse." Deep lines appeared between his eyes as he explained the serious nature of his former student's charge and the damage it could do to his career.

Could a teenager really be that calculating?

"I dismissed her threat and refused to change her grade. She was crying and making a big scene when she left my class. The next day I had lunch with the school counselor. He mentioned she'd been in to see him. At first he seemed hesitant to talk about Marla's accusation, then he launched into a story about a wounded veteran who worked as a playground supervisor at the elementary school Marla had attended. She'd accused him of slapping her. Her little circle of friends supported her story, and the fact that no one else saw this supposed incident was deemed irrelevant by the school detective, who never got around to investigating her story for almost a month. A few kids saw Marla kick his cane one day, causing him to fall, and he may have bumped her as he fell, but the jury seemed to think that if he needed a cane, he shouldn't have been a playground supervisor. Without a shred of evidence, they found him guilty of class B child abuse."

"Do you think he was comparing that man's experience to Marla's accusations about you?"

"Yes, I think he was giving me the same warning as Marla's threat. Any time a kid makes an accusation against an adult, whether there's evidence of wrongdoing or not, the adult loses."

"Isn't that a cynical view?"

"Yes, it is, but it's also realistic. I spent some time before coming over here tonight Googling and found some gloomy statistics. Terrible things happen to too many children—child abuse is at an all-time high—but when a case is ambiguous and there is no proof to support the claim, juries nearly always find in favor of the child's claim. Children are notorious for making up stories, telling lies to get their way or to get out of trouble, yet when set before a jury, every word they say is accepted as truth." She'd found Ford to be an optimistic, easy person to be with, but now he sounded pessimistic and depressed.

"I've heard of women getting a divorce and wanting sole custody of their children making up stories of sexual abuse and even getting their children to lie about their fathers, but do you think children really invent abuse stories on their own and get away with it?" She couldn't believe a child would do such a thing, but was she just conditioned to believe children were innocent and naive about sexual matters in spite of the steady barrage of explicit TV, Internet, and movies they watch in today's world? Was a modern child really incapable of lying about abuse? The idea was troubling.

"I'm a teacher," Ford went on. "I chose teaching as a career because I like kids. Growing up with four younger siblings and more than a dozen younger cousins made teaching a natural choice. I had great youth leaders and teachers as I grew up as well, but I always knew some of my friends weren't as fortunate. I served a mission for the Church in a large Eastern metropolitan area, where many young people didn't have the opportunities or relationships I had. Too many didn't even know who their fathers were. I felt like I made a difference for some of them, but I soon learned that lying came as naturally as breathing to many of them. Either that or they'd learned it as a survival skill."

"Did Detective Daley accuse you . . ." She couldn't say it. It was unthinkable.

"No, he didn't come right out and accuse me of anything, but he made it clear I'm on their suspect list."

CHAPTER SIX

SLEEP DIDN'T COME EASILY THAT night. Kira tossed and turned and wondered if she could be wrong about Ford. She went over and over in her mind everything she knew about him. He'd arrived within moments after she'd started to scream. She wasn't naive enough to believe that just because a man was attractive and she liked him, he couldn't be capable of doing something terrible. But something deep inside her insisted Ford would never hurt a woman and certainly not one of his students. It would be difficult to refute a dead girl's charge, but somehow she must help him do just that.

The problem was how could she help him? She didn't know anyone who attended Murray High School, where Ford taught. He'd implied he was active in the Church, but she didn't know anyone other than him in his ward. She didn't even know his family. When it came right down to it, she knew little of his background, and they had no acquaintances in common. Still, something deep inside her assured her she hadn't misjudged him.

The next morning she continued wondering how she could help as she fastened her running shoes. She opted to run in her neighborhood since Ford had decided on an early start to grading finals so he'd be free to see her that evening. Four blocks from her condo, she passed an elementary school, and something clicked in her mind. The news article she'd read about the murder had mentioned the victim had attended this elementary school. It wasn't in the Murray School District, which surprised her and left her wondering if the girl might have once lived in the neighborhood.

Thinking of Marla living and attending a school so close gave Kira a creepy feeling.

If the girl had gone to school here, she and her family must have lived nearby. Her family might still live in the area, but something didn't add up. Murray High School was in a different school district than this elementary school. She'd heard some of the women in Relief Society mention that their area was in Granite School District. *If Marla Hayden went to elementary school here, why did she attend high school in a different district?*

Kira continued to run, but her thoughts returned to the school, and she remembered Ford speaking of his conversation with the school counselor. The elementary school in her neighborhood was likely where the events with the military veteran occurred. That event happened three or four years ago; could it possibly have a bearing on the murder? It didn't seem likely but also seemed the only direction she could explore. Was there a chance she could find that man? The story of the veteran continued to trouble her all morning as she vacuumed her apartment and washed a couple loads of laundry.

Seeing a neighbor planting petunias shortly after lunch inspired Kira to dress up her own small patio. She hesitated, considering how long it would take Jasper to trample and destroy any tender little flowers during his frequent visits. Earlier she'd planted a border of petunias around her patio. They hadn't survived Jasper's first visit. Perhaps some of those big ceramic pots would keep the plants safe. It was worth a try. Grabbing her purse, she made a quick trip to a nearby nursery for a couple of ceramic pots and a hanging basket.

As she approached the checkout counter with her purchases, she recognized the man behind the counter as a customer she often saw at the credit union.

"Hello, Mr. Andrews!" She smiled as she began unloading the plants from her cart onto the counter.

"Why, Miss Paxton! Nice to see you." He rang up the plants then reached into her cart to scan the two heavy porcelain pots so she wouldn't have to lift them out.

"It's good to see you again too. I decided it was time to do something with my patio. Do you think these pots will keep my brother's dog from tramping on the flowers I set out?"

The elderly nurseryman chuckled. "It would take a high-stepping tramp to trash anything in those pots. The daisies you picked out will look lovely in them. You'll need to water them every day and add a little fertilizer now and then." He busied himself ringing up plants, potting soil, and the hanging basket. Then he looked around as though assuring himself no other customers were waiting. He spoke in a sad, softer voice. "I'm sorry you had to be the one to find the Hayden girl. That must have been quite a shock."

She felt another moment's irritation that the television station had released her name as the person who had discovered the body. "It wasn't a pleasant experience," she acknowledged.

The old man shook his head. "I wasn't surprised to hear something bad happened to Marla. She ran with a rough crowd." His frank statement took her by surprise. She hadn't considered that if Marla had gone to school in her neighborhood, other people nearby might know her and her family. It occurred to her that they also might know the veteran accused of striking her. Perhaps Mr. Andrews could give her a lead on finding the man.

"How well did you know Marla Hayden?" Kira wondered if this might be exactly the opportunity she'd been looking for to learn who might have disliked Marla enough to kill her or if she should just ignore the man's obvious invitation to gossip.

Mr. Andrews lowered his voice again. "She grew up on the street I live on. I've known the family since her mother's fourth or fifth marriage. She got to keep the house after her last divorce. When she married again, her new husband moved into the house with her. He seems okay, not too friendly and kind of quiet, but he's stuck around longer than her other husbands." Mr. Andrews fussed with her purchases then, apparently making up his mind to confide in her, resumed talking about his former neighbor. "Nita's last marriage seemed to work out okay, but she had just the one baby, Marla. Not like her sister, who lives near here too. She has half a dozen young ones, and I don't think she married any of their fathers." He shook his head as though something displeased him. "That oldest one, Luis, is something else, but he and Marla were close as two peas in a pod and always in some kind of mischief. They scribbled dirty words all over my fence a few years back. I saw them, but when I reported it to the police, her mother swore they were both at her house watching TV that night, so nothing was done."

"Do you have any idea who might have killed her?"

Mr. Andrews glanced from side to side again and lowered his voice further. Perhaps she was being too direct. "I think it was that cousin of hers. He's a big shot in one of those gangs, and he was mean even when he was a little kid. Once he threw a couple of baby chicks that a little neighbor girl got for Easter into the canal and laughed when she cried and screamed. She would have gone in after them if her mother hadn't grabbed her in time. I told the detective to check on Luis, but I don't think he believed me."

"Why not?" The cousin sounded like a strong suspect to Kira.

"He hasn't been arrested. I saw his jacked-up truck parked in the Haydens' driveway last night." That answered her question whether Marla's family lived in her neighborhood.

"That doesn't mean they aren't investigating him." Kira wanted to believe the police had more and firmer suspects than Ford. She couldn't think of a subtle way to ask him about the veteran, so she plunged in with a direct question. "Someone told me she had trouble a few years ago with a playground supervisor at the elementary school. You wouldn't happen to know his name, would you?"

"Sad business that was." He shook his head as though commiserating with someone. "It wasn't right he was treated like that. Young Warren fella got messed up right bad in that war over in Iraq. He spent a coupla years at Walter Reed Hospital; then he moved here with his wife and little boy. Couldn't do regular work anymore and walked with a cane. The school asked him to help out supervising the playground during recess. David caught Marla and her friends breaking some playground rule, and she claimed he hit her. She made a big production out of it though there wasn't a mark on her. Her teacher tried to protect the school and her job, so she went along with it. My grandson said she kicked his cane and he fell, but that lazy school detective wasn't interested in anything my grandson had to say. He wasn't sure if David bumped her as he fell, or if she made the whole thing up. She always was a liar and a bully, bad as Luis."

"Excuse me. Do you have any flowering crab trees?" The large woman who stood at the end of the counter spoke in an angry voice. Kira hadn't noticed that she and Mr. Andrews were no longer alone.

"Yes ma'am." Mr. Andrews became all business. "Good talking to you, Miss Paxton. You won't need to worry about that dog anymore." He dismissed Kira as he turned to help the waiting customer.

Kira hesitated a moment then reached in her purse for one of her business cards. She hastily scribbled on it and set it on the counter. "Call me if you remember anything else."

Trundling her cart to her car, she took her time loading her purchases into the trunk. The pots were heavy, and she didn't want to risk breaking any of them. As she worked, Mr. Andrews's words kept repeating in her head. The police were looking into the cousin's possible involvement in Marla's death. Could it be the police were closer to solving this crime than she'd previously thought? And now the story the school counselor told about Marla and a playground supervisor had been confirmed. She even had the veteran's name. She couldn't wait to tell Ford what she'd learned. Her hands began to move faster as she transferred her purchases to her car. She slammed the trunk closed and hurried to return the cart to the store. After sliding the cart into place, she practically ran back to her car. She'd call Ford as soon as she reached home.

Arriving at her condo, it didn't take long to unload the plants from her car. The pots could wait. As soon as she finished moving the plants to a shady spot on her tiny patio, she stopped to call Ford. When he didn't answer, she sent a quick text. *Heard something interesting today. Can't wait to tell you.*

By the time she finished planting her pots and had hauled a ladder from the garage to hammer in a hook for the hanging basket, she had only enough time for a quick shower and to dress before her date with Ford.

Ford arrived promptly at seven. He looked tired, and worry lines showed at the corners of his eyes. She wondered if it might be better to stay at her condo and watch a movie than to go out, but when she suggested it, Ford insisted he really wanted to hear the band playing at the park that night. "An old friend plays the drums for the group, and I promised I'd be there."

"In that case we'd better go." She locked the door and pushed the key into the small change pocket of her jeans.

As they drove toward the center of the city, Kira related all she'd learned that day, and they discussed the possibility of a gang connection to Marla's death.

"Mr. Andrews, the man I talked to, suggested her cousin may have killed her," Kira concluded.

"If she and her cousin were close, it's possible she was shot by a rival gang, especially if she was affiliated with a gang too," Ford added another possibility. "I'll pass this information on to Detective Daley."

When they reached the downtown park where the concert series was being held, Ford pulled a small cooler and a blanket from behind his seat, then took her hand to walk across the grass. They circled dozens of blankets until they found a spot where they could spread their blanket on the grass near a large tree. Once they were seated, Ford opened the cooler and handed her a sub sandwich and a bag of chips. She noticed most of the occupants of the other blankets were also enjoying picnics from coolers or sharing buckets of chicken.

The music had started when Ford drew her back against his chest and wrapped his arms around her. The night was clear and warm. A feeling of peace filled her heart. Through the canopy of overhead trees, Kira caught a glimpse of a single star, and she wished this happiness, this man could be hers forever.

CHAPTER SEVEN

KIRA SNUGGLED CLOSER TO FORD with her head resting against his shoulder. She was glad his truck had a bench seat. Sitting close seemed like a continuation of sitting on the blanket in the park listening to his friend's band. She'd never attended a concert in the park before and had been pleasantly surprised that the large crowd was generally well behaved. A few people had even brought small children. It was like a big picnic, and she'd enjoyed the music.

"Uh-oh!" Ford squared his shoulders, and she could feel his muscles tense. She lifted her head to see they'd entered her street. Parked in front of her condo, with red-and-blue revolving lights, sat a police cruiser. Almost simultaneously she noticed glaring streaks of black paint on her garage door.

As Ford pulled into her driveway, she fumbled for the door handle.

"Just a minute." He reached for her arm to stop her from bolting out the door. "Let's check this out together. There could be danger."

She knew he was right, but seeing ugly graffiti on her garage door made her angry. She wanted to find the jerks who defaced her property and . . . She couldn't think of anything terrible enough. Ford pulled her closer, and together they slid out his door. Before they could take a step, a light shone in their eyes.

"Miss Paxton? Kira Paxton?" A voice came from behind the light. She lifted her arm to shield her eyes, and immediately the light was lowered. With the light no longer blinding her, she realized a police officer was addressing her. She nodded her head and gave him a stammered affirmative. He asked to see ID, and she fumbled in her purse for her wallet. Ford reached for his as well.

"What's going on?" Ford asked when the officer turned to him.

"You are . . ?" the officer asked. Ford gave his name and provided his driver's license to verify his identity. The officer looked it over then handed it back.

"We got a call a short time ago from one of your neighbors, followed by a report of breaking and entering from your security company. I responded at once to a reported crime in progress and I was less than a mile away, but I was unable to catch the vandal. I spotted a figure running across your backyard, but I was too late to apprehend him. Your neighbor said she heard glass breaking and looked out. She felt certain there was only one person involved."

"He was in my house?"

"I don't know if he actually got inside or not. There's a broken window in back. You might want to check to see if anything else was broken or stolen." Another police car pulled into her driveway, and two more officers stepped out.

Kira hurried toward her front door, freeing her key from her pocket with her fingers as she ran. She unlocked the door, but before she could open it, one of the officers barred her way.

"Just in case there is a second person, let me go in first," he ordered. "I'll let you know when it's safe for you to enter." The other two officers hurried around the side of the house toward the backyard.

Standing on the doorstep, she could feel herself begin to shake. *How did this happen?* She'd never had any trouble before, and the homeowners association had always been security conscious. Ford put his arm around her, offering his support. It was only a few minutes before the officer who had entered the house returned.

"The house is empty. There's no sign of anyone hiding. Be careful where you step; there's glass all over the floor," the officer warned them. He waved the strong light he held, indicating they could enter, and they stepped inside Kira's front room. She flipped on the light switch then stared in dismay at the sight of shattered glass glittering like spilled sugar across both her living room and kitchen floors. Even her upturned sofa and armchair sparkled as light found tiny bits of imbedded glass. Graffiti marred the side of her refrigerator then ended abruptly as though the vandal had been interrupted. A slight breeze rattled her ripped blinds, revealing a gaping hole in the large picture window that overlooked her backyard and the wooded area behind the condo.

After a quick check, Kira concluded that nothing obvious was missing, but she felt sick over the terrible mess. The two main rooms seemed to bear the brunt of the damage, while the bedrooms and bathroom appeared untouched. The officer speculated that the neighbor's call and the quick arrival of the police had interrupted the burglar before he could cause further damage or take items he might have otherwise stolen. She followed the officer outside to find that her new ceramic pots had been smashed, the hanging basket ripped from its hook. The plants she'd purchased had been thrown against the side of the house. Dirt and broken daisies littered her patio. Black paint had been sprayed and drizzled across her grill and patio set. She felt like crying, but anger froze her tears.

"No other houses in this complex were vandalized," the first officer commented. "This seems kind of personal. Have you had words or a disagreement with anyone recently?"

"No, I get along with all of my neighbors. Mrs. Gleason, next door, was nervous of my brother's dog when I took care of him a few weeks ago and accused him of chasing her cat, but she knew I wasn't happy about caring for the dog and that it was a temporary situation."

"I doubt she would have called us if she'd had anything to do with this." The officer dismissed Mrs. Gleason as a suspect. "She sounded concerned for your safety. Can you think of anyone else who might have a grudge against you?" the officer continued his questions.

Kira shook her head. She got along well with most people. Well, she did fight with Tracy quite a bit, but that was because he was overly protective and because he often needed a sitter for Jasper.

"This couldn't have anything to do with Kira discovering Marla Hayden's body a few weeks ago, could it?" Ford, too, seemed to be searching for an explanation for the attack on Kira's home.

"That was you?" The officer appeared startled.

"Yes, but I don't see how there could be any connection." Kira didn't know why Ford had even mentioned the discovery of the body. "I didn't see anything, and I didn't know the girl or anyone connected to the case. Whoever killed her would have no reason to come after me."

"Just the same, I think it would be a good idea for you to stay somewhere else until this mess can be cleaned up and your windows repaired." The officer made the suggestion sound like an order.

"He's right," Ford backed him up. "With that broken window it isn't safe for you to stay here tonight."

"I can always stay at my dad's place." She sighed, feeling discouraged. After all the battles she'd fought with her family for independence, she had no choice now other than to do as they'd wanted all along. "He never wanted me to move out in the first place, and between him and my brother, I'll have a difficult time leaving there again."

"I'll need an address and a phone number where you can be reached." The officer pulled a small notebook from his pocket, and she quickly rattled off her father's address.

As soon as the police officers left, Mrs. Gleason, who lived in the adjoining condo, tapped on her door. "Oh, my dear, are you okay?" She hugged Kira, and Kira had to swallow several times before she could speak. At times like this she missed her mother intensely, and Mrs. Gleason's motherly efforts to offer solace meant a great deal to Kira.

"Thanks so much for calling the police. Your quick action probably saved me from far worse damage."

"I called the homeowners association. They should be here soon with plywood to cover that window. I don't suppose anyone from the insurance company will get here until Monday."

"Pack what you'll need for a few days and anything of value," Ford advised. "I'll follow you to your father's house to make sure you get there safely. You can put anything that won't fit in your car in my truck."

"The biggest items I have are my TV and my computer. They aren't too big to fit in my car. I can't believe someone broke in and didn't take either of them." She shook her head, still unable to fathom why such a thing had happened to her and dreading the call she'd have to make to let her dad know she was on her way to his place.

An hour later she closed the trunk of her car and walked back inside to examine the window that Ford and a man sent by the HOA had covered with plywood. She looked around, and her shoulders sagged. Would she be back? She'd struggled with her family over leaving home in the first place. Dad and Tracy would do everything they could think of to keep her from leaving again. She'd have to make it clear this was only a temporary change of address.

"Don't forget this." Mrs. Gleason held out the shoe box that had rested undisturbed throughout the evening on Kira's coffee table. On seeing the box that held her new slippers, she couldn't help wondering—if Jasper had been there when the vandal invaded her home, would the dog have attacked him? With her luck Jasper would have licked the intruder's face and helped him rampage through her house.

CHAPTER EIGHT

"Because I live there! That condo is my home now." She was wasting her breath, and she knew it. Both Dad and Tracy were determined she should stay in the large family home near Sugar House, where she'd grown up. She continued packing her suitcases. A week had passed since the graffiti and window-breaking spree had chased her from her home, and though she'd enjoyed many things about the time with her father, it was no longer home in the same way her tiny condo had become. She was anxious to return to her own space.

"There's no reason to take chances." Her dad spoke in that I'm-trying-to-be-reasonable-and-think-you-should-be-too voice that drove her crazy. "There's plenty of room here, and you're in no danger of some crazy gangbanger breaking in. You're loved and secure here. And think how much you could save by not making house payments or buying groceries."

Kira shook her head but didn't speak. They'd been over the same points so many times she couldn't count them anymore. For a short time having someone else do the cooking and cleaning, leaving her free of responsibility, was like a vacation, but in the long run it left her feeling like a child. In the week she'd been at her dad's place, she'd been late for work three times due to heavy, cross-valley traffic; she'd been stuck caring for Jasper four days; and she'd been able to run with Ford just one morning. That run had only been a few laps around nearby Sugar House Park. She'd faced her dad's head-shaking inquisition each time she was late returning from work because of her visits to her condo where she stopped each evening to check on the progress being made there. Besides, Tracy insisted that Jasper should have the free run of the house in order to deter any would-be burglars, and she was down to one pair of shoes she could wear to the office. After he'd chewed up the second pair of shoes, she'd resorted to stowing her shoes in a top drawer instead of the closet, which Jasper had long ago learned to open. She certainly didn't dare slip off her shoes when she curled up in an armchair to read or watch television.

She picked up her suitcase and set it on the floor. When she reached for the strap to pull it toward the stairs, her father took it from her hand and spoke again. "I think you're making a big mistake."

"Dad, can't you see?" She was almost in tears. "I love you, and I have happy memories of growing up here, but I'm twenty-four years old. I need to be independent. I need my own space. I'm no longer a little girl. Yes, some scary things have happened lately—finding that body and having my home vandalized—but whether you think so or not, those things could happen anywhere."

"If you'd just take Jasper with . . ."

"No way! Anyway, it was Jasper, not me, that found that body." She reached for her smaller bag. Looking defeated, her father helped her carry her things to her car. He checked her engine and reminded her to visit the dealership where she'd purchased the car to have the oil changed.

Ten minutes later her rearview mirror still showed her father standing on the front porch watching her drive away. She hated feeling guilty because he was lonely. She wished he'd make a greater effort to maintain a social life outside of his work. His brother lived halfway around the world with a wife and two children, Tracy was seldom home, and with Kira gone from home too, he really needed something besides work to fill his time. As a teenager she'd pitied a friend who lived with her father and a stepmother. Now she wished her father had found someone else to fill his life.

She hadn't seen Ford as much the past week as she would have liked, but they'd talked on the phone every day. High school graduation was scheduled for tonight, so soon there would be less demand on his time. She was looking forward to spending more time with him, even though she knew he would begin teaching a couple summer school classes in two weeks. A smile chased away the melancholy remaining from her parting with her father when she saw Ford's truck parked in front of her house. He greeted her with a kiss that wiped away her remaining gloomy thoughts, and he wasted no time helping her carry her bags into the house.

Kira wandered about inspecting the repairs made to her living room. New carpet and drapes had been installed, and she'd paid an additional amount to upgrade her windows to ones that were shatterproof. She hoped she'd made the right decision on the carpet. Hardwood floors seemed to be the in thing, but she hated stepping on bare floors in the winter, even with central heating. There was just something warm and comforting about bare toes on a deep-pile carpet, and she liked the way the dark-brown leather of the sofa and love seat contrasted with the lighter tan carpet.

"Come here." Ford seated himself and patted the puffy leather cushion of her new sofa. Smiling, she joined him, and he placed an arm around her shoulders, drawing her closer. "I can't stay long," he whispered. "I just had to assure myself you were back and that you're okay. I missed you."

"It was as difficult as I expected to leave my dad," she confided. "He tried every argument he could think of to persuade me to move back in. He's always had an exaggerated protective streak toward me. If I didn't love him and know he really is concerned for me, it would be easier to refuse him, but disappointing him makes me feel guilty even though I know the time has come for me to live my own life. I'm afraid he'll always think I'm his baby and he should continue to take care of me."

"I've heard most fathers feel that way about their daughters."

"I think if Mom were still alive, she would have helped him ease into letting me grow up. They used to talk about going on a mission together or traveling after their family was raised. He often said he would turn the company over to Tracy so he could retire early and see the world with Mom. Because of his job, he's always traveled a lot, but Mom wasn't often able to accompany him. There are places all over the world he wanted to show her." She felt a lingering sadness for her parents' dreams that would never come true.

"I've always thought serving a senior mission with my wife would be a terrific way to start my retirement years." The look Ford gave her seemed to imply more than his words and brought a warm flush to her skin.

"You're kind of young to be talking about retirement." Kira giggled and cuddled closer, thankful he'd lightened her mood.

"Hey! I believe in planning ahead." He tickled her side, and when she squirmed away, he followed, sending teasing kisses up her neck. Delicious shivers raced up her spine. They laughed like playful children. Then their laughter stopped, and for one long, heart-stopping moment, they simply stared at each other. Ford made the first move, and a sigh surfaced from deep in Kira's throat as his lips claimed hers in a sensual, shattering kiss. One hand swept up her back and cradled the back of her neck. With the other hand he pulled her closer. His heart beat an erratic rhythm next to hers. Heat exploded like fire through her entire body, making coherent thought impossible. Her hands roamed his back, tugging him closer.

When he at last pulled back, Kira stifled the automatic protest that trembled on her lips. His hands brushed up and down her arms several times, and she sensed he was as stunned as she felt. He swallowed several times before whispering, "It's a good thing I have to leave, though I don't want to."

She nodded her head in agreement though a part of her didn't agree at all. She was glad he shared her views on no intimacy outside of marriage, but she'd never realized keeping those standards could be so hard. Struggling to change the direction of her thoughts and cool her emotions, she asked, "Would you like something to drink before you go?"

"That would be great." She suspected he was as anxious as she to slow their explosive reaction to being together after seeing so little of each other over the past week. Struggling to keep her legs and hands from shaking as she moved unsteadily toward the kitchen taxed her self-control. Not wanting to risk spilling the soft drinks she'd placed in the fridge more than a week ago, she carried two unopened cans back to the sofa where Ford waited. She handed him one, and instead of resuming her seat beside him, she sat on the loveseat that formed an *L* with the sofa, their knees not quite touching.

Quietly sipping her drink, she tried to appear calm and relaxed, but when her eyes met Ford's she understood the message there. Their relationship had just passed some silent milepost. It wasn't the strong physical pull between them that made the difference. It was more a sense of belonging, a cord of commitment that stretched between them. She wasn't ready to explore the direction her thoughts were taking her and was grateful when Ford turned her thoughts back to the damage to her home.

"Have you heard any more about who vandalized your condo?" He didn't remark on her choice of seats or the fire that had exploded between them.

"No. It doesn't make sense that anyone would target me, but the HOA feels certain someone went to a lot of effort to bypass security and specifically choose my home to vandalize. They're considering putting up a fence between our backyards and the grove of trees that separate the complex from the canal."

"That might improve the security a great deal. It could be a safety feature too for any of the families on this side of the road who have children."

"I know, but I enjoy the feeling of almost living in the woods. I often run on the canal road. It's not much more than a dirt trail, but it's a handy place to run."

Ford stood, then paused before stepping toward the door. "I had another meeting with Detective Daley earlier today. I asked him if he thought there was any connection between the vandalism and Marla's murder. He suggested it was more likely gang related because of the signs that were part of the graffiti on your garage door. He said they might have gotten the wrong address and thought a rival gang member lived here. He said there have been some serious confrontations over the past few months between Luis Vincent's gang and another local gang."

Kira also rose to her feet. "I can't stop feeling like whoever did it intended to scare *me* specifically. What I don't understand is *why*? Remember, I met a neighbor of Marla's family last week. Mr. Andrews said Marla was close to her cousin Luis, but even so, why would he target me when all I did was stumble on her body? Somebody else killed her several hours earlier."

"I don't know. I don't understand how kids who join gangs think." He sounded frustrated. "I've read up on it because I work with teenagers, so I know that some kids join because they need that sense of family they get from being part of a group, some join for protection, and some are angry and gangs give them an outlet for violence. But gang mentality is complicated and not easily explained." He walked across the room to stand in front of the new window, staring into the trees at the back of her tiny yard. His fingers played with the cord that opened and closed the deep maroon drapes.

Ford appeared uneasy. He might be worried about her, but she feared something more troubled him. "Why did Detective Daley talk to you again? He doesn't still think you had anything to do with Marla's death, does he?"

"I'm not sure. He didn't really accuse me. I suspect the police are still exploring every possibility, and I'm just one of multiple persons who may have had a reason to dislike Marla."

"I can't help thinking that for some twisted reason the person who killed that girl is behind the attack on my house. I hope Detective Daley is looking into that possibility." Her voice shook. *How could anyone think Ford might do something so awful?* That someone could consider Ford a suspect aroused a spurt of anger when she was already feeling emotionally off balance.

Ford reached for her trembling hand. Probably mistaking anger for fear, he said, "Maybe you should have stayed at your dad's house. If someone is targeting you, you'd be safe there."

She couldn't believe he said that. She pulled her hand away from his and took a few steps back. "You sound like my dad! I'm perfectly safe here, and the homeowners association assured me they've arranged with the security company to patrol more frequently. You know how much more convenient to my work I am here. I thought you'd be happy I'm back closer to you and to places where we can run together."

He returned to her side and put an arm around her waist, drawing her close. "I'm sorry. I really do like having you back closer.

It isn't just fathers and brothers who have an ingrained protective streak when it comes to the women we care about." His head bent toward hers, but before their lips touched, he leaped toward the back door, sending her staggering back. "There's someone out there hiding in the trees!"

Ford tore out the back door and disappeared into the trees. Kira followed him to the edge of the lawn. With her nerves on edge, she peered into the wooded area and listened intently for sounds of movement. All was quiet.

Twenty minutes passed, and she became more worried that Ford would miss graduation than over the possibility that someone was hiding in the trees. She should have warned him that walkers and runners sometimes strayed from the canal road into the trees.

She'd just made up her mind to lock up the house and go look for him when Ford emerged from the trees, looking disheveled.

"He's gone. I heard a vehicle take off fast, but I wasn't close enough to identify it or the driver."

"It was probably just a runner who stopped to take a break in the trees." She attempted to downplay his concern. "You'll have to hurry now to be on time for the graduation ceremony."

"I don't know . . . Maybe I should skip—"

"Don't even think it. You need to be at the ceremony, and I'll stay inside unpacking. I'm sure there's nothing to worry about." She wished she felt as certain there was nothing to worry about as she attempted to convince Ford.

CHAPTER NINE

SHE SUPPOSED SHE'D NEVER KNOW whether Ford really saw someone hiding in the trees. He'd searched a considerable distance but found no one. It could have been children from the nearby subdivision playing there. It wouldn't be the first time one had climbed over the block wall that surrounded the development and crossed the canal to play in the trees. The vehicle Ford heard might not have had any connection to the figure he saw. Occasionally an animal found its way into the grove of trees as well. In the two years she'd lived in her home she'd caught glimpses of several stray dogs, a raccoon, and more geese than she could count in the trees. Whatever he'd seen had served to make her leery of spending time in her backyard, and she'd had shutters installed over her new window.

Switching on her turn signal, she watched for an opening in oncoming traffic then pulled into the parking lot surrounding the Fashion Place Mall. The lot was a sea of cars. It was evident she wasn't the only one who had decided to spend Saturday afternoon shopping. Once parked in one of the few open parking spots, she took a deep breath and reached for her purse. It was much too large to lug around the mall, but she hadn't wanted to take the time to switch purses so she was stuck with it.

She really wasn't in the mood to shop for shoes, but she didn't have much choice. She'd put it off too long. Unlike some of her friends who liked nothing better than shopping for shoes, to her it was a chore—one she had to endure far too frequently thanks to Jasper. She wasn't sure how he did it, but he seemed to have a sixth sense for shoes, and no matter where she hid her footwear, the dog found them and used them as chew toys. Currently she was down to one decent pair of shoes she could wear with a suit and the dated pair of sandals she'd worn to church last Sunday. On her feet were her only running shoes. If only she could convince Tracy to leave the dog home when he dropped by or at least convince him to find another babysitter for the beast when he had to go out of town. Tracy was good about footing the bill for the shoes his dog ruined, but she hated sacrificing the time shoe shopping required and she didn't always share Jasper's escapades with her brother.

Two hours later she shifted six shoe boxes to the trunk of her car and slammed the lid closed. "I wonder how long these will last!" she grumbled as she moved to the side of her car and reached in her purse for her keys. Thinking a few words she'd never say aloud, she dug to the bottom. As she pulled the keys free, a credit card she'd dropped loose into her purse after her last painful purchase slipped to the pavement. Stooping to pick it up, she heard something swoosh over her head followed by the sound of shattering glass. Too shocked to stand, she watched as the driver side window of her car crumbled to tiny bits of shattered glass that rained down on her. Unable to move, she crouched beside her Jetta wondering what had happened. She had no idea how long she'd remained in the cramped position when she heard someone speak.

"Lady, are you hurt?" She looked up to see a boy standing near the front of her car. He looked to be about seven or eight years old. When she lifted her head, he took an uncertain step toward her.

"Look out for the broken glass," she warned. It took a surprising amount of effort to stand.

"Braxton, I told you not to get so far ahead." A woman with red bouncing curls, who didn't appear to be much older than Kira, hurried toward the boy. She was pushing a stroller that held an infant and a toddler. Clinging to her pant leg was a little girl with fiery-red pigtails, who had to run to keep up. The woman stopped abruptly when she saw Kira then noticed the shattered glass on the ground. "What happened? Are you hurt?"

"I-I'm not sure. Uh-h, no, I'm not hurt." Her voice sounded strange to her own ears. "I was about to get in my car when I dropped something. I bent down to pick it up, and I'm not sure if

I heard something or felt it pass over my head. Then the window shattered." She could feel the sharp edges of the plastic card she still gripped in her hand.

"You better call your insurance company. Here, use my phone." The woman plunged a hand into a voluminous diaper bag and produced a cell phone, which she held out to Kira. Kira couldn't help marveling that the woman could unerringly produce what she sought in that bag on her first try.

"I'm okay. Really. And I have my insurance company's number in my phone." Kira reached into her own purse and fumbled for her phone. A vigorous search at last produced the phone. She held it up as though announcing victory.

"Well, okay. If you're all right, we'll be on our way." The redhead took a few steps then turned back to add, "I'll stop by the security office to report this. I don't suppose there's anything they can do, but your insurance company might want a report for their records."

"Thank you," Kira called after the woman. Just mentioning insurance added to her gloom.

She stared at her phone for several minutes. She really didn't want to make this call. With trembling fingers she dialed her father since a division of his company handled her insurance.

Speaking to her father was as difficult as expected. Every word he said sounded like *I told you so*. Knowing he wouldn't send someone but would come himself, she made one more call. She needed moral support. The phone rang twice, and Ford answered. In a shaking voice she explained what had happened.

"You're not injured?"

"I'm fine. Just a little rattled," she assured him.

"My apartment is only a few blocks from the mall. I'll be right there." He hung up, and she clicked End.

Mall security arrived first. There were two men dressed in simple tan uniforms who pulled up beside her car in a golf cart–like vehicle with the name of the mall blazoned on the door. An older officer who appeared to enjoy his dinner breaks a little too much asked questions while the younger one opened the Jetta's door and checked inside. Kira had just finished telling all she knew of the incident to the mall security man, who seemed determined to capture each word she spoke in his notebook, when Ford arrived. He immediately wrapped his arms around her and held her while she fought the urge to cry.

"Are you all right?" He stroked her back, and she reveled in the warmth that spread through every part of her. A low whistle reminded her they had an audience and that she had resolved to be strong. She backed up a step and sniffed back the tears that threatened. Ford kept an arm about her shoulders.

"Look at this!" The younger officer who had crawled inside her car pointed to something Kira couldn't see, but his reaction convinced her it wasn't good.

The other officer leaned in as far as his girth and his fellow officer's presence would allow. She couldn't quite hear their animated conversation, but whatever was happening she felt certain meant more trouble.

"You better leave it," the older mall cop advised as he backed out of the narrow space. "It looks like we turn this one over to Murray's finest." He was punching in numbers on his phone as he spoke.

Kira craned her neck trying to see what they had found that warranted calling the police. They were both standing between her and her car, and unless she asked them to move, she couldn't see what they'd found. She wasn't certain whether it was being reluctant to interrupt their whispered conversation or that she didn't want to walk through shattered glass that kept her silent. Perhaps she just didn't want to leave the shelter of Ford's arms.

Detective Daley along with three other officers and Kira's father arrived at about the same time moments later. Kira straightened, putting some space between her and Ford. She wasn't going to let the detective see her fall apart again; neither was she going to let a rock tossed through her car window drive her back to living in her dad's house. She knew before he said a word that would be his solution to any problem.

"Sweetheart, don't worry about a thing. I'll take care of it." Garrett Paxton leaned over to kiss his daughter's cheek. "We can deal with a broken window as long as you're safe. Go wait in my car."

Daley merely raised an eyebrow and nodded his head in a brief acknowledgment of recognition when he saw her, or maybe it was Ford he recognized.

The first words out of the security guard's mouth as he greeted the detective almost buckled her resolve to be strong. "Looks like a bullet lodged in her dashboard, Daley." He hitched up his tool belt with his forearms. "Kids these days have no idea how much trouble they can get in for firing random shots. With the number of shoppers here today, this could have been a real tragedy." Daley merely grunted and began issuing orders to the uniformed officers who accompanied him.

One of them snapped several photos of the car. He leaned inside and took a couple more of the interior. Garrett peered over his shoulder and made a few suggestions. The officer dutifully produced a notebook and jotted down several notes.

"Okay, that's enough." Daley sounded frustrated. "The tow truck is on its way."

"Tow truck? I don't think that will be necessary for a broken window." Kira's father took a step toward the detective. "I'll call my mechanic to have someone drive the car back to his garage to have the window replaced. After Kira's doctor checks to be sure she isn't in shock, I'll take her home."

Now Kira was fuming. She had no intention of allowing her father to take her to a doctor. She hadn't been hurt, and she resented the way her father assumed decision-making authority over her and her car.

"Forensics will need to dig that bullet out to determine what kind of gun it came from. They'll need the car for a few days." Daley turned his back on Garrett as though to dismiss him and spoke to Kira. "I assume one of these gentlemen can give you a ride to my office. You'll need to fill out a report, then we'll talk about why trouble seems to follow you around."

CHAPTER TEN

SHE WANTED TO BE ALONE. Neither Ford nor her father had left her side since they had arrived at the mall. She felt smothered. Worse yet, Tracy had shown up and promised to empty her trunk and take her packages into safekeeping for her. Once Jasper got a whiff of those packages, she'd be back shoe shopping! She hoped Tracy would heed her warning to keep them in his trunk until he could deliver the packages to her house tomorrow morning. She was grateful he'd also offered her his car to get back and forth to work.

She had to believe there was a connection between the attacks on her and the body she found, but why? It made no sense that the murderer would want to punish her for finding the body where it had washed up, but what else was she to think? Actually she didn't find Marla; Jasper did, and no one was running around attacking Tracy's dog. Now she was being ridiculous.

She was tired, angry, and confused—and without her car for who knew how long. Being without her car had been the major factor that impelled her to agree to Tracy's deal. She'd use his car for the next week while both he and Dad were out of town. In exchange for her brother's generosity, she was stuck with Jasper. She sighed, anticipating almost another full week of Jasper's presence again.

Ford hadn't said anything since she'd refused her dad's offer to drive her home and climbed into Ford's truck instead, but she hadn't missed the look the two men had exchanged. She glanced at Ford's firmly set jaw. She wanted Ford and her dad to like each other, but she didn't want them to become allies. She didn't need one more man in her life who saw her as a helpless baby. Instead of feeling sorry for herself, she needed to put all the pieces together, be more observant, and find out as much as possible about each of the troubling incidents she'd experienced in the past few weeks. Talking to Ford might help her think through all that had happened and help her formulate a plan to learn more.

"Do you think Detective Daley is right that there's no connection between the shot today, the break-in, and Marla Hayden's murder?" She began with the thoughts circulating in her mind.

"Everything he said could be right, but my gut doesn't believe it." There was a hint of frustration in his voice. "Sure the attack on your house could be completely random. The bullet could be a stray fired by some irresponsible gun owner. It's even possible, but unlikely, there's a serial shooter out there who just happened to hit Marla and almost hit you. I believe there's some kind of weird connection; I just don't know what it is."

She was glad he thought there was a tie-in too. She'd begun to worry he might think her as incapable of rational thought as her father and the detective both seemed to. Even she had begun to question whether she might be going crazy.

"I can't help feeling they're connected, but why would someone target me?" She voiced her inability to make sense of the seemingly random crimes.

"At least Daley promised to check out the gang angle. He said they'd already looked at that cousin of Marla's, Luis Vincent, and he is a leader of a group the Unified Metro Gang Unit is keeping an eye on. But Marla attended a school dance the night she was killed, and neither he nor any of his gang members were there, according to her friends and the dance chaperones. Besides, both her friends and their parents insist the two were almost inseparable and there's no way he'd kill her."

"You mentioned once that she had a boyfriend. Is he a possible suspect?"

"The police seem to consider everyone a suspect at this point, but Daley said they checked him out. He said the boy is quiet, a nice kid, and that his mother wasn't too thrilled that he was dating

Marla. She said Marla often made fun of him and said mean things to him. Marla encouraged him to be more like her cousin, whom she admired. Her girlfriends said she often called him names both to his face and behind his back. He wasn't in any of my classes, so I don't know him well. My impression of him is he's shy and was a little too quick to do whatever Marla told him to do. Her girlfriends said Marla attended the dance with them that night. She didn't have a date, which reinforces Aaron's mother's claim that he was studying and watching television at home the night Marla was killed."

Ford drove his truck into her driveway. She looked around and breathed a sigh of relief, seeing no graffiti. It was impossible to not wonder if she'd ever again be able to arrive home without fearing she'd be greeted by painted slogans and damage to her property.

Instead of getting out of his truck to open her door as he always did, Ford sat still. His only movement was to pick up her hand. He acted hesitant to speak. "Kira, I know your independence is important to you, but if there's any possibility that shot was meant for you specifically, it might be best to do as your father asked and stay at his house for a while."

She shook her head in refusal without verbally saying no to his advice. She couldn't go back to her childhood home, and she didn't know how to explain her refusal to do so to Ford. She was scared, but to give in to that fear could mean she'd never have the courage to leave again and she couldn't go through life being nothing more than Garrett Paxton's little girl. She couldn't let the frightening things that had happened cripple her ability to think and act for herself. She'd fought too hard for her independence to throw it aside now.

"I know you and Dad are concerned for my safety, and I appreciate that concern, but I can't do it." She spoke carefully. She didn't want to argue with Ford. "I can't go back to living under Daddy's thumb. I know he means well, but ever since Mother died, he's done everything for me—or hired someone else to do it. Even this past week, he had his housekeeper sleep at the house instead of going home each night; he had a security firm drive by every hour. He even arranged a doctor's appointment for me—which I cancelled."

She'd never doubted her father's love for her, but his hovering parenting style had left her feeling like a prisoner. Not once had he allowed her to sleep over at a friend's house while she was growing up. He'd refused to permit her to attend summer camp, even with her church group, or to date before she turned eighteen. She could have told Ford of her father's refusal to allow her to attend public school, that he'd accompanied her or sent the housekeeper or Tracy with her when she'd shopped, and if she sneezed he rushed her to a doctor. He'd opposed Kira's desire to attend BYU in Provo, though it was only forty-five miles away, after refusing to consider the out-of-state school that had been her first choice, so she'd attended nearby Westminster College instead. Ford had the distinction of being the first boyfriend her father and brothers hadn't chased away—yet.

"Come inside," she invited. "I'll fix dinner and try to explain."

As Kira mixed a batch of muffins and prepared vegetables for a stir-fry, she shut thoughts of the disturbing events out of her mind. With Ford tucking a towel in his waistband and endeavoring to help in her tiny kitchen, they found plenty to sidetrack their thoughts. It was only later, when they sat on the patio as dusk turned to darkness, that her thoughts returned to their earlier conversation. Gathering her years of frustration into words, she explained that she'd been pampered and cared for all her life but allowed few choices. It had taken a major tantrum and all of the courage she could muster to move out of the family home, accept a job offer, and begin a life of her own after her college graduation. Resorting to sneaking away while her father and brother were at work had been her only recourse for finding a job and purchasing her tiny condo.

"At some point everyone needs to grow up," she explained. "I need to make my own choices, whether I choose right or wrong. I can't spend my life feeling like a doll being manipulated by some-one else."

"I understand your need for independence. I'm a firm believer that this life is our time to prove ourselves, and we can't do that if our lives are rigidly controlled by some person or force other than ourselves. At the same time you need to realistically examine whether or not you're safe here by yourself." His words were reassuring, giving her a sense that he understood. Still his frequent glances toward the trees told her he wasn't convinced that the figure he'd seen the previous evening was harmless or that she could protect herself if the intruder returned. The gunshot added another level of tension.

"The homeowners association installed dead bolts on my doors, and my new window is shatterproof," she reminded him. "If there's even a hint of trouble, I won't hesitate to call the police."

"Instead of running alone or meeting me somewhere to run in the mornings, I could pick you up until this is resolved," he offered. "Would you feel okay with that?" His hand gripped hers, conveying a sense that he was concerned for her safety but wouldn't overstep her boundaries.

"Tracy is bringing over Jasper in the morning. He's going to be out of town again most of this coming week. Me agreeing to keep Jasper was the only way he'd agree to loan me his car, and since bus service isn't conveniently located near here, I need a car."

"That's okay. Jasper can run with us." He leaned back in his chair without releasing her hand. There was something soothing about sitting in the dark beside Ford, watching the moon rise and a smattering of stars prick the darkness above the mountains. The weight of worry that had rested on her shoulders for what seemed a long time now slipped away.

The night brought a cool breeze, and she felt herself begin to unwind. She'd be okay. Thinking a rock had struck her car was bad enough, but learning that a bullet had narrowly missed her had turned her emotions into a turmoil. A niggling fear crept into her thoughts, overriding the peaceful night. *After Ford leaves and I'm alone, will all my brave words mean anything? Will I be able to sleep, or will I lie awake all night cringing at every sound?*

CHAPTER ELEVEN

FORD DIDN'T LIKE LEAVING KIRA alone, but it was a little after eleven, and she needed some sleep. He was well aware that sometimes an emotional upheaval could tire a person as much or more than a physical workout, and she'd had a rough day. He sensed it wouldn't be a good idea to mention they might both sleep better if he took her to her father's house. He understood her need to escape her father's smothering control, but he shared the older man's concern for Kira's safety. That bullet today was a little too coincidental.

She accompanied him to the door and snuggled into his arms like a sleepy kitten when he kissed her good-night. She was a perfect fit, and he'd have liked to keep her there all night. He loved the way she felt in his arms, the smell of her shampoo, the easy way they could talk about anything together. He was beginning to suspect he loved everything about her. He hadn't known her long enough to be contemplating a future together, yet more and more his thoughts were turning in that direction.

Forcing himself to pull away, he reminded her he'd pick her and Jasper up for their run in the morning. What he really wanted to do was stay. It was with great reluctance that he opened the door and stepped outside. He'd had a number of girlfriends, but never one that affected him the way Kira did. He hadn't imagined marrying any of them. He paused beside her closed door until he heard the click of the dead bolt before walking to his truck. Before climbing inside, he scanned up and down the street. All appeared quiet.

Half a block away he noticed a white Audi parked against the curb. He couldn't be sure, but there seemed to be a single occupant inside. A vague memory of seeing the same car earlier came to mind and filled him with a niggling concern. He might have only imagined someone in the trees the previous night and he might be blowing the incident at the mall out of proportion, but he wouldn't get any sleep all night if his thoughts were centered on someone possibly watching Kira's house, waiting to catch her alone. He debated with himself for another block and then pulled his truck to the side of the street.

From where he sat, he could see the white car, but he couldn't be certain if it was occupied. He needed to get closer, but if someone was watching Kira's house, he didn't want to reveal his own presence. Reaching up he loosened the small overhead cab light then opened his door just far enough to allow him to slip out. Keeping the truck between himself and the Audi, he crouched low until he reached the deep shadow of a tree in the median strip. Sticking to pools of darkness beneath trees and behind shrubs, he worked his way toward his target. His spy tactics left him feeling a little silly, but he reasoned he'd rather risk looking foolish than regret an attack on Kira he might have prevented.

Only three houses separated him from the Audi when head-lights warned of a car moving slowly down the street toward him. Scrunching deeper into the hedge where he hid, he waited. The rough edges of clipped branches scratched his face and arms. Something tickled the side of his face, and he hoped it was only a leaf. The oncoming car slowed even more as it passed the white car. Ford held his breath, but the car continued on its way.

When the car was out of sight, Ford moved out of the thick shrubs far enough to have a better view of the Audi. His suspicions were confirmed when he spotted the dark shape of a head rising from where the occupant had ducked to avoid the scrutiny of whoever was in the car that had passed. It was too dark to make out features, but Ford could read the license plate number and memorize it. He'd see if Detective Daley would run a check on it tomorrow.

Resigning himself to getting little sleep that night, he began working his way back to his truck. He'd keep an eye on the Audi, but unless the person inside it got out or drove toward Kira's house, he'd just watch. It wouldn't be a smart move to confront the person unless he made a move toward Kira.

By the time Ford made his way back to his truck, thirty minutes had passed since bidding Kira good night. Was doing nothing the best way to deal with a possible threat? He considered calling to warn her, but what could he say? Yes, the car was suspicious, but he had no way of knowing if the person in the car was watching her. Was there another explanation for a guy sitting in a car alone in the middle of the night?

He had Detective Daley's card, and the officer had practically ordered him and Kira to call if either noticed anything out of the ordinary. He reached for the card.

* * *

Kira stood at her darkened bedroom window. She was tired, but no matter how hard she tried, she couldn't fall asleep. The street was quiet; not even a stray cat wandered into sight. A quarter moon drifted behind wispy clouds, casting strange shadows up and down the street. A car drifted down the street, and she wondered if it was just her imagination or if it moved more slowly as it passed her house. She reminded herself the HOA had promised to patrol the street at night.

This is ridiculous! she scolded herself. *I can't stay up all night worrying about what might happen.* Turning her back on the window, she marched to her bed. Before climbing between the sheets, she knelt. She'd learned as a small child that prayer could calm her fears and help her face the unknown.

Praying did help. When she finished she felt calmer. She climbed into bed and closed her eyes. Sleep came almost at once.

* * *

Ford rolled down his driver side window and leaned forward to speak with the officer who pulled up beside him in a well-marked Unified police car. He'd noticed the police car stop beside the white car a short time ago, then had watched as the Audi pulled away. If the police weren't concerned, perhaps he shouldn't be either. He'd been reaching to start his truck when the officer pulled up beside him.

"Did that guy in the Audi check out?" he asked before the patrolman could voice his own question.

Without responding to the question, the officer asked to see his driver's license. Ford had it ready and handed it through the window. He'd expected he'd need to prove his own identity. Handing it back to him with a brief smile, the officer instructed him to follow him to the homeowners association clubhouse.

It seemed like an odd request. It was after midnight, and if the guy in the parked car had a legitimate reason to be sitting in his car in the middle of the night, then Ford would like to return to his own apartment and get some sleep. He wondered what reason the man had given the officer. Had he come home late or drunk and his wife locked him out of the house?

Ford parked his truck next to the patrol car and was surprised when the officer signaled for him to get out instead of coming to the window again. He'd taken two steps from his truck when he noticed the white Audi parked a short distance away. Warily he watched the driver slide out of the car and step toward them. When he got closer, Ford could see the other man was only a few years older than himself. They were also of a comparable height and weight, though the other man's hair was several shades lighter than his own. The other man was dressed in sweats and a polo shirt that shouted comfort over style, an outfit that suggested the man had expected a long night in his car.

"Gentlemen," the officer addressed them both. "I think you two should meet. Dispatch got calls from the both of you within minutes reporting the other for suspicious loitering. Stan Martel." He turned to the man eyeing Ford in a suspicious manner. "Stan, this is Rutherford Kettering. According to Detective Daley, whom you both got out of bed tonight, Mr. Kettering has been dating Miss Paxton for a month or so. Mr. Kettering, Stan here is well known to the officers in this area. He's a security agent and private investigator currently employed by Garrett Paxton."

Ford hesitated a moment, then extended his hand.

A slow grin spread across the other man's face. "I'm glad to see you're taking Kira Paxton's safety seriously."

"I'll sleep better tonight knowing someone is keeping an eye on her. I should have guessed Paxton wouldn't go away quietly when his daughter demanded she be left alone."

"He's a little paranoid when it comes to his only daughter," the investigator conceded. "I'll admit I was skeptical when he first asked me to watch her. It's not the first time he's hired me to check on her safety, but after learning someone vandalized her home and took a shot at her, I decided to assign myself to her case. I or one of my employees will be keeping an eye on her house every night until the threat ends."

"She may not be too pleased to learn her father has hired you to watch her." Ford suspected she'd object strenuously. On the other hand, he'd sleep better.

"She has a legitimate complaint about the high-handed treatment she gets from Tracy and Garrett. They've walked over her wishes so often, I'm afraid she'll put herself at risk before accepting their help when she needs it." Stan turned away, and Ford watched as he opened his car door, started the engine, and turned back toward Kira's street.

CHAPTER TWELVE

KIRA STRETCHED HER LEGS, DETERMINED not to slow Ford down. She knew his long legs could easily outpace her much shorter ones and that he deliberately ran slower when they ran together to stay abreast of her. She couldn't help noticing that he seemed preoccupied. Usually they talked while they ran, but he'd said little this morning. Guilt raised its head. He may not have slept any better than she did. Her stubborn refusal to spend the night at her dad's house may have cost him a good night's sleep.

She'd gotten a lecture about her selfish attitude from Tracy this morning when he dropped off his dog and his car. He assured her both he and their father would be distracted worrying about her while they were on their respective business trips. Her eyes traveled to Jasper, and she felt a small measure of exasperation. The lab was running smoothly at Ford's heels, never fighting the leash or attempting to stray from the path. He never behaved that well for her.

Ford kept glancing sidewise at her. She smiled, encouraging him to say whatever was on his mind. They were facing a long straight stretch of the trail. He took a deep breath and began. "Uh, there's something I think I need to tell you." Ford hesitated, and she felt a stab of concern. Whatever he was going to say couldn't be good with that kind of beginning. She hoped he wasn't going to say he didn't want to see her anymore or that he'd met someone else. He wouldn't try to guilt her into moving back in with Dad and Tracy, would he? She tried to appear calm as she waited for him to continue.

"Last night after I left your house, I noticed a white Audi with a single person inside parked down the street about half a block from your house."

A chill raced up her spine.

He continued. "I contacted the police and, in an embarrassing turn of events, discovered the person in the car is a security agent hired by your father."

"What!" She stopped in the middle of the trail. "Daddy hired a security agent to spy on me?" Ford nearly tripped over Jasper as he too came to an abrupt stop. He reached out his hand as though he wished to comfort her. She ignored the gesture.

"I doubt your father thinks of it as spying. You said he was protective. I think it's just his way of making certain you're safe, especially while he's away, but he certainly should have told you."

Ford flashed her a rueful smile and attempted to make light of his encounter with the security agent. "A heads-up also would have saved me from an embarrassing encounter with Stan Martel."

Her shoulders sagged. "Why can't he trust me to look after myself?"

"Probably for the same reason I didn't want to tell you. He knew it would upset you. I debated whether or not I should say anything, but I had to tell you before you discovered for yourself that someone is watching your house. I've been worried you would fear the worst if that happened. I didn't want you to be frightened like that if you caught sight of some stranger hanging around your place. The cop who checked him out introduced us. He's a pretty nice guy, and I think you can just ignore him."

Kira sighed and began to move forward again. She had mixed feelings about Ford's revelation. It was true she'd get more sleep knowing no one could sneak into her house, but she couldn't help resenting her father for hiring someone and saying nothing about it.

Soon they both resumed their former pace. Several times she caught Ford stealing quick glances at her, but he didn't speak. He probably thought she was sulking. She wasn't happy about the situation, but she was trying to be fair. This wasn't an ordinary situation like the other times she'd objected to her father's meddling. She admitted that both her father and Ford had grounds for concern. As hard as it was to admit, whatever was happening was beyond what she could handle by herself. She mulled over in her mind all that Ford had said, and as her burst of anger cooled, it left her wondering if Ford had been hinting that she was reacting childishly to her father's concern for her safety. She knew her father loved her and that it was hard for him to let her go. She'd even concede that she needed to have more patience with him, but she wouldn't give up her hard-earned independence even if the present situation meant accepting his security agent.

"I appreciate his concern. I really do." She broke the silence, knowing Ford would know to whom she referred. "But I don't believe I'm in any real danger, and I've taken appropriate precautions with securing my home. The homeowners association and the sheriff's department are both patrolling my area more frequently. Since school let out, I haven't run alone. Nevertheless I won't make a fuss about Daddy hiring someone to watch my house."

A large tree with heavy branches cast a shadow across the path. Ford placed an arm around her shoulders and pulled her off the trail into the deep shade. He held her close for a long time. Then cupping her face with his hands and looking deeply into her eyes, he said, "I'm glad you've decided not to fight your dad on this point. I care an awful lot about you and couldn't bear to lose you. I understand your need to live your own life, a life I'm hoping will include me in the future. Sometimes risks go beyond what one person, even the strongest person, can handle. If you ever feel something isn't right or suspect you're in danger, promise you'll call me?"

She nodded. Just before his lips met hers, she wondered why Ford's strong protective instincts didn't annoy her the way her father's and brother's did.

* * *

FORD FELT AT LOOSE ENDS. With school out, he'd have time to collect his brothers and take that backpack trip they'd talked about into the Big Horns. He knew he only had to pick up the phone and his brothers would start packing. Instead he sprawled on the couch after showering and stared at the television without turning it on. Running his fingers through his still-wet hair, he admitted he didn't want to leave town. He wanted to be close enough to see Kira every day. The presence of the security agent provided some assurance she was safe, but he still felt reluctant to be more than a few minutes away from her. He marveled at how quickly she'd become an integral part of his life.

After he'd returned her and Jasper to her condo that morning, he'd driven around trying to make sense of the death of a young girl and two attacks on the woman he was becoming more and more attached to. It was hard to see what connection there could be to the events, but some impulse told him there was a connection. He'd driven past the elementary school that Kira had discovered was the scene of the story about the man who had been the victim of Marla's lies four years ago. He wondered if the man still lived in the neighborhood. He didn't know whether Marla's family still lived in the area. Had the family moved into Murray High School's district, or was she a transfer student? He thought about checking on that.

Opening his laptop, he searched for any David Warren within a half-mile radius of the elementary school. He found plenty of Warrens but no David Warren anywhere near that location. There were at least a dozen listings for that name throughout the state, but he wasn't certain how to go about narrowing down the list, short of calling each one. Giving up on the computer search, he decided to go to the nursery where Kira had met the man who'd told her about the veteran. The longtime neighbor of Marla's family might know more than he'd shared with Kira. Besides, it might be nice to replace the ceramic pots and flowers the vandal had destroyed.

He took a moment to hang up his towel and finish dressing before leaving his apartment. Traffic was light, and it didn't take long to reach the nursery located a short distance from Kira's condo. He wished she were with him instead of at work that morning. She hadn't been enthused about going to work and had been worried about leaving Jasper alone in her house all day. He should have volunteered to keep Jasper for her. That would have saved her concern about the damage the dog might do shut up in a small space all day. On the other hand, the dog might discourage another break-in.

Flashing red lights caught his attention as he slowed to pull into the parking area in front of the strip mall where the flower shop and greenhouses were located. He watched as a gurney was loaded onto an ambulance and a woman was helped into the ambulance and buckled into a jump seat beside the gurney. Another woman, who looked like she might be close to retirement age, was speaking animatedly to a pair of police officers, and a small crowd had gathered near the door to the nursery.

Ford found a parking spot a short distance away from the activity taking place near the front door. He shifted into park and shut off the engine but continued to watch as the ambulance slowly pulled away. The siren began its shrill scream just before merging with traffic on the busy street.

He sat a few minutes longer, debating whether or not to go inside in search of Mr. Andrews or to leave. If there had been an accident or someone was ill, Mr. Andrews might not want to chat, he reasoned. Eventually he climbed out of his truck but continued to hesitate until the woman who had been talking to the police officers hurried in his direction. Her keys were in her hand, and she pressed a button to unlock the doors of the van he'd parked beside.

"What happened? Did someone get hurt?" Ford took advantage of her proximity to enquire. He didn't have a good feeling about what he'd seen.

The woman looked up, and he could see traces of tears on her face. She wiped at her eyes before speaking. "It's Mr. Andrews. Someone attacked him and beat him severely. The police don't know yet when it happened; the shop was closed yesterday, and he's unconscious and can't tell them." She wiped at her eyes again. "Lucy Jackson found him this morning when she and her husband came in to open the shop. They've worked for Mr. Andrews for almost forty years, even when he had the old store. I just can't bear thinking of how long he might have lain there suffering." Her shoulders shook as she struggled to control the sobs that shook her entire body.

Feeling numb, Ford struggled to control his own shock. He extended his hand toward her then slowly withdrew it. The woman was a stranger and might not welcome his touch. He knew no way to comfort her. "Was it a burglary?"

She shook her head. "Lucy said she put the money in the office safe herself Saturday night, and it's still there. A few things are knocked over like there was a scuffle, but neither the Jacksons nor I noticed anything missing."

"You work here?"

"Yes, I've taken care of the books ever since Alice Andrews passed away back in eighty-eight." She glanced at her watch. "I'd better be going. I promised Lucy I'd meet her at the hospital and fill out the admission papers for Mr. Andrews. And I need to speak with his insurance company. The police are trying to locate his daughter to notify her, but she doesn't know anything about the business."

"Be careful," he admonished. "I'm not sure you should be driving when you're upset."

"I'll be fine." Her chin took on a firm posture as she ducked into her car and started the engine.

Ford climbed back in his truck and waited until the woman's car disappeared into traffic before backing out of his parking spot. He found a creeping sense of horror invading his thoughts. Was this another coincidence, or was this attack connected to the events surrounding Marla Hayden's death and the attacks on Kira?

* * *

At five o'clock Kira shut down her computer and cleared her desk. It took five minutes to reach home. Traffic was light, and for once the lights all seemed to cooperate. As she turned onto her street, she felt the same nervous tension she'd felt lately each time she returned home after being gone for a few hours, wondering if her house would be untouched by the vandals that had attacked it before. She breathed a sigh of relief that all looked as she'd left it that morning. The next challenge would be the inside of her house, where Jasper had been cooped up all day. Why couldn't Tracy see that the big dog would be happier in his own fenced backyard with the housekeeper or a neighbor checking on him? She wasn't sure someone who traveled as much as her brother did should even own a dog.

Stepping from the garage to the kitchen, she punched in the code to shut off the alarm before daring to look around. Jasper came galloping toward her with bits of white speckling his face and clinging to his coat. With a sinking heart she peeked into the living room. Tiny flecks of foam were everywhere. They littered the carpet, clung to the drapes, and lay on every surface. Seeing what appeared to be several rags on the floor, she realized Jasper had demolished the decorative pillows from her sofa.

She sighed in frustration. Scolding the dog would do no good now; he'd have no idea why she was upset or what he'd done wrong. However, cleaning up the mess promised to be a major chore.

The dog raced toward the back door, warning her she'd better take him out or she'd have more to clean up than pillow filling. Once outside, Jasper did his business then leaped and raced around her tiny yard reveling in much needed freedom. Kira sank down in a lawn chair and watched the dog play. She was tired. She'd dealt with several complicated accounts that day, necessitating a shortened, rushed lunchtime. Besides, she hadn't slept well the previous night. She closed her eyes, wishing she could take a brief nap instead of going back inside to tackle cleaning up the mess Jasper had made.

The feeling of something vibrating in her pocket alerted her to an incoming call. She groped for her cell phone and mumbled hello without checking the caller ID.

"Kira? Are you all right?" She perked up at Ford's voice.

"Yes. I'm just tired."

"Rough day?"

"Kind of. I had a couple of complicated accounts to deal with, then came home to a big mess Jasper made." *Jasper!* She looked around frantically for the dog. "I've got to go. I can't see Jasper anywhere." She pushed End and shoved the phone back in her pocket.

"Jasper!" she called. There was no sign of him in the neighboring yards, so she headed for the trees and nearby canal calling his name. Like most Labradors, Jasper loved water and never missed a chance to go for a swim. The canal wasn't large, but she knew from previous experience that it drew Jasper like a magnet. She shoved tree branches out of her way, ignoring the havoc to her suit and shoes. At last she reached the canal bank and looked both ways. There was no sign of the big black lab.

Heading north, she hurried as fast as she could, wishing she'd taken time to change her shoes. Strappy sandals with two-inch heels were both chic and comfortable for work but not so great for following the narrow dirt and gravel trail that paralleled the canal.

Wondering if she'd chosen the wrong direction for her search, she turned back, rushing toward the bridge that spanned the canal to the south, where cars rushed by on the busy highway. She was almost to the bridge when she heard both splashing and wild barking. Trying to move faster, she brought her foot down in a small hole, sending her sprawling in the dirt.

Kira lay stunned for several seconds before trying to pull herself upright. Her skirt hiked almost to her waist, making her glad no one was around to see her. She struggled to stand and was dismayed to see dirt clinging to her skirt and that the seam from under her arm to the hem of her jacket was ripped. Once on her feet, she noticed blood dripping from one knee and the heel missing from one of her shoes. The roar of traffic on the bridge had grown louder, and she could still hear a dog barking. She had to get to Jasper before he ran into traffic. Pulling both shoes off, she hurried on in spite of her tender, scraped knee and the rocks that gouged her feet.

Rounding a corner, she spotted a dark head in the water. Jasper! He seemed perfectly happy swimming about in circles, splashing with abandon, and snapping at bits of debris floating in the water. After being confined to her tiny house all day, he hadn't been able to resist the urge for a cool dip, but how was she going to get him out of the water and persuade him to return to her house?

She edged as close to the water as she dared, feeling the grass and marshy edges of the canal bank through her tattered stockings.

"Jasper! Come here, boy," she called. The dog made no indication he'd heard her. As she stared at the water wondering what to do, another head popped up closer to shore. This one didn't belong to a dog but to a man. She couldn't see any indication he was in danger of drowning. And since he didn't seem to be in trouble, she hung back watching as he grasped a handful of grass and reeds, near where she stood, to pull himself from the water.

"Are you all right?" She hesitated to offer him a hand to assist him in climbing out of the water. He was a stranger, and enough scary incidents in the past month had made her wary of strangers.

He stumbled to his feet and shook his head, much like she'd seen Jasper do, sending water flying in every direction from his slightly longish hair and saturated clothing.

"I'm fine." He sounded angry. After looking around as though searching for something, he walked a few steps away then sat down to pull on a pair of shoes Kira hadn't noticed earlier. Since he'd removed his shoes before jumping in the canal, it clearly wasn't an accident he was in the water.

Why he'd jumped in the canal fully clothed wasn't her concern; coaxing Jasper back to shore and getting him back to her house was. She took a step closer to the canal.

"Jasper!" she shouted.

He barked and lunged as though playing a game and inviting her to join him. She'd had enough of his disobedience. Her suit and shoes were ruined; she was tired, and she had three pillows worth of foam shreds to clean up. This nonsense had to stop!

"Jasper! Come here this minute!" She wanted no more of the dog's nonsense. To her surprise, the dog swam toward her and crawled from the water like a naughty child who knew he was in trouble. He stood with his head hanging down and his tail between his legs for just a moment, then gave a mighty shake, showering her with dirty canal water.

"Oh!" It came out like a startled scream.

"He won't hurt you. I've had plenty of experience with this dog, and I can assure you he can be a pain in the b—uh, neck, but he doesn't bite."

Kira whirled about to face the man she'd seen in the water. "You know Jasper?"

"Oh, no." He looked mortified. "You're Kira Paxton." It wasn't a question. "I didn't recognize you at first since I've only seen a picture of you."

"Why have you seen my picture?" Kira took a step closer to Jasper and found herself teetering on the edge of the canal bank.

"Look out!" The stranger reached out a hand to steady her. Regaining her balance, she glared at him until he withdrew his hand.

"We've gotten off to a bad start," he apologized. "I'm supposed to be watching you and keeping you safe from the person who's behind the recent attacks on you and your home." He held out his hand again. "I'm Stan Martel."

"The PI Daddy hired," she finished the introduction in a flat voice.

CHAPTER THIRTEEN

"I don't need a babysitter!" Kira spit out the words as she reached for Jasper's collar, determined to put as much distance as possible between her and this man. She began walking back the way she'd come as fast as her shoeless feet would allow. Jasper was unusually cooperative about staying beside her. One look at the dog sniffing her shoes explained everything. Actually she was surprised to find she still held her broken shoes in one hand.

"Your father warned me you'd try to fire me." Stan grinned as he caught up to her and kept pace with her angry steps. She wanted to hit him. Instead she attempted to ignore him. It was probably his fault Jasper took off and ended up in the canal. No, to be fair, Jasper didn't need any encouragement to run off or jump in the canal.

When they reached her condo, he asked if he might borrow a towel. She was tempted to refuse, but she really had no cause to be mean to him. She supposed he was just doing his job, and since both her dad and the police trusted him, it wouldn't hurt to loan him a towel.

"Wait here." She indicated her kitchen. Without waiting for a response, she hurried across her living room to the tiny hall that led to her bedroom and bathroom. Returning with a couple of thick towels in hand, she found Stan leaning against the bar that separated the kitchen from the living room surveying the bits of foam covering every surface.

He whistled. "Courtesy of Jasper, I assume?"

She nodded once and handed him a towel. He immediately began wiping down his face and scrubbing at his hair. She stooped to towel off Jasper, fearing that if she didn't, he'd jump on her new furniture, leaving it wet and muddy. Her kitchen floor already bore evidence of three sets of muddy footprints—four, if she counted all of Jasper's paws.

"How do you know Jasper?" Curiosity got the best of her, and she had to ask.

"Tracy and I go back a long way. We met in college, and when he's in town, we play handball, tennis, or hike together. Jasper usually accompanies your brother wherever he goes on weekends."

Just her luck! Her babysitter was none other than a close friend of Tracy's. She'd heard Tracy talk about his friend, Stan, but she hadn't connected him with the PI Ford told her he'd met the previous night.

"I think you're making matters worse." Kira looked at Stan critically. "You've smeared mud all over you instead of wiping it off. Here!" She took the towel from him and wiped at his face and arms.

"Why were you in the water?" she asked as she scrubbed at his mud-soaked shirt. What he needed was a shower! "Surely you weren't attempting to rescue a Labrador retriever."

Stan looked sheepish. "I wasn't exactly trying to rescue him, but I knew he was staying with you and it appeared he'd gotten loose. I tried to coax him to shore, but he wouldn't come. I should have known he wouldn't pay any attention to anything I said to him. I was afraid he'd go under the bridge into a faster current and be swept too far away to find his way back to your place, so I planned to wade out to where I could grab his collar then take him back where he belonged. Unfortunately the water is deeper than I'd thought, and Jasper had moved farther from shore." His voice held an apologetic note.

"Don't tell me you just happened to be walking by when you spotted Jasper in the canal!" She scrubbed a little harder than necessary at a streak across the PI's cheek.

"Uh . . . no." He took the towel from her hand. "Your boyfriend spotted my stakeout last night, so I thought it would be best to park farther away and hike up the canal path to keep watch tonight. I planned to be in place before you returned from work."

She made a disgusted sound. "I don't want someone watching my house or spying on me. Wait a minute!" She remembered the figure Ford thought he saw hiding in the trees a couple of nights ago. "How long have you been spying on me? Were you hiding in the trees behind my house Sunday night?"

"Your dad hired me the day you left his house to come back here, and yes, that over-zealous boyfriend of yours almost caught me that night. But I'm not spying on you. You've had your house vandalized and someone took a shot at you. I'm just trying to keep you safe. That's all your family wants."

"Sure, that's why no one bothered to tell me you'd be hanging around."

"You didn't seem surprised when I told you my name."

"No thanks to my dad or brother. Ford told me about meeting you last night." She picked up the towel she'd used on both Jasper and Stan before pointing down the hall. "The bathroom is down there. It's going to take soap and clean water to get that muck out of your hair."

* * *

Ford tapped a finger against the side of his phone. *She should be answering her phone by now unless something serious has happened to Jasper. It's been almost an hour since she went looking for that dog.* He'd been trying to reach Kira for the last half hour. *Of course, she might have stopped to talk to a neighbor or had some errand to run, but what if someone took Jasper or he was injured?* He paced as far as the window that overlooked the park and gazed across the broad expanse of lawn. *She could have accidentally turned her phone off or dropped it while searching.*

The attack on Mr. Andrews had left him feeling jittery all day. He couldn't just sit by, waiting and hoping all was well. Making up his mind, he checked to make sure he had his wallet and keys, then rushed down the stairs to his truck. In less than ten minutes, he pulled onto the street leading to Kira's condo.

He surveyed the area and saw nothing amiss, but he couldn't dismiss the uneasy feeling in his stomach. In moments he was pressing the doorbell and heard Jasper bark, but no one came to the door. He pressed the doorbell again. This time he heard a male voice order Jasper to be quiet, increasing his sense of unease. Kira's father and Tracy were both out of town. He tried the knob, but the door was firmly locked. Forcing the door crossed his mind, but he knew breaking down a door wasn't as easy as it looked on TV. Before he could race around to the back, the front door was flung open, nearly jerking his arm out of its socket.

There, in Kira's front room, stood the security agent he'd met the previous night, looking like he'd just taken a dip in the pool, clothes and all. In addition to wet hair and damp clothes, his shirt was buttoned wrong. An almost irresistible urge to connect his fist with Stan Martel's jaw took all of his willpower to subdue. If he'd hurt Kira . . .

"Kira!" they both shouted. It sounded almost like a duet. Jasper came bounding toward them, leaping up to swipe his tongue across Ford's face. Behind the dog, the room was a disaster with bits of white fluff sticking to every surface and muddy tracks across the pale carpet.

"Sit!" Ford pointed at the floor. Jasper sat.

"How'd you do that?" Stan stared at the dog, now resting on his back haunches, his tongue lolling from one side of his mouth, and his eyes resting soulfully on Ford.

"I thought you were supposed to *watch* Kira's house, not make yourself at home in it! What happened here?" Ford wanted some answers. Stan looked far too comfortable in Kira's house. Before Stan could respond, Kira walked into the room.

"Ford! I didn't know you were coming over." She looked from Ford to Stan then back at Ford. She didn't meet his eyes, and he couldn't tell if she looked more embarrassed to be caught with another man or disturbed by Stan's presence.

* * *

"I guess you two already met." It was a dumb thing to say. She didn't know what was going on between the two men, but both were behaving a bit oddly. She couldn't help feeling awkward as well. It was bad enough having Stan see her in torn, dirty clothes and windblown hair earlier, but she hadn't anticipated having Ford find her barefoot with wet, uncombed hair and her house looking like a tornado had struck.

"Jasper escaped, and I was trying to help . . ." Stan's voice trailed off as though he realized no one was listening to him. Ford and Kira's attention was focused solely on each other.

"I was worried and decided to check . . ." Ford's explanation was left incomplete as well.

Kira didn't know what to say, but a sudden loud sneeze from the PI ended her dilemma. She turned to Stan. "You need a hot shower and to get into dry clothes. Perhaps you should go home."

"I can't. I contracted with Mr. Paxton to keep an eye on your house and make certain no one *questionable* can get close to you."

"I hope you don't consider me in that questionable category."

Kira detected an almost belligerent undertone in Ford's voice.

She decided to ignore the exchange. "Stan, you can't sit in your car all night in those wet clothes! Use my shower, and I'll throw your clothes in the dryer. If you need it, my robe is hanging behind the bathroom door."

"I'm not sure that's a good idea." Stan gave Ford a quick look.

"What if I take Kira out for something to eat while you shower and keep an eye on the house and Jasper?" Ford spoke to Stan, but she wasn't sure whether he was trying to be helpful or if he was amused by the prospect of Stan wearing her robe while his clothes dried. Whatever the case might be, she welcomed a chance to escape both Stan and Jasper.

* * *

Kira accepted the A&W root beer can Ford handed her and turned her attention from the view of a small mountain lake to the man seated across from her on a corner of a shabby quilt he'd pulled from a zipped plastic bag stashed behind the seat of his pickup.

She hadn't missed the tension between Ford and Stan when she returned from the tiny laundry and storage room in the basement, but she sensed Stan had nothing to do with whatever was bothering

Ford. In spite of their serene surroundings, Ford had something on his mind other than the PI. He held his sub sandwich in one hand but hadn't eaten much of it. He met her eyes and gave her a sheepish grin.

"Sorry," he murmured. "I'm not being moody; I just had a few things to think through. Seeing the condition of your living room and a disheveled man answer your door scared me into thinking something had happened to you. I think, too, I got bit by the green-eyed monster when I saw Martel answer your door as though he owned the place. It really was nice of him to agree to watch your house and Jasper so we could go out."

Kira laughed. "I'm not sure he was being as generous as he made it sound. He's being paid to sit in his car and watch my house all night, and the prospect of doing so in wet clothes wasn't something I think he looked forward to. By sending me off with a male protector for a few hours, he can shower and dry his clothes while still doing his guard thing. As for Jasper! That dog doesn't listen to him any more than he does to me. But I couldn't pass up his offer to clean up the mess Jasper made tearing my pillows apart."

"I'm still not sure I understand why he jumped into the canal after Jasper. If Jasper is anything like other dogs of his breed, he can swim circles around most people." He shook his head and took a large bite out of his sandwich. She was glad he'd suggested getting sandwiches and going up one of the canyons to eat instead of heading for a restaurant. They could talk without the distraction of other diners, and she loved watching the changing colors of the aspens as the wind stirred their silver-green leaves.

She passed on Stan's explanation. "I think he meant well and assumed that because the canal looks like an overgrown ditch, it would be shallow. He only planned to wade out far enough to grab Jasper's collar and return him to me. Slipping under the water was a surprise and coming up to find me searching for Jasper was another."

Ford moved closer and reached for her hand. "Jealousy wasn't the only reason I snapped at Stan. I was worried something might have happened to you or to your brother's dog."

"It's good to know I rate as high as Jasper on your worry scale." She couldn't resist pretending to pout. A giggle broke out. "Poor

Stan! I wasn't very nice to him when I discovered his identity, then you growled at him. To top it all off he's stuck babysitting Jasper and cleaning my front room!"

"Hmm. I'd say you rate much higher than Jasper." He bent forward to brush his lips across the ticklish spot just below her ear. She squirmed away then turned so that her lips met his, and a now-familiar warmth spread its way through her. Scrambling to keep her wits about her, she remembered his earlier call.

"I cut you off so quickly earlier when I realized Jasper had run off that I didn't find out what you were concerned about. You sounded a little upset."

He leaned back, taking a deep breath. "I was upset, and I still am. Over the weekend someone attacked that old man at the nursery, Mr. Andrews. His employees found him on the floor unconscious this morning and called an ambulance."

"Oh no, is he going to be all right? Did he see who hit him?"

"I don't know. Hospitals only give out information to family members. I spoke with his bookkeeper. She said they had no idea if he'd been lying there since sometime Sunday or if he'd gone in early this morning and been attacked when he opened the door. He was unconscious, so no one knows whether or not he can identify his attacker. She said Mr. Andrews never got around to installing a security camera."

Kira felt tears brimming in her eyes and wiped them with her fingers. Mr. Andrews was always kind and had an old-fashioned air of courtliness about him when he came into the credit union. He'd greeted her like an old friend and been concerned about her when she'd spoken with him a few days ago at the nursery. He lived alone and enjoyed visiting with his customers. An uneasy thought sent a shiver down her spine.

"You don't think he was attacked because he talked to me, do you?" Was she becoming paranoid? It was crazy to think the attack on Mr. Andrews had anything to do with her, wasn't it?

"I don't know, but there have been too many questionable attacks on or around you since you found Marla's body. I don't want to interfere with a police investigation, but perhaps we should see if we can find a connection or confirm there isn't one." Ford remembered his reason for looking up Mr. Andrews had been to see if he could find further information concerning Marla's cousin Luis.

"I've been thinking about tracking down that playground supervisor the school counselor told you about." Kira wiped at her eyes again. "That incident happened three or four years ago, but if he still lives in the area he might know something helpful. Mr. Andrews told me his name and I Googled it. I didn't find anyone with that name in my neighborhood, though I did find six David Warrens in the state."

Clearly they were thinking along the same lines. "That's a good place to start. We can check by telephone to see if any of them are the person we're looking for." It would be a big task, but Ford felt certain it was one they should undertake.

* * *

When they arrived back at Kira's condo, all was quiet. She didn't invite Ford in since she had to work the next day and the events of the day had left her feeling in need of a good night's rest. She was impressed with the thorough job Stan had done cleaning up her living room; even the bathroom had been left neat and orderly. Jasper's appearance suggested he'd been bathed and brushed as well. For just a moment she wondered where Stan was spending the night. She hadn't noticed a white Audi parked along the street when Ford brought her home. She hoped he wasn't spending the night crouched in the trees behind her condo.

She was too tired to wonder about Stan for long. She brushed her teeth and changed into pajamas before taking Jasper outside one last time. Keeping him on a leash while he did his business, she gave him no opportunity to run off.

Once Jasper was settled in the kitchen on the folded quilt she used for a doggie bed, she double-checked the locks and made certain the alarm was set before climbing into bed and switching off her bedside lamp. She lay for several minutes, staring into the darkness. Sleep didn't come as quickly as expected. If such a thing were possible, she suspected she was too tired to fall asleep. Perhaps if she read for a few minutes, her mind would unwind and she could sleep.

Switching her bedside light back on, she reached for her scriptures. It was as difficult getting into the story of Jared and his brother as it was to simply relax, but after a few minutes she felt her eyes closing. She closed the book and switched off the light once more. This time she drifted into much needed sleep.

Something woke her. She couldn't tell if she'd been asleep for two minutes or two hours, but the deep darkness of night still surrounded her.

Realizing her telephone was ringing, she fumbled on the nightstand until her hand brushed against it. Putting it to her ear, she mumbled, "Hello."

"Next time I won't miss," a voice hissed in her ear. "You're dead."

CHAPTER FOURTEEN

KIRA GASPED AND DROPPED THE phone. Some part of her consciousness heard it hit the floor, and for just a moment, she cringed back against her bed. It took only seconds until a spark of anger took over. She lunged for the switch to turn on the lamp. In the dim light she scrambled beneath her bed searching for her phone. When she found it, she gripped it with both hands and shouted, "Leave me alone! I'm calling the police!"

No sound came from the device. Either she'd cut the connection when she dropped the phone, or the caller had hung up after delivering his message. Kira hunched forward, cradling the small phone between her hands and tried to think. Her stomach cramped, and she feared she might be sick. What had she done to make someone hate her so much he wanted her dead?

Should she call the police? She doubted there was anything they could do. They'd probably dismiss the call as a prank. She started to punch in Ford's number, then stopped. "There isn't anything he can do either." It didn't seem right to disturb his sleep when there was nothing he could do.

She wondered if Stan might be close enough that she could attract his attention. He was supposed to be awake and watching her house. She had no way to signal him, and she wasn't about to set foot outside her door.

An ominous scratching at her bedroom door sent shivers up her spine. She held her breath as the door slowly swung open. Before she could scream, Jasper stuck his head through the opening. On seeing she was awake, he padded toward her and lay his head in her lap. For the first time in her life, she was glad to see him. She wrapped her arms around his neck and pressed her cheek against his shiny black head.

"Oh, Jasper, what should I do? I'm so scared."

The dog seemed to understand in some unexplainable way. He licked her arm and sidled closer. Tears spilled unchecked down her cheeks.

Jasper gave a soft woof and backed off a few steps. He cocked his head to one side before beginning the most mournful howl Kira had ever heard.

"Hush!" she whispered. "You'll wake up Mrs. Gleason." The dog continued to howl despite her efforts to shush him. "Please!" she begged to no avail. He stopped abruptly when the sound of someone hammering on her door reached her ears. He cocked his head to one side then tore from her bedroom to the front door barking exuberantly. Indecision kept her feet glued to the floor. Had the caller come to make good on his promise? Or was an irate neighbor complaining about her howling dog? She tiptoed into the living room and attempted to gather her courage enough to peek through the tiny viewing spot in her front door.

A hoarse whisper reached her ears. "Kira! Are you okay?"

"Stan!" She lunged for the door, fumbling with the security chain in her rush to open it. At last the lock was free. She jerked the door wide and threw herself into a startled security agent's arms.

"Uh, what happened?" He seemed unsure what to do with his hands. His awkwardness reminded Kira she was wearing only short, almost-sheer pajamas. She slowly backed away, crossing her arms across her body. "Come in," she stammered, continuing to retreat. Her face burned, and she knew it was flushed from embarrassment. She'd only met Stan a few hours ago, and here she was, practically naked, throwing herself in his arms. She looked longingly at an afghan draped over the arm of the sofa. "I'll be right back. There was a telephone call . . . I have to . . . uh . . . get a robe." She fled down the hall.

When she reached her bedroom, she rushed to her closet. No bathrobe. She remembered suggesting Stan use it earlier. He probably left it in the bathroom or downstairs in the laundry. She grabbed a pair of jeans and the first shirt she laid her hands on.

Returning to the front room, she found Stan seated on the edge of the recliner with Jasper sprawled at his feet. Determined to pretend she hadn't embarrassed them both, she squared her shoulders and moved forward. He jumped up when Kira walked in.

"I checked your doors and windows. Everything seems to be okay."

"It was a telephone call." She struggled to keep her composure. Just mentioning the call brought back the horror of that threatening voice. She took a deep breath before continuing. "He woke me out of a sound sleep."

"It's okay." Stan spoke in a soothing voice. "Tell me about it."

She struggled to keep her voice steady. "The caller said, 'Next time I won't miss. You're dead.' I dropped the phone, and I couldn't get Jasper to stop howling." Tears pricked her eyes again.

"It's okay." Stan attempted to console her. "Did you call the police?"

"No. What can they do?"

"Perhaps nothing, but there needs to be a record that a threat has been made. It might spur them to delve deeper into the shot that was fired at the mall and to run a background check on anyone you or even your father has had problems with."

"But that's just it. I haven't had a problem with anyone since Alice Brewster in the eighth grade." She reached for a tissue and found the box empty. Stan handed her a crumpled one he dug from his pocket. After wiping her eyes and blowing her nose, she sniffed a couple of times and straightened her shoulders. She had to stop falling apart. Where was the strong, independent woman she prided herself on being?

She only half listened while Stan placed a call to the Unified Police Department. An officer would be at her house to speak with her shortly, and Stan would stay close by through the remainder of the night. She heard him explain that he'd been hired by her father to keep an eye on her home from the time she got off work each afternoon until she left again in the mornings. He'd known something was wrong when her light came on at two o'clock in the morning and her dog began howling.

Something didn't make sense. Her only telephone was her cell phone. How did the caller get her number? Several people in her ward had it, as did her supervisor and some of her coworkers. Ford, Detective Daley, her dad, and Tracy. A sudden picture of scribbling the number on the card she left with Mr. Andrews came to mind. She felt confident he hadn't shared it with anyone, but if he'd left the card sitting on his counter or if his wallet had been stolen . . .

* * *

Ford arrived fifteen minutes early for their running date. The sun was just casting its first rays over the mountaintops. He knew something was wrong the moment he spotted an unfamiliar car parked in Kira's driveway. As he drew closer, he noticed the red-and-blue lights in the window. Parking quickly on the street, he jumped from his truck and hurried toward Kira's front door. Once again Stan answered the door when he pushed the doorbell.

Looking past Stan he saw Kira hunched on the edge of the love seat across from Detective Daley, who sat on the sofa beside his partner, Officer Chetfield. Chetfield was busy taking notes in his ever-ready notebook. Jasper sat at Kira's feet with his big head resting on her knee. She looked up and, seeing Ford, rose to her feet and hurried toward him. The dog followed, wagging his tail in a welcoming gesture. Almost of their own volition his arms circled her slender body, and he held her for several seconds before grasping her upper arms and looking into her face. She looked exhausted, and he could see she'd been crying.

"What's wrong? Did something happen?"

She nodded, taking several moments before speaking. "I got a threatening phone call in the middle of the night. Stan got worried because Jasper was howling, so he came to check on me and called the police. Some uniformed officers came, then Detectives Daley and Chetfield came a few minutes ago."

He acknowledged the two officers, who were both standing now. They motioned for him to be seated, and still supporting Kira with one arm, he made his way with her to the love seat across from the sofa where the two officers had resumed their seats. Stan laid claim to her recliner. As Ford looked at the grouping and studied the serious faces surrounding him, the inconsequential thought crossed his mind that it didn't look like he and Kira were going to enjoy their usual run that morning.

* * *

Thank goodness the weekend was finally here. Kira hadn't had a decent night's sleep since that awful phone call earlier in the week, though all had remained quiet since then. She'd worked out a signal with Stan should she need his future assistance, and Tracy was due to arrive any minute to get his dog and take her to pick up her car.

She paced the floor and jumped when the doorbell sounded. She remembered to peek outside before opening the door and was surprised to see Mrs. Gleason standing on her front step instead of Tracy. Unhooking the security chain, she opened the door.

"Come in." She smiled warmly at her neighbor. The older woman stepped inside, giving Jasper a disapproving glare. Kira mentally groaned, fearing her neighbor had come to complain about the night the dog had howled and two sets of police officers had arrived none too quietly. She'd expected a visit and a complaint much sooner. "Have a seat." She motioned toward the sofa.

Mrs. Gleason seemed to be checking for dog hair on the cushions before seating herself with her ankles primly crossed. She surveyed the room for several minutes before getting to the purpose of her visit. "LeRoy Andrews asked me to give you a message."

"LeRoy Andrews?" She couldn't place the name or guess why he'd sent a message by her elderly neighbor. Suddenly the name Andrews registered in her mind. "Mr. Andrews from the nursery? You're acquainted with him?"

"Oh my, yes! He and I have been friends since his dear wife and I were classmates more than fifty years ago." She puffed up as though her friendship with the Andrews somehow made her important. She sighed and appeared to deflate. "Such a terrible thing, that young thug beating LeRoy like that."

"Is he conscious? Is he going to be all right? I haven't known who to ask and had no idea you were friends with him." She leaned toward her visitor, anxious to hear if the elderly man was recovering.

"He's awake now but has several broken bones. Broken bones don't heal so quickly at our age, and he has no one at home to help him, so it may be a long time before he's back at his nursery." She pursed her lips, and her eyes sparked with anger. "That daughter of his can't wait to stick him in a nursing home and get back to her big important job at that hotel in Miami. LeRoy isn't the kind of man who can sit around doing nothing. A nursing home will be the death of him. What he needs is a live-in helper until he's back on his feet."

An awkward silence followed, and Kira wasn't sure how to fill the silence, but her visitor did it for her.

"That's neither here nor there. I didn't come to complain about LeRoy's daughter. He wanted me to tell you to be careful. I don't know what's become of this neighborhood. I've become nervous about even working in my flowerbeds or walking to church after what happened to you and now to LeRoy. The person who attacked him wore a mask like those skiers, but he's pretty certain it was Luis Vincent. He thinks Patricia Dilworth may have overheard him talking to you about Luis, and she told her nephew. She's a friend of Nita Hayden and Julie Vincent, you know. Also after she left the nursery the day you two talked, he couldn't find the card you left for him."

Kira swallowed a gasp as she sat up straighter. She could only vaguely recall the woman who had interrupted her conversation with Mr. Andrews, and she certainly hadn't known the lady was connected to the dead girl. That could explain how the anonymous caller got her telephone number. It was also a piece of information she should pass on to Detective Daley.

"I'm sure I don't know why LeRoy was worrying about one of your business cards or that crazy woman meeting the person who discovered her cousin's daughter. You'd think she'd want to thank you. If you hadn't found her, heaven only knows how long that girl might have lain there rotting in the water and sand. I've known all three women since I moved to this neighborhood almost twenty years ago and none of them ever did show good sense. Always stirring up trouble and telling lies about people. Most everyone in the neighborhood has gotten tired of them putting on airs and pretending to be better than everyone else. Nita's daughter was getting to be just like her mother. It was a relief when they moved to the other side of the river."

Kira didn't like the picture Mrs. Gleason's words brought to mind. Clearly Mrs. Gleason didn't like the Haydens—mother or daughter. It was almost like she was saying Marla got what she deserved. Before she could think how to respond, her doorbell rang again.

Welcoming the excuse to end Mrs. Gleason's tirade, she hurried to the door. Jasper followed her. On seeing Tracy, he gave a couple of happy barks and jumped up to lick his face.

"Okay, boy. That's enough. I'm happy to see you too." Tracy playfully ruffled the dog's fur. "Ready to go?" As he turned to Kira, he noticed Mrs. Gleason. "Oh, hello. I'm sorry to interrupt. I wasn't aware Kira had company."

"I just came to deliver a message." The woman rose to her feet. "I'll be going along now."

Tracy held the door, and once Kira's neighbor reached her side of the front porch, he closed it and turned to his sister. "What did she want? More complaints about Jasper?"

"No, she didn't even mention him, though I've been expecting to get an earful all week."

"Why? Jasper didn't chase her cat again, did he?"

"No . . ." She felt reluctant to tell her brother about the phone call. It would be more ammunition for him and her dad to try to persuade her to move back home. On the other hand, it would be impossible to keep them from finding out since Stan was sure to report to her dad and he and Tracy were friends.

"Something happened. Let's hear it." His face turned stern, giving her a glimpse of the man who had risen to a position of power and responsibility in an international securities firm before his thirtieth birthday. His position wasn't entirely due to being Garrett Paxton's son. Once again she repeated the events of the night she received the phone call.

"Don't say it!" she finished. "I'm not moving back into Dad's house."

"Something has to be done!" He stomped around the room. "You're too stubborn to see Dad and I only want to protect you, so . . ."

"I'm safe here." She attempted to stand up to her brother. "Dad hired Stan and that's enough."

"He's only here at night. What about the rest of the time?"

"I run with Ford, and the credit union employs a security guard." She took a deep breath and resolved to stay calm. "I'll admit I've been a little paranoid about losing my freedom to live my own life and that you and Dad are only trying to keep me safe, but you have to understand I'm an adult now. I have to make my own choices and decisions. If I spend the rest of my life with a nursemaid following me around, I won't really be living."

"All right, I'll talk to Dad. I understand better than you think I do, but remember too, accepting help when you need it doesn't make you weak or dependent. There's a time to take charge, and there's a time to lean on others."

After Tracy left with Jasper, Kira decided there was one thing she could do to take charge of the situation and hopefully get a good night's sleep again. She'd call her cell phone service provider and change her telephone number. Then she'd let her family, Ford, and a few critical people know about the change. Then she'd track down David Warren.

CHAPTER FIFTEEN

DAVID WARREN HADN'T MOVED FAR away. Kira located him in a nearby suburb on her third call. He'd been suspicious at first but had finally agreed to meet with Ford and Kira at a West Jordan park. It was nearly seven that same evening when they pulled into the parking area. A lone figure sat at a picnic table nearby; a dog wearing a service harness lay at his feet, and a walking stick leaned against the table.

"Mr. Warren?" Ford extended his hand as they approached the man, who didn't attempt to stand. Instead he gestured for them to be seated.

"Dave is fine."

"I'm Ford, and this is Kira." Ford completed the introductions.

"What's this about?" Dave asked. "I've put all that nonsense with the Haydens behind me, and I thought they had too. She stalked me for nearly a year until I got a court order to stop it."

"Ford finds himself in much the same situation you were in four years ago, accused of inappropriate behavior with Marla. Only this time she isn't around to pursue her false charges," Kira began the explanation. "She was murdered in early May."

"I heard something about that." Dave scratched his dog's ears and was silent for several minutes. "She cost me and my wife a lot financially and emotionally at a difficult time in our lives. I was wounded in Iraq and suffering from PTSD. My wife had to go back to work, and Marla's lies cost us the possibility of adopting another little boy. At first her lies made me angry, but I got over that and found that more than anything I pitied her. Her death is another tragedy in a wasted young life."

"Because of her charge against me, I've become a suspect in her death," Ford spoke matter-of-factly.

"And that's why you want to talk to me." Dave shook his head, implying he was at a loss to know how he could be helpful. "I don't know anything that could be of help to you. In my case, Marla was just eleven or twelve, still in grade school. She was breaking a playground rule, and I stopped her. She demanded candy, and I refused. She threw a tantrum and knocked my cane out from under me. I've no idea whether I bumped her as I fell or not, but she claimed I slapped her. Kind of hard to do while falling backward, but it doesn't matter anymore. Her so-called friends—who all seemed afraid of getting on her bad side—backed up her story, and the detective who was supposed to be investigating her complaint didn't get around to it for a month. Even so, the real problem was her mother. Now there's a woman you don't want to cross."

"Her mother?" Kira sent Ford a puzzled look.

"I finally had to get a court order to stop her from harassing me and my family. She followed me to stores, to restaurants; she drove past my house, screaming obscenities. When she scared my little girl and made her cry in a restaurant where we were having lunch, I decided that was enough. I got the security footage from the restaurant and filed a complaint."

"Did you have any further trouble with either Marla or any of her family after that?" Ford asked.

"No, not really. The whole mess made it impossible for us to adopt another child or have much confidence in the school district. I wasn't comfortable working at the school any longer or having our son there, so we moved to another school district. How about you? Are you being harassed by Mrs. Hayden?"

"No, I've had no contact with Marla's mother, but Kira, whose only connection to Marla is that she found the body, has had her life threatened and her property damaged since discovering the body."

"That's weird—even for Marla's mother."

"I don't think Mrs. Hayden is the one threatening me. I think she told her nephew Luis some garbled version of my involvement and he's the one causing trouble. I'm sure it was a man's voice on the phone," Kira attempted to clarify. "But our real concern in speaking to you is hoping your experience can help us clear Ford of the charges she made against him and encourage the police to look harder at other suspects in her death."

"I'm willing to help if there's anything I can do, but other than my experience suggesting Marla had a habit of making false claims when she didn't get her way, I don't see how I can be much help." Dave rested both hands on his walking stick and appeared regretful. "It's sad, really. Marla had been in a number of scrapes already at that young age and had a reputation as a thief and a liar, but I never really blamed her. Her parents provided no moral guidelines to help her. Still I feel sorry for them. I have two children, and I can't imagine anything worse than losing a child."

* * *

Ford took Kira's hand as they walked slowly back to his truck. She wasn't sure they'd learned anything that could be of use in finding Marla's killer, but if Detective Daley knew about Dave's experience with the girl, he might be inclined to look more closely at her cousin and remove Ford from his list of suspects. At least, she hoped that would be the case.

"It's hard to believe a girl that young could cause so much trouble." Ford, too, was mulling over the things Dave had said. "It doesn't seem right that those who give so much for our way of life are often the ones short-changed the most in the way of justice."

"She may have been a troublemaker and certainly not a nice person, but she didn't kill herself. Someone out there murdered her." Kira gestured widely as though encompassing the whole world.

"I've always found that old 'blame the victim' mentality ridiculous. Yet in a way, I guess that's what I've been doing." Ford unlocked his truck and helped Kira make the big step up into the cab before he went around to the driver's side. Instead of starting the engine, he continued with his thoughts. "I've been offended by Marla's accusation and angry that anyone might believe her lies. In a way I've felt like she brought this on herself by the way she treated others. Maybe it took talking to Dave to set my thinking straight. No matter what she did, she didn't deserve to be shot and dumped like garbage in the river."

"I think I've been guilty of the opposite thinking. Because everyone refers to her as a murder *victim*, I've had a difficult time accepting the idea she might not have been an innocent kid. After all, doesn't the word *victim* imply someone took advantage of her?"

"Her behavior may have placed her in a position that endangered her, or she could have just been in the wrong place at the wrong time." He twisted the key, and the engine roared to life. "I just hope I can be as compassionate and forgiving as Dave." As he pulled out of the parking lot, he waved to the veteran, who still sat at a picnic table staring off into a distance only he could see.

They didn't say much as Ford drove back toward Kira's condo, but as they approached her home, Kira caught a flicker of movement beside her garage.

"Did you see that?" She leaned forward for a better view. The half-light of dusk shrouded the neighborhood in shadows. Another shadow separated from the corner of Mrs. Gleason's garage and disappeared into the deeper darkness behind the condos.

"Call the police!" Ford switched on his high beams as he pulled into the driveway, highlighting a third figure, who hurled an object toward the truck before ducking around the side of the garage. The object hit the hood of the truck with a loud clang.

Digging out her phone, Kira punched in 911.

"This is 911. What is your emergency?"

Kira quickly relayed the information to the 911 operator and was assured the police were on their way. She turned back toward Ford in time to see him ease out of his seat. She heard the click of the door locking behind him as he pressed a button on his remote key. She reached for the door beside her. Ford shook his head and motioned for her to stay inside the truck.

She watched as he made a dash for her front door. Stepping up to the door, he twisted the knob, then jiggled it, but the door didn't open. She hoped that meant no one got inside.

She held her breath when Ford ducked around the side of her condo, remembering the shattered window from the last time an intruder made his way inside her home. She didn't want to go through that again!

All remained quiet for what seemed a long time. Her fingers inched toward the door handle, and ugly pictures crept into her mind. Was Ford safe? Had he been attacked? Surely he hadn't followed those shadowy figures into the trees! And where was Stan?

A loud crack broke the silence, and she cringed, ducking below the window line of Ford's truck. After a few seconds—which seemed like an eternity—she raised her head to peer into the darkness. Was it a gunshot she'd heard? She honestly couldn't say what sound had accompanied the shot fired at her in the mall parking lot. Biting her lip, she considered whether she should continue to sit in the truck or go looking for Ford. What if he was lying bleeding in her backyard?

Her concern for Ford's safety overruled her fear. Trying to avoid making any sound, she opened her door, just wide enough to slip out. Shock rippled through her when a hoarse voice whispered, "Police! Don't move! Keep your hands where I can see them."

She stood as still as her trembling knees would permit. A large shadow loomed out of the darkness. As it drew closer she could detect the figure wore a uniform. She relaxed a little.

"Miss Paxton?" the officer questioned. She nodded her head. Then realizing he might not see the motion in the darkness, she whispered yes. *What's wrong with the lights that usually come on at dusk on either side of the garage door?* She feared she knew the answer to her own question.

"My friend, Ford Kettering, went around to the back after them. I heard a shot." The officer muttered something unintelligible. He was close enough she could see him now when he turned his head to speak into the phone attached to the shoulder of his uniform.

Several officers ran toward the side of her house.

"Get back in the truck, and keep the doors locked," the officer who stood a few feet away ordered. She obeyed, then sat squirming, not knowing what was happening. The sound of that gunshot kept echoing in her mind. She needed to know if Ford was hurt or—

No, she wouldn't think about that.

She'd just made up her mind to go see what was happening when she spotted a figure running toward the truck. She crouched low, hardly daring to breathe. Her heart pounded, and fear drowned out rational thought.

"Kira! Kira, it's me." She recognized Ford's voice. She glanced up. It was Ford's face she saw peering through the window. In seconds she had the door open and was leaping into his arms. He pulled her to him, running his hands up and down her back as he swept her closer.

"I heard a shot," she sobbed. "I was so afraid you'd been hit."

"I'm fine. The bullet lodged in one of the patio pillars, and a police officer is busy now removing it for evidence. Most of the others are pursuing the guys down the canal bank."

"Did they break into my house?"

"No. I didn't see any damage; I think they must have arrived just minutes before we did and hadn't got started yet. The officer who spoke to me said it would be all right for us to go inside now." With his arm around her, he led the way to her front door.

Not more than five minutes after they entered the house, there was a knock on the back door. Ford peered out before thrusting the door open and stepping aside to permit two uniformed officers into Kira's kitchen. Between them, they supported a rumpled and blood-smeared man.

"Stan!" Kira's hands flew to her mouth in shock. The hired guard slumped onto a kitchen chair. He seemed barely able to hold up his head. His left arm dangled at an awkward angle, and one side of his face was purple and swollen. He was as wet and bedraggled as the first time she'd seen him. A trickle of blood escaped from a gash over his right eye. His clothing was torn and covered with mud.

"We've called for an ambulance, but he refuses to go without seeing you first, Miss Paxton, and seeing for himself that you're safe." The officer reached for the roll of paper towels that hung just under the cupboard. He tore off a broad strip and handed it to Stan, who daubed weakly at the blood that trickled toward his eye.

Kira rushed toward him and knelt beside his chair. "Let me do that." She took the paper towel from his hand. "What happened?"

"Half a dozen punks came sneaking down the canal road. When I realized they were heading for your house, I intercepted them and told them to leave. Two more I hadn't seen rushed me from behind. I got the worst of the fight, but I wasn't the only one knocked into the canal."

"You likely saved Kira's house from being damaged again by delaying them until we arrived." Ford rested a hand lightly on Stan's shoulder. Silently he added an apology for the ill will he'd felt earlier toward the battered man and vowed to find an opportunity to thank him for possibly saving Kira's life. There was no way to know what might have happened if Stan hadn't been there.

"The ambulance is here." An officer opened the back door and made the announcement.

"I can't leave," Stan protested when the officers stepped forward to help him to his feet. "What if they come back while Kira is alone?"

"Go," Ford told him. "She won't be alone."

CHAPTER SIXTEEN

FORD STIFLED A YAWN. HE needed sleep, but he refused to be the first to abandon Kira's condo. Not only had he sat up in Kira's front room all night, but he'd been joined by Tracy and Garrett shortly after the police left. Ten minutes ago he'd answered the door to find Stan, his arm in a cast and stitches on the gash above his eye. The only one not there was Kira.

Kira had insisted on going to work that morning. Tracy had followed her to make certain she arrived at her office without mishap and to have a few words with the security guard. Ford understood their concern, but he also sympathized with Kira, who had whispered to him before she left, "Don't let Dad and Tracy pack up my stuff and move me back in with them while I'm gone." He ached for Kira both because of the uninvited vendetta against her and because of her well-meaning family members who were making her feel trapped.

He hoped she had gotten a little sleep. She'd sat up for some time with the three of them, swearing she was too keyed up to sleep, but either she'd grown tired or had heard enough of her family's insistence that she quit her job, give up her condo, and move back into the family home where they could protect her better. Regardless of anything she said, they adamantly refused to listen to any solution other than moving back in with them. He hadn't said much, though he'd tried to convey his support to Kira.

The doorbell rang once more, and as he made his way to the door, Ford found his movements stiff from sitting so long. He intercepted the disapproving glance that passed between Garrett and Tracy. He didn't care whether they approved of his assumption of host duties. He strongly believed Kira would prefer he play that role to either her father or brother doing so.

Though the caller was expected, he checked the security window before undoing the dead bolt. "Come in, Detective." He gestured for Bruce Daley to join the men occupying the sofa and love seat in Kira's front room. Daley stood in the entry for several seconds as though searching for someone.

"Where is Miss Paxton?"

"I tried to dissuade her, but she insisted on going to that job of hers." Garrett stood and extended a hand toward the detective. "This kind of thing wouldn't happen if she'd come home and accept the job I offered her."

Daley shook Garrett's hand then turned back to Ford. "Is there someplace we can discuss what happened here last night?"

Both Garrett and Tracy looked affronted but didn't protest being excluded from whatever the detective had to say.

"Will the patio do?" Ford had gone over and over the events of the previous evening both in his mind and with the officers who had responded earlier to the call. Nevertheless, he'd expected to review the incident again with the detective.

"When we finish"—Daley turned to Stan—"I'll need a few minutes with you."

"I'll be right here." Stan made no effort to stand, and Ford could see he wasn't as pain free as he'd insisted earlier.

Ford took a step toward the patio doors. Before Daley could follow, Garrett confronted him. "Kira has been in constant danger for over a month. If the police can't protect my daughter better than I've seen so far, I'll move her to—"

"Your daughter is an adult and can't be moved without her consent no matter how secure the facility or what your intentions may be," Daley cut Garrett off. "Now if you'll excuse me, I have a job to do." The detective indicated Ford should precede him through the kitchen to the patio.

Garrett appeared about to explode when the detective turned his back on him. Ford hid a smile. He suspected not many people stood up to Garrett Paxton.

"Just so you know," Daley began as they settled in two of the chairs that surrounded the patio table, "I'll be interviewing Miss Paxton at her place of work as soon as we finish here."

"Good," Ford responded with one word. After a slight pause he went on. "Kira is under a great deal of pressure to move in with her dad and brother. She'll likely place the best possible light on last night's incident to sugarcoat it. I'm worried about her, though, and question whether she should continue living here alone, even with a security guard watching at night. Although, most of the things that have happened seem intended to scare her more than harm her—even that shot at the mall—but what if whoever is doing this gets tired of playing around and makes a serious attempt on her life?"

"That's the department's concern exactly. Why don't you tell me about last night? Perhaps something you noticed will shed some light on why this is happening." He set a small recorder on the patio table between them. "Tell me everything that happened from the time you met Miss Paxton after she left work yesterday until the police arrived here last night."

Ford leaned forward, adding emphasis to his words. "Kira and I met David Warren at a park in South Jordan in the late afternoon. David used to live around here and was the victim of trumped-up charges Marla Hayden made four years ago. He's a wounded veteran with PTSD. She accused him of slapping her. After speaking with him, we drove back here." He went on to describe the figures they'd seen hanging around Kira's house.

Daley didn't interrupt, so Ford went on. "I made my way to the back corner of the house and almost reached the point where the two condos' garages meet, when the woman in the other condo opened a window and yelled, 'Get out of my yard!' I saw several shadows disappear into the trees, then a shot was fired. I'm not certain if it was meant for me or for Mrs. Gleason."

"From the trajectory of the bullet, we assume it was meant for you," Daley observed in an emotionless voice. "Go on."

"There isn't much more to say. The police arrived about that time, and I went to check on Kira. A few minutes later two officers brought in the security guard, who had been roughed up pretty badly."

"Could you identify any of the people you saw?"

"No," Ford admitted. "It was dark, and I didn't get a good look at anyone."

"How about clothing? Did you notice colors, insignia, anything?"

"Not really. Their clothing appeared to be dark, but I can't say whether it was actually black or not. I've heard Luis Vincent described as medium height with a wiry build, but if he was one of the people here last night, I didn't see him. The ones I saw all appeared to have builds more like men than boys. One had a definite paunch." Ford attempted to remember details blurred by darkness and fear.

"That fits with our findings." Daley shook his head, and his mouth turned down in a grim frown. "Indications are the attack last night did not come from the gang Vincent leads but from a rival gang. We found a partial spray paint mark on Miss Paxton's garage door that looks like whoever began painting it was interrupted. We also got a description of a suspicious car from a neighbor. It fits the description of a vehicle known to be used by this other gang."

"Kira has no connection with any gang. Why are they targeting her?"

"I don't know, but I plan to find out. Chances are the second gang has no interest in Miss Paxton and is simply protecting its turf from Vincent's gang." The detective leaned back in his chair. "Would you mind sending Stan Martel out?"

Clearly Ford had been dismissed. His mind swirled as he made his way back inside. Detective Daley hadn't said anything about the allegations Marla had threatened to make against him. He hoped that meant he was no longer a suspect. But what about Marla's cousin? If he and his gang weren't involved in whatever had been planned for last night, were his suspicions concerning the boy wrong?

Placing his concerns on hold for the moment, he helped Stan to the patio then returned inside, closing the door behind him.

* * *

Kira had difficulty concentrating. Twice she had to start over on the papers she was preparing for a major client. She'd be out of a job if she messed up on such a large account. Leaving her desk, she walked to the water cooler in an attempt to settle her thoughts. It was hard not to think about the gang that had surrounded her house when she and Ford arrived there the previous night. It was equally hard not to feel scared when she thought about what might have happened if she'd been alone and if the police hadn't arrived promptly. She didn't know what to do. She just couldn't move back in with her dad and brother. Neither was she brave enough to stay in her condo any longer. She considered checking into a motel, but could her finances handle that? She didn't want to ask her dad for money. And what if she were followed?

"Miss Paxton?"

Startled, she whirled around to see Detective Daley standing a few feet away.

"Good morning, Detective." She attempted to appear poised and self-confident but feared she failed miserably. She hadn't expected him to come to her office.

"I'd like to discuss what you saw and heard last night. Do you have a few minutes?" Though he phrased it as a question, she suspected speaking with the detective was more of an imperative than a question.

She led him to her cubicle and invited him to sit while she claimed her own chair behind the desk. The detective was a large man who barely fit in the chair usually occupied by credit union clients. He'd intimidated her when she'd first met him in April following the discovery of Marla's body, but in time she'd grown more comfortable with him, more able to ignore his brusque manner and appreciate his sharp mind.

"You don't mind if I record our little talk, do you?" Daley set his small recorder on her desk between them. She nodded her permission but then remembered from their previous interviews that he needed verbal approval; she gave it.

"I've gotten statements from both Stan Martel and your friend Ford Kettering, but I'd like to hear your take on all that happened last night. Why don't you start with your visit to that retired soldier?"

She was a little surprised that he knew about the visit to David Warren, but she obliged him by telling him about David and her favorable impression of him.

"How did you learn about this Warren guy?" Ford asked. Anyone listening to their conversation would assume they were sharing a casual chat, but she knew something she'd said had raised a flag in the detective's mind.

She gave a quick review of her trip to the local nursery and her talk with Mr. Andrews and followed with the graffiti attack and break-in at her condo and the beating that put Mr. Andrews in the hospital.

Without commenting on her story, Daley urged her, "Tell me about last night."

"There isn't much to tell. I noticed someone standing at the corner of my garage when we pulled into the driveway. Whoever he was, he quickly disappeared around the corner. Ford insisted I stay in the truck with the doors locked while he investigated. I called the police, and they arrived a few minutes later. One officer stayed behind the truck while the others ran toward the back of the house. I didn't see anyone else until Ford returned to tell me it was safe to go inside. Nothing inside was damaged, but we'd only been inside a few minutes when a couple of officers brought Stan in. He'd been hurt pretty badly and was taken to a hospital."

"Both Stan and Ford are doing fine." The detective pushed a button on his recorder and returned it to his pocket. "They're both tired, in need of some sleep, and worried about you."

"I suppose my dad and brother are still there too." She couldn't keep the sound of defeat out of her voice.

"They're worried too."

"I don't know what to do," Kira admitted. "I can't face going back to live at my dad's house. He means well, but he makes me feel like an incompetent, helpless child. When I'm treated like a brainless twit, I begin to feel like one. I don't really want to go back to my condo, but I'm afraid of what I'll become if I do what Dad and Tracy insist I do."

"Let me tell you something." The detective leaned closer and spoke in a whisper. "I suspect Ford will do almost anything to keep you safe. You could move into his apartment."

She felt the instant burn of embarrassment flush her face. Before she could say anything, the big detective went on. "I'm not suggesting you move in with him. You could just trade spaces. Come to think of it, that security man your dad hired could move into your apartment too. As for being scared, let me share a little something somebody said came from John Wayne, 'Courage is being scared but saddling up anyway.'"

CHAPTER SEVENTEEN

FORD WAS SURPRISED WHEN KIRA called to ask if he and Stan could meet her for lunch. He was even more surprised when she suggested they switch apartments.

Stan snorted then began to laugh. "Well, that's one solution." His laughter faded, and he grew serious. "Actually it's not a bad idea. In fact, it might work well for me since I'm not handling stairs too well." He pulled up his pant leg to reveal a hinged support on his right knee. "My arm hurt so much last night I didn't realize I'd suffered the consequences of a boot against my knee until after I reached the hospital."

"I'm really sorry." Kira looked like she might cry. "You should be home resting."

"What! Don't take back your offer. I live on the fourth floor of a building without an elevator!" He grinned, and Ford wasn't sure whether he was serious or not. Kira's suggestion had taken him by surprise, but he could see the merits of their switching places.

His building required that he either enter a code or be let in by someone from an apartment. In addition each apartment had a separate alarm which was monitored 24-7. He'd worry much less with her in his third-floor apartment, and since he still had a couple of weeks of summer school left before the fall quarter began, driving the short distance between Taylorsville and Murray would be no problem.

"That sounds like a workable solution." Ford spoke slowly, still mulling over the details in his mind.

"Actually, it was Detective Daley's suggestion. He also said if we decide to do it, we shouldn't tell anyone where I'm staying. He thinks it would be best for just the three of us and him to know where I'm staying."

Ford could see the sense in that suggestion and thought they should go a step further and make certain no one was ever followed to the apartment. He didn't want anyone finding Kira because they followed one of them to his apartment.

"My family will go nuts not knowing where I am." Kira sighed.

"You can call them, and I'll be staying in touch with them." Stan was all business now. He looked around as though assuring himself no one could overhear their conversation. "We need a plan. Ford should go home, pack up everything he's going to need, then head back to your condo. I'll call Kaitlin and have her go shopping." Seeing Kira's raised eyebrows, Stan added, "They didn't tell you, did they? Your brother's fiancée is my niece. Her mom is my big sister. Anyway, it's probably best if she doesn't spend any time at your condo packing. Give me a list of your sizes, and she'll have everything ready by the time you get off work this afternoon. I'll have someone drop her purchases by here and switch cars with you."

Ford wondered if Stan's precautions were necessary, but he'd go along if it would ensure Kira's safety. He wrote down the apartment number and codes she would need to get in. "The apartment will be ready for you to move into by the time you get off work this afternoon."

* * *

Her ability to concentrate didn't improve when she returned to work. She found herself watching the clock and hoping she didn't mess up any of the accounts she was working on. She couldn't help wondering about Ford's apartment; she hadn't been inside it. And what would Kaitlin consider appropriate work attire? Some of the outfits her future sister-in-law picked for herself didn't come close to something Kira would choose. Thinking of work, she wondered if the person threatening her might know where she worked and follow her from the credit union to Ford's apartment. Then there was church on Sunday. Would she be able to attend her meetings? She even found herself worrying about Ford's and Stan's safety. With his injuries, Stan wouldn't be much help if someone attacked them at her condo.

The wall clock ticked off the last minute, and Kira reached for her purse. Just as promised, a man dressed in jeans and a sky-blue Western shirt approached her in the parking lot. He handed her a set of keys and pointed out a nondescript white sedan. She handed over her own car keys and took the few steps to the strange car. It took her a few minutes to familiarize herself with the instrument panel before putting the car in gear and leaving the parking lot.

She turned left instead of right and wove her way through several subdivisions as per Stan's instructions before heading for Ford's apartment. Each time she glanced in her mirror, Detective Daley's words echoed in her mind. *Courage is being scared but saddling up anyway.*

At last she turned in at the entrance to the apartment complex. Instead of a parking garage, there was only a long carport, open on the sides. She pulled into the parking stall with the number that matched Ford's apartment. After she removed the large suitcase from the trunk, she locked the car. Glancing up at the modern building, she eyed the third row of windows where she knew she'd find the apartment that would be home for however long Detective Daley thought she should stay away from her own home. She wasn't certain whether she felt a measure of relief to leave her own house and the recent attacks behind or nervous about beginning a sojourn in unfamiliar surroundings.

It was almost six when she punched in the last digit of the door code and heard the click that signified the apartment was unlocked. She twisted the knob and carefully pushed the door open. She stood for several minutes just looking. Two black leather couches faced each other in front of a large window. Between them was a chrome-and-glass coffee table covered with a clutter of books and magazines. On the wall were brightly colored framed geometric designs. Somehow she'd expected historical prints in Ford's living space. A familiar-looking sweatshirt lay on the floor where its owner had missed tossing it on the arm of a sofa.

Stepping inside the room, she turned to close the door and set the dead bolt in place before she walked slowly toward the window, which overlooked a wide expanse of park. Grass and trees covered acres of land, and she caught glimpses of a stream running through it. Ford would meet her there in the morning for their run.

Leaving the living area, she opened the door that led to Ford's bedroom. Standing in the doorway, she first noticed a patchwork quilt that covered a queen-sized bed. A bookcase filled with well-worn books of varied colors and sizes and an oversized recliner formed a cozy nook in one corner. On the wall opposite the bed, a series of framed historical prints took pride of place. Kira smiled to herself. Above the bed was a simple painting of the Jordan River temple, and on a small bedside table sat a clock radio and a snapshot of Ford and his younger brothers. She picked up the small picture to more closely examine it. Their matching grins made her smile.

It was time to shake off worry and uncertainty. She needed to find something to eat and then let Ford and her family know she had arrived and was fine. She stepped into a small kitchen and found it wasn't terribly different from her own. It held the basic appliances, stainless steel where hers were white. She opened the refrigerator and was surprised to see it was fully stocked with 2% milk, her favorite brand of orange juice, and an assortment of the ice cream novelties she had a weakness for. Front and center sat a sub sandwich. Knowing Ford had taken the time to stock his apartment with groceries for her touched her, bringing a lump to her throat.

* * *

Ford hadn't had a roommate since his college days, and he wasn't sure how he felt about sharing Kira's home with Stan. Thank goodness Garrett and Tracy had finally gone. He and Stan had agreed to take turns watching while the other one slept, and since Stan had suffered serious injuries the night before, Ford insisted Stan sleep first. They reheated a casserole they found in the refrigerator and sat at Kira's small dining room table to eat it. When they finished, Ford loaded their dishes into the dishwasher, and Stan disappeared into the bedroom. He supposed he was being foolish, but he found he didn't like the picture that came to his mind on seeing Stan go into Kira's bedroom and close the door behind him.

Ford left the television off and spent some time on his computer. At short intervals, he peered out the windows and checked the doors. All remained quiet. By midnight he resorted to compiling a list of actions that might be related to the discovery of Marla's body, and a few hours later, he discovered a Sudoku puzzle book Kira had left on an end table and began working out one of the puzzles.

A sound caught his attention, and his eyes searched the darkness beyond the front room window. He jumped when Stan spoke to him.

"It's three o'clock, man. I thought you were going to wake me at two." Stan stood beside him rubbing his eyes and looking thoroughly rumpled.

"Nothing was happening, and you needed the rest." Ford's attempt at nonchalance was interrupted with a wide yawn.

Stan laughed. "Go get some sleep." He dropped onto the love seat and reached for a briefcase he'd left beside it.

Ford removed his shoes but didn't undress when he reached Kira's bedroom. He noticed the spread was wrinkled, but it didn't appear Stan had crawled between the sheets. He didn't either. He flopped face down and was rewarded with the scent of Kira's shampoo on her pillow. He expected to fall asleep at once but didn't. Instead his mind flew to his own apartment, and he wondered if Kira was comfortable sleeping in his bed and whether they'd succeeded in keeping her location hidden from anyone who might want to harm her. The sky he glimpsed through the bedroom blinds was just beginning to turn a lighter shade of gray when he finally drifted to sleep.

* * *

Feeling foolish for behaving like some guy out of a TV whodunit, Ford made his way through yet another subdivision. When he felt confident no one was following him, he pulled into a parking lot at the back side of the park. He pulled off his outer shirt, locked his truck, and hurried toward a trail that disappeared into the trees.

It didn't take long to reach the spot he'd selected for a rendezvous with Kira, and he only had to wait a few minutes before she appeared. There was a bounce to her step that emphasized her oversized T-shirt and baggy shorts. It was like a load had dropped from his shoulders when he saw her looking fresh and alert. On closer examination he discovered there were still dark shadows beneath her eyes, but she was smiling and appeared happy to see him.

She brushed his lips with hers then grinned. "Ready?" she asked. "We can talk while we run."

He returned her smile and picked up his pace. Even with the small amount of sleep he'd gotten, it felt good to stretch his muscles. Perhaps it was just being with Kira that added zest to his steps.

"Were you able to sleep?" he asked as they loped along a trail barely wide enough for two.

"Yes. It felt strange at first to be in a different apartment and a different bed. Maybe it was just being so tired, mentally and physically, but I fell asleep much faster than I expected and woke up just a few minutes before we were supposed to meet. Oh, and thank you for stocking your kitchen with food you know I like."

"I didn't think making a shopping trip would be a good idea for you just now."

"What about you? Any problems? Could you sleep? Is Stan feeling better?" Her questions echoed the rhythm of their breaths as the pair rounded the south corner of the park.

He laughed. "One question at a time. Everything is fine. We didn't see or hear any trouble all night. But I'll admit I had a difficult time falling asleep in your bed. Perhaps if you'd been there . . ." He waggled his eyebrows, and they both laughed. "Stan is stiff and has quite a few tender bruises, but he insists he feels fine and can do his job."

The morning felt brighter and fatigue slipped from his shoulders. The park was green and lush with only a few early risers running around the perimeter. He glanced at his running partner and knew just being with her lightened his day.

Several runners passed them, and Ford took her arm to lead her off the path into a copse of trees that provided them some privacy. His arms closed around her, and they held each other tight for several minutes. His lips sought hers, and he knew there was nothing he wanted more than to be able to hold Kira and love her forever. Feeling her in his arms and tasting her sweetness was something he was quite definitely growing addicted to. At last she pulled away, and he resisted the urge to pull her close and kiss her again.

"I'll be late for work if we don't finish our run. I need to shower, and I hope I can find something suitable to wear to work."

"You got the clothes Kaitlin picked out for you, didn't you? Do they fit okay?"

Kira chuckled as she pulled at the baggy shirt she wore and pointed out the safety pin holding her shorts. "If they all fit like this outfit, I definitely need to go shopping myself. I was thinking of heading for the South Towne Center after work. It's not likely I'll run into anyone who might recognize me there. Or you could just pack a bag for me with the clothes in my closet."

"Stan thinks if one of us was spotted carrying a suitcase out of your condo it would increase the odds we might be followed and would tip off the vandal that you're not there. I could meet you at the mall after you get off work tonight if you'd like." Her dubious look clearly told him she doubted he'd be much use on her shopping trip, or maybe she was remembering the men in her family supervising her teenage shopping trips. "I promise to keep my opinions to myself unless asked for."

She laughed, and they made arrangements to meet after work; she turned to trot toward his apartment and he toward his truck. Once in the trees he looked back, watching until she disappeared inside the apartment building that overlooked the park.

* * *

Kira pushed her sleeve up for the hundredth time and reached for a blouse that caught her eye. It wasn't exactly what she wanted, but at least it was in her size. Finding clothing that fit both her small size and her taste wasn't easy. She glanced over at Ford, who calmly sat in a chair beside the fitting room. True to his word, he hadn't commented once about any of her selections. Nor had he attempted to hurry her.

Gathering up her selections, she moved toward the cash register. Behind her she heard a young feminine voice. "Mr. Kettering!" A smattering of giggles followed.

Turning she saw two teenagers standing with Ford. They were dressed in micro mini-skirts and halter tops and wearing way too much makeup. So much for her theory that they wouldn't run into anyone they knew at a mall at the south end of the valley.

After paying for her purchases, she turned back to Ford and was surprised to see he was still talking to the teenagers. He looked up and motioned for her to join them. When she reached his side, he introduced her before reaching for her shopping bag and suggesting they visit the food court for a drink.

She still needed to purchase a good pair of running shoes, and it seemed a bit odd that Ford would include some of his students in their shopping trip when he'd expressed concern for anyone discovering her whereabouts. She supposed she could have him find shoes in her closet and bring them to her when they ran together again. Besides, she was curious about the girls. She didn't know many teenagers who would willingly spend their free time with one of their teachers. It might be her imagination, but something about Ford's invitation suggested there was more involved in this get-together than was apparent on the surface.

It was a short walk to the food court. Once they were settled at a table with creamy milkshakes, paid for by Ford, he turned to the more flamboyant of the two girls. "Heather, you said you had something to tell me about the shoes Marla was wearing the night she was killed. I think Kira would like to hear it too, since it was her brother's dog that found the shoes."

"Wow! You're the lady that found her?" Heather turned to Kira. "Was it really awful?"

"Uh," she mumbled, unsure how to respond. She certainly had no intention of rehashing the gory details of that horrible experience. "It was really Jasper, my brother's dog, that found her. I think it was the shoes. He has a thing about shoes." She wasn't certain her words even made sense.

"Oh, the shoes. They were really pretty, and they just matched her dress. That's why she took them. It wasn't fair to put them in my backpack so it looked like I was the one who swiped 'em." Heather took a big sip of her shake, making a slurping sound. She didn't act unduly upset over the situation she described.

Kira stared at the girl. "Are you saying Marla's shoes were shoplifted?"

"Well, sure. Marla did it all the time, but she never got caught because she never hid the stuff she took on herself. She always made sure they were hidden in someone else's bags."

"Did you report this?" Kira asked, and Heather shook her head. "But why didn't you tell someone?"

Heather gave her a look that suggested she didn't think Kira was too bright and spoke in the same tone. "If junk is found in your bag, there's no way to prove you didn't take it, and it's her word against yours. Just like the story she made up about Mr. Kettering having a thing for her. He can't prove he *didn't* put the moves on her. Anyway she'd kill me if I ratted."

Kira felt as if she'd just stepped off one of the wilder rides at the amusement park. All she could think to say was, "Did you consider Marla a friend?"

"Sure. We did stuff together, and we had lots of fun. I miss her." She stirred her milkshake with her straw.

Kira didn't know what to say. To her it was incomprehensible that anyone would remain friends with a thief and a liar who didn't hesitate to set her friends up to take the blame if she were caught.

While Kira was trying to process Heather's words, Ford brought the other girl into the conversation. "Jessie, did you know about this?"

Jessie kept her head lowered and took her time answering. Nervous fingers pinched her straw. Kira could barely hear her when she at last offered a mumbled yes. The girl glanced up, and Kira caught the sheen of tears in her eyes.

"Don't be such a baby!" Heather taunted Jessie. "You knew what she was doing. If you didn't want her to put stuff in your bag, you shouldn't have gone shopping with her."

"After I got sent to juvie, she promised she wouldn't do it anymore. I believed her, but she lied. She did it to me all the time. We were only in the fourth grade the first time a clerk at Walmart said I took some candy and the store detective found it in my jacket pocket. I had to go to juvenile court the last time she put a bra in my backpack. I tried to tell them it wasn't even my size. I couldn't tell them Marla took it because she said if I got her in trouble she'd make sure the ring she took from our teacher's desk would be found where everyone would think I took it. She made me lie too. She said if I didn't swear in court that Mr. Warren at our old school slapped her, she and her cousin would burn our house down and it wouldn't matter if I escaped or not because everyone would know my mom left me alone at night and they would put me in foster care."

Kira scooted closer to the girl and put her arm around her shoulder. "She can't lie about you, hurt you, or get you in trouble anymore. I think you should go to the police and tell them what you just told us."

"I can't. Marla's mom is my mom's boss. She said it was important for me to be Marla's best friend. She even made me change schools when Marla did."

"Why did Marla change schools?"

Heather made a loud snorting sound. "It was because of Aaron. She wanted to go to the same school as that wimp, and she got in some kind of trouble at her old school. Most of her friends got split up and sent to different schools."

"Aaron isn't a wimp." Kira was surprised when Jessie defended the boy.

"You just stand up for him because you like him and he was your boyfriend until Marla took him away."

"That's not true. Aaron is nice to everyone, and he didn't deserve the mean things Marla always said to him. She called him a coward because he didn't want to be in her cousin's gang, but he doesn't like to fight or drive fast or steal stuff." Jessie paused to wipe her eyes. "You don't understand because you're mean, just like Marla, and I'm going back to Kohl's and telling someone about the shirt you stuffed in your purse!"

Heather stood. "Maybe you're the jealous creep who shot Marla! I just might call the police and tell them you're the one they should arrest!"

CHAPTER EIGHTEEN

"Wait!" Jessie ran after Heather. "I won't tell. You know I won't."

Kira watched in disbelief as Jessie disappeared into the crowded mall hall chasing after Heather. For just a moment she wondered if she should try to catch the girl, but what could she say or do if she did? When Ford began gathering up cups and napkins to deposit in the trash can, she became aware of her own unfinished drink and the clutter the girls had left behind. Absently she reached for her cup then set it back down.

"Do you think . . . ?" She couldn't finish her question. It just wasn't possible. Heather, possibly, but Jessica couldn't have killed the friend she'd followed like a loyal puppy. "I guess I assumed the killer was a man . . ."

"Don't take Heather's accusation too seriously." Ford set down the clutter he'd collected and reached for her hands, seating himself once more. "Heather is almost as good as Marla was at manipulating people and creating dramatic scenes. And poor Jessie is one of those people who has been controlled all of her life, first by her mother then by Marla. She's basically a good kid, but her eagerness to please too often makes her a victim of less scrupulous people. I was surprised she told us as much as she did."

"That's sad."

"Perhaps she was prompted in a way. Heather may have been goading her into telling us things she didn't want to say herself."

Kira had found the two girls' relationship strange, and even during Jessie's outburst she'd sensed Heather was taking some kind of perverse revenge on Marla by pushing her loyal shadow into revealing her true character.

"The question now is what do we do about it?" Ford stood once more to clear their table. When he returned he picked up Kira's purchases with one hand and held out his other hand to her. She took it. With her bag in the opposite hand, they made their way to the parking lot. She found herself nervously watching passing cars and eyeing strangers with suspicion. It would take a long time to get over the shots aimed at her the last time she visited a mall.

"We should call Detective Daley." Kira answered his earlier question, pausing before entering the car Stan had loaned her.

Ford merely nodded his head before punching in the number on his phone. He spoke briefly into the phone, giving a bare outline of the events that just occurred.

Kira followed Ford from the mall to the Murray police station where Detective Daley arranged to meet them. They were ushered immediately into his cramped office. He stood to greet them and invited them to be seated in two chairs in front of his desk. She couldn't help remembering how sick and nervous she'd felt the first time she'd sat in the detective's office. She wasn't entirely without the jitters this time, but she felt optimistic that the conversation they had to report would aid in clearing Ford.

Daley turned to Kira first.

When she had finished reiterating all that had been said during their encounter with the two girls at the mall, Daley turned to Ford, who had little to add.

"It won't be difficult to check out whether the shoes were purchased or stolen." The detective spoke in an absentminded tone as though he were deep in thought. "I appreciate your bringing this matter to my attention, and you can be sure I'll be doing a little checking on their story." He asked a few additional questions then excused them.

* * *

"What more can we do?" Kira leaned against the rail that separated the viewing platform from the river. It had been a week since she and Ford had told Detective Daley about their conversation with Heather and Jessie. They'd heard nothing about how the case was progressing or even if the girls' statements had helped to clear Ford of suspicion. She was tired of jumping at loud sounds, worrying about being attacked. Most of all, she wanted her own things around her and the freedom to go when and where she wanted. She strongly suspected Ford was also anxious to be back in his apartment since school would be starting soon and he'd mentioned several times that he needed to make preparations for his classes.

"I don't think we can do anything but wait and hope Detective Daley is still following up with Luis Vincent and that he's talked to Mr. Andrews and all of Marla's friends. Neither Stan nor I have seen anyone hanging around your house. I'm not sure whether that means the harassment is over or that whoever is responsible knows you're not staying there."

Kira felt like she should apologize to the cluster of ducks gathered below the platform. She usually carried a few scraps of bread to feed the birds when she ran along the parkway, but Ford had surprised her by driving to a distant section of the trail for their run instead of circling the Murray park as they'd been doing since they'd traded apartments. She had to admit she'd loved the change of scenery. There was something about the parkway that always felt more open and free than other parks or high school tracks.

"I'm not good at doing nothing," she lamented.

Ford laughed. "Instead of doing nothing, how about going to church with me tomorrow?"

She accepted. The previous Sunday hadn't felt like Sunday without attending church.

It felt strange to walk into a chapel the next morning where almost everyone was near her own age. Even as a college student, she'd attended the same family ward she'd gone to all of her life. After buying her condo, she'd gone to the family ward a few blocks away even though she'd been told there was a singles ward she could attend. She hoped Sister Walker, the Primary president, hadn't had any difficulty finding a substitute teacher for Kira's class of active four-year-olds. She felt guilty for not finding her own substitute, but Detective Daley had cautioned that she should avoid telling more people than necessary that she would be away for an undetermined time.

A young man wearing a bright-pink shirt and a flamboyant teal tie walked up to Ford, greeting him with a fist bump. "Who's the good-looking chick?"

She felt her cheeks flame.

Ford's arm circled her shoulders, pulling her a little closer to his side. "This is Kira." She noticed he omitted giving her last name and that he found a quick excuse to move them toward another cluster of young people.

They were welcomed warmly by several others, and she noticed quite a few envious glances directed their way. She suspected that behind some of the disappointed looks were girls who were speculating that Ford's eligible bachelor status was over and they had missed their chances to catch his attention.

Ford led the way from the foyer to a bench inside the chapel, where he introduced her to the couple who had scooted over to make room for them. "Kira, this is Lisa Roberts and Daniel Ottley. Daniel lives in the same apartment complex I do." Lowering his voice, he explained to Daniel that Kira was temporarily living in his apartment while her apartment was undergoing some repairs and he was staying with a friend. She wasn't certain whether his explanation constituted a lie or not, but she was glad he'd offered an explanation other than the conclusion someone might assume for finding her living in his apartment.

When the meeting started, she basked in the familiar warmth of the opening hymn and listened intently to the speakers. She felt gratitude to be able to partake of the sacrament. She closed her eyes and pleaded for an end to the fear and uncertainty she'd experienced all summer.

She enjoyed the adult Sunday School class, but when it came time to introduce herself in Relief Society, she hesitated. Should she give her last name? Each time Ford had introduced her, he'd simply called her Kira. But deciding it would sound odd if she didn't use her full name, she said as confidently as she could manage, "I'm Kira Paxton."

"Any relation to Garrett Paxton over at Paxton Enterprises?" someone asked.

She automatically nodded her head, admitting the relationship and ducking her head to avoid revealing a self-deprecating smile. She'd been so concerned someone might connect her name with the discovery of Marla's body that she'd forgotten the attention her surname had garnered all of her life. Her father was well-known for his successful businesses and his philanthropic donations to numerous causes.

Sinking into her chair, she tried to look as inconspicuous as possible. She tried to concentrate on the lesson given by a nervous young woman who didn't look a day over sixteen, though to be in the singles' ward she had to be. Kira's mind kept returning to the innocent question asked about her family connection. Could her father be right? Was someone singling her out for harassment, perhaps even harm, because she was Garrett Paxton's daughter? All along she'd believed there was some kind of connection to the body Jasper found. Was it possible the only connection was one that some disgruntled fanatic had made to her name when it was given out in news stories related to that discovery? Could the harassment and threats be because she was her father's daughter? But that didn't explain the attack on Mr. Andrews.

All of her life she'd resented the restrictions her father had placed on her. Was it possible that the impediments to her independence had more to do with protecting her from the kind of warped people who had vandalized her home and threatened her life instead of simply a refusal to see her as a strong, healthy woman capable of managing her own life?

CHAPTER NINETEEN

UNABLE TO SLEEP, KIRA STOOD at the bedroom window looking out over the park. She hadn't bothered to turn on any lights. Since moving into Ford's apartment, she'd found she often did her best thinking in the dark with no distractions and only the serene beauty of the dark shapes of trees and the silvery glint of the distant stream interrupting her focus.

A movement caught her eye, and she watched as a large figure moved from one group of trees to another. Her heart raced, and she wondered if the vandals had discovered her whereabouts. Seeing no further movement, she chided herself for jumping to conclusions. Even though the park was officially closed at night, it was likely lovers, vagrants, or those bent on mischief were still inside after the general public had gone for the day.

Once more her thoughts returned to her father. Did she owe him an apology? Had he only been thinking of her safety all those times she'd accused him of trying to keep her a dependent child? If that were the case, why had he never explained his actions? Had there been kidnapping attempts when she was a child—which would explain his extreme protectiveness? As an adult she knew money was a powerful motivator behind most crimes and that the children of successful people were more vulnerable to kidnapping and the demented revenge actions of disgruntled employees than the offspring of the average person, but she wasn't certain her father fell in that category. Sure, he owned an international company, lived in a large home and hired people to care for it, and drove an expensive car, but she'd never thought of her family as being rich. Had she been unrealistic?

Since moving out of her father's house and being responsible for her own livelihood, she'd discovered that many things she once took for granted were now beyond her means. She'd learned that some people did without necessities. She wasn't naive; some did without because of poor decision making, but others lacked the necessities of life through no fault of their own. She knew, too, that some people preyed on others to gain what they couldn't or wouldn't earn honestly.

Thoughts swirled about in her mind, alternately justifying her father and brother for coddling her and blaming them for her lack of independence and preparation for real life—factors that undermined her self-confidence.

She didn't want to think about it anymore. She returned to bed, determined to think of something pleasant until she drifted to sleep. It was Ford Kettering that filled her mind as she imagined she could still catch a faint whiff of his aftershave on the comforter she pulled up to her chin. She was almost asleep when she remembered the large hospital almost across the street from Ford's apartment complex. Tomorrow she'd go there to see if Mr. Andrews was allowed visitors. As far as she knew, no one had been charged in the attack on the elderly man. Intellectually she knew what had happened wasn't her fault, yet she felt a guilty kind of responsibility for his injuries.

* * *

Ford awoke with a vague sense of uneasiness. He listened for any sound of trouble. Hearing nothing, he stepped out of bed and moved to the door that led to the hall. Easing the door open, he listened once more. This time he could detect voices coming from the living room. He felt certain it wasn't the TV. Stan never turned the television on during his shift, which was usually from two in the morning until noon. They'd agreed to keep sound at a minimum while one slept and one watched, a pattern which would benefit both of them. He caught the tone but not the words Stan spoke.

He didn't sound alarmed, but there was a placating note in his voice. The other voice had a familiar ring to it, though he couldn't immediately place it.

Ford moved with caution down the hall until he had a view of the space in front of the door, pausing when he recognized Garrett Paxton. He listened a moment and determined Garrett sounded angry. He didn't want to tangle with the man, but if Stan needed backup, he supposed he'd better go in there.

"Ed reported that she left the apartment at nine thirty this morning, crossed the street, and entered the hospital. She hasn't been seen leaving. The hospital refuses to verify if she's been admitted."

Ford rolled his eyes. No doubt about it—he'd better go in.

"It's okay." Ford strolled into the front room, hoping Kira's father would assume that his casual attire was evidence everything was under control. He chose not to comment on two facts the man's words revealed: one, Garrett's words made it clear he knew where Kira was staying; and two, he had someone watching her. Stan wasn't the only security man Garrett had brought in. He wondered if Detective Daley had been informed. It was certain that if he and Stan hadn't been told, Kira didn't know.

"An old man Kira befriended is a patient at the hospital. She called earlier this morning to say she'd be visiting him before going to work." Ford kept his words casual.

Stan picked up the cue and added, "She's been concerned about him being alone." He hesitated. "You never mentioned you were going to bring in Ed." Stan didn't sound happy at this turn of events.

"With you laid up, I figured I couldn't take chances, especially with this lamebrain plan to just trade living spaces. Kira needs around-the-clock protection until those hoodlums are caught. I want her back in my house today! Is that understood?" He glared at Stan then turned on Ford.

"I expected better of you. I had a thorough background check run on you or I wouldn't have allowed my daughter to continue seeing you, but I won't have you encouraging this kind of dangerous rebellion. Be out of here by four o'clock." He turned to

include Stan. "You can pick up your check from the HR office. Ed
will take care of returning Kira home, where she belongs."

"Whoa!" Stan's face didn't reveal any alarm over his dismissal or
the older man's tantrum. "Kira won't go willingly, and I don't think
you want kidnapping charges brought against you. The press would
have a field day."

"Don't you threaten me!"

"I'm not threatening, just reminding you that your daughter
is an adult, not a little girl. She doesn't want you running her life
and interfering with her right to make her own decisions. The
Murray Police Department won't take kindly to your interference
either. And by the way, you can dismiss me from this case, but you
can't fire me from my own firm. You don't own Zumbrowski and
Martel Security; my partner and I do. And I hope you're aware that
trusting your daughter to your company security man is putting her
life at risk."

"Come on, Mr. Paxton." Ford attempted to play peacemaker
when inside he was seething with anger. "Sit down. Let's talk about
this rationally."

"Dad?" The door behind Garrett burst open, and Tracy,
followed by Jasper, rushed into the room. Tracy looked around in
confusion before turning to his father. "What's going on? I heard
you yelling as soon as I pulled into the driveway and thought you
were in some kind of trouble."

"Nothing is the matter. I was letting these two know they're
to stay away from Kira and that from now on I'll see to her
protection."

"Oh, really?" Tracy looked amused. "You might think Kira is
still your sweet little girl who will do anything Daddy says, but let
me assure you, she's as bullheaded and determined as her old man.
I've seen the way she looks at Ford Kettering, and I'd be willing
to bet that if you make her choose between the two of you, you'll
lose."

CHAPTER TWENTY

As she approached the desk, Kira noticed a nurse pressing a telephone to her ear. She paused, and when the nurse finished her call, Kira asked which room Mr. Andrews was in.

"It's early for visitors."

Kira hadn't considered that the hospital might have set visiting hours. She'd only thought ahead enough to send Ford a text and to let the credit union branch manager know she'd be late. Dressing to go straight to work after a short visit, she hadn't considered whether an early-morning visitor would be welcomed by the hospital.

The nurse seemed to hesitate, then added, "But I'm sure he'll be happy to see you. He doesn't get many visitors." She checked her chart and then pointed to a room directly across from her desk.

When Kira stepped into his room, Mr. Andrews wasn't lying in bed as she'd expected. Instead he was sitting in a large, comfortable-looking armchair. His leg, covered by a cast, was propped up on the footrest. His face showed heavy bruises that were turning interesting shades of green and purple. He smiled in spite of a split lip and motioned for her to come closer.

"Hi! I'm glad you're feeling well enough to sit in a chair." She set down a box of chocolates she'd purchased in the gift shop. "I've been worried ever since I heard someone attacked you."

"The punk should have been locked up a long time ago. That young officer they sent here to ask me questions said he'd get a warrant and he'd be in jail in no time, but I haven't heard whether or not he's been arrested."

"Was it Luis Vincent who did this to you?"

"I hadn't turned the lights on yet and he was wearing a ski mask, so I didn't get a good look, but I'm sure it was Luis. I think Patricia Dilworth heard us talking and garbled everything we said when she reported it to Nita Hayden. Nita likely blew it up further to her sister and Luis." He shook his head in disgust.

Kira's shoulders slumped. She wasn't the only one to suspect a connection between the body found along the river's edge, the attacks and threats she'd received, and the brutal attack on poor Mr. Andrews. "If it was him, I hope the police get him soon. I'd like some answers too. Like, why has he been harassing me when all I did was scream and nearly pass out when my brother's dog found Marla? Surely he doesn't think I had anything to do with her murder." She vented her frustration.

"I don't know how that crazy kid thinks. He and Marla were close, and I suspect you're just the first person he could find to take out his anger on with any kind of connection to her death."

"But why you? You had nothing to do with it."

"Sit down." He motioned to a chair. She sat, folding the jacket that matched her new slacks across her lap.

Mr. Andrews went on, "I've asked that question a hundred times. That young policeman asked too. All I could tell him was something Luis said when he hit me. 'That's for shootin' your mouth off.' That's why I think Patricia heard us talking and repeated a twisted version of what I told you, and Luis took exception to it."

They visited for a few more minutes until Mr. Andrews began to look tired. Kira stood.

"Should I call a nurse to help you back to bed?"

"No, I'm fine. I'll just snooze in this chair for a few minutes. My daughter will be back any minute."

"I'm glad I got to see you, and I hope you'll be back home soon." She touched his shoulder in a brief farewell gesture.

The old man's shoulders slumped. "I won't be going home. As soon as the doctor gives the okay for me to travel, Carrie is taking me back to Florida with her."

Kira felt sad to think the elderly man would have to leave behind his business and the people he'd known and loved most of his life, but she could sympathize with his daughter too. Carrie's home and job were on the other side of the country. To care for her elderly father, she had little choice other than moving him closer to her.

Sliding her purse strap over her shoulder, Kira left Mr. Andrews's room and walked toward the elevator. As she walked, she reached for her phone, but when she pulled it out, she remembered she'd turned it off when she'd entered the hospital. She'd turn it back on to call Ford once she was out of the building. He should be up by now. Perhaps they could still get in a short run later this evening. She slid the small phone back into her purse and folded her jacket over her arm.

Exiting the elevator, she followed the hall to a set of automatic doors and fumbled in her purse for her car keys.

"Don't create a scene. Your father sent me to get you." A large, meaty hand closed around her upper arm. Startled Kira attempted to pull away from the man. His fingers dug into her arm, tightening his grip. He looked vaguely familiar, but she wasn't certain where she might have seen him before.

"Leave me alone," she hissed. "I'm not going with you."

"You don't have a choice. Daddy is calling the shots this time." He relentlessly propelled her toward a van parked in the hospital's loading zone. A flash of memory told her she'd seen the man from behind on one of the rare occasions she'd visited her father's office. Anger replaced fear. Her father had gone much too far this time. No way would she quietly go along with his high-handed takeover.

Digging in her heels and refusing to walk did no good. The man, who was several inches over six feet tall and solidly built, picked her up and shoved her in the back of the vehicle. She landed painfully on her knees, and her head struck the opposite wall, leaving her too winded to scream. As soon as she could catch her breath, she searched for a door handle. There wasn't one, and the van was moving.

"Let me out," she screamed at the two men seated in the front.

"Your father warned us you'd make a fuss. It won't do any good. Just relax. You're safe now." The big man didn't bother to turn around to speak.

"I'm sure Daddy will be thrilled to see the bruise on my arm, my scraped knees, and a goose egg on my forehead."

The big man who'd dragged her from the hospital entrance shrugged. His attitude angered her, and she vowed that she'd make certain her father knew about every scrape, bruise, and indignity she'd suffered at the hands of his security goon. Though she'd caught a glimpse of Ed Ellsworth once, she'd never actually met him. This big ape certainly fit a laughing description Tracy had once used to describe the man hired to oversee security at the company headquarters in Salt Lake—a gorilla with more muscles than brains.

"Here! Maybe this will cool you off." The big man handed her a bottle of water. She was tempted to refuse it, but it was hot in the van, and her useless screams had left her throat dry and scratchy. She unscrewed the leaky cap and took a long swallow. With the bottle in her hand, she considered dumping the contents on the infuriating man's head or using it as a weapon to hit him. Neither action would realistically gain her freedom. She took another swallow.

Tightening the lid, she took stock of her situation. The back of the van held nothing but her and what looked like a worn pad from a patio lounge chair. There were no seats, just as there were no door handles. Thank goodness she'd put on pants this morning instead of the pleated skirt or dress suit she usually wore to work. She suspected Ed hadn't run this part of their plan past her father.

Her head felt funny, and her vision seemed blurry. Was it possible she had a concussion from hitting her head? She rubbed the sore spot on her forehead. As soon as they reached her father's house, she'd put some ice on the lump she could feel beneath her fingers. A wave of dizziness swept over her. She must have hit her head harder than she thought. It occurred to her they should be at the house by now. Raising her head, she peeked through the windshield in time to see a sign for the Draper exit. They were on the freeway and should have turned off a long way back. Something wasn't right.

She'd call . . . Daddy wouldn't allow them to treat her like this. Her phone was in her purse. She groped in the dim light for her purse. Her purse! Where was it? It had been on her shoulder when she left Mr. Andrews's room at the hospital. That awful man, the one she thought was Ed, must have taken it. Or she dropped it on the ground when he grabbed her. She opened her mouth to demand the return of her purse, but nothing came out.

She remembered sliding her phone out back at the hospital. Perhaps she only thought she'd put it in her purse. Her hands moved sluggishly searching for her jacket. Nothing. It was gone too.

The light was growing dimmer, and she was so tired. Ford would worry when he called and she didn't answer. She felt cold—and tired. If only Ford were with her, everything would be all right.

* * *

Ford paced the floor. There was no way Kira could still be at the hospital. She wasn't answering her cell phone, and Garrett's security man insisted she hadn't left the hospital. Something was wrong. Some sense told him she was in trouble and needed him. He turned to Stan. "I'm going over there."

"I'll go with you," Stan volunteered. "We'd better lock up and notify Detective Daley that there won't be anyone here for a while." He gave Kira's father and brother a pointed look.

"Come on, Dad." Tracy reached for the door. "There's nothing we can do here." Without a word, Garrett stomped out the door. Tracy gave Stan and Ford an apologetic shrug and followed his father.

Stan called the detective while Ford made certain the house was secure. In minutes they were in Ford's truck driving as fast as he dared. Still when they reached the hospital, both Daley and the Paxtons were already there and embroiled in a sharp exchange with the hospital's head of security. Garrett's security man wasn't with them.

"Go check with Mr. Andrews," Stan whispered to Ford. "See if the old man has any idea how long ago Kira was here. I'll look around for Ed." Ford thought Stan added under his breath, "He's probably hunkered down in the cafeteria." It didn't take much brainwork to figure out Stan didn't have a high opinion of Ed Ellsworth.

Twenty minutes later they met in the first floor waiting room. "Mr. Andrews has no idea how long ago Kira left, but he thinks it must have been a couple of hours," Ford reported. "He said he fell asleep right after she left. I spoke to the nurse at the desk. She said she's pretty sure she saw Kira waiting for the elevator about nine."

"I never found Ed or anyone who's even seen him." Stan looked grim.

"Okay, what do we do now?" Ford asked. He was at a loss to know what to do, but one thing was certain. He wouldn't simply wait around for the police to act.

"Let's check out your apartment and see if she went back there. She probably turned her phone off in the hospital and may have forgotten to turn it back on."

"Stan! Ford!" Both men turned as Detective Daley approached them. "You haven't located Miss Paxton either?"

They shook their heads in glum acknowledgement. "We were just getting ready to go to my apartment to see if she may have gone back there."

"I'll tag along." The officer joined them for the brief walk to Ford's apartment building, where everything appeared neat and in order—but there was no sign of Kira.

Remembering his friend Daniel Ottley on the floor above him, Ford punched in the number for his cell phone. It rang several times, and he was about to hang up when Daniel picked up. Skipping their usual teasing chat, Ford got right to the point. "Have you seen Kira this morning?"

"Kira? No, she was probably still sleeping when I left for work this morning—it was about four thirty when I left the apartment. Is something wrong?"

"She isn't at the apartment, and she's not answering her phone."

Daniel was quiet for a moment. Ford started to say good-bye, but his friend continued in a thoughtful voice. "I didn't see Kira. I seldom see anyone when I leave for work—even you early-morning joggers—but this morning I did see a couple of guys hanging around those trees that separate our driveway from the park."

"Can you tell me what they looked like?" Ford waited for a description of the gang members who had been identified by some of Kira's neighbors.

"I didn't pay close attention, but I'm sure they weren't dressed as runners. One was a big guy. I'd guess he was well over six feet tall and close to three hundred, three fifty pounds. The other guy was smaller, normal height and weight."

"Thanks! If you think of anything else, give me a call." They ended the call, and Ford turned to the detectives to share the description.

"None of the guys in Luis's gang are that big," Daley mused. "One kid is tall but skinny. Anyway if you're thinking some of the gang members were hanging around after Kira left the hospital, you can forget that theory. I've been in touch with someone from the Salt Lake City Gang Unit. He says Luis Vincent's gang has been jittery all week, and they met behind the bowling alley for some kind of confab this morning. Their man couldn't get close enough to hear what was being said, but he suspects they're planning a confrontation with another gang that's been encroaching on their territory. The officer I talked to said there was a drive-by shooting last night. Fortunately no one was hurt, but it has the gang unit on edge."

"Why hasn't Luis been picked up for assaulting Mr. Andrews?" Ford wasn't ready to let go of his suspicion that Marla's cousin had something to do with Kira's disappearance.

"Andrews can't positively identify his assailant. He *thinks* it was the Vincent kid, but it was dark and he can't be sure."

"Any word from ballistics on the bullets found in Kira's patio post and her car?" Stan asked a question of his own.

Daley hesitated as though uncertain how much information he could share. He seemed to decide and answered, "They're the same caliber, but the markings indicate they were fired by different guns. And before you ask, neither matches the slug found in our young victim. The murder weapon wasn't found, and the gun owner can't be traced without it."

An air of dejection seemed to surround the three men; then Stan straightened his shoulders. "Where do we go from here?" he asked. "I'm off Paxton's payroll, but I owe Kira. I also owe the creeps who attacked me and threw me in the canal."

"I've never given up on a case yet." Daley's voice was grim but determined.

Ford took heart. He wasn't alone in his determination to find Kira.

CHAPTER TWENTY-ONE

KIRA LAY STILL, TRYING TO get her bearings. Without opening her eyes, she knew she wasn't lying on the bed in the room that had been hers since she was a toddler. She wasn't in her own bed at her condo nor the bed she'd been sleeping in for the past week at Ford's apartment. Not only did the bed feel wrong, but the single blanket wrapped around her was rough and smelled of stale smoke and perspiration. She could hear the murmur of voices, but they weren't close enough to make out the words.

Lifting her lashes a tiny bit, she endeavored to look around her. When she was convinced she was alone, she opened her eyes wider and attempted to sit up. The room seemed to revolve, and she had to grip the edge of the cot to keep her balance. It took several minutes for the haze to clear enough so that she could make out the room's features. The walls looked like rough-hewn logs with cementlike chinking. Bare planks in need of a good sweeping made up the floor. The only window consisted of four narrow, dirty panes of glass, shuttered from the outside. The cot was the only furniture in the room. She'd never before seen such a dingy room.

She eyed the single wooden door. She assumed the voices she'd heard came from the other side of it. Surely her dad had no idea what kind of accommodations Ed had made for her. With as much care as he'd always taken to make certain she had whatever she needed, with the comfort and grace he'd surrounded her with all her life, she suspected he'd throw a fit when he saw this place.

Attempting to sit up, she struggled with nausea for several moments. All she needed to add to her discomfort and the stench of the wretched room would be losing her long-ago breakfast. Once her stomach settled, she cautiously rose to her feet. After standing in place until she felt her legs would bear her weight, she placed one hand on the wall to begin her journey toward the door.

Inching her way along the wall seemed to take forever, but at last she reached the door. A shove against it produced no result. She grasped the doorknob and twisted. It didn't move. She tried again with the same result. The door was locked! A shiny new lock caught her eye; it looked as though it had been recently installed. The door itself also appeared to be new. She couldn't believe it. Daddy would never give his approval for locking her in!

She opened her mouth to scream at the men to unlock the door, but only a whisper came out. Frustrated she hammered on the door but only succeeded in bruising her fists. Drawing back her leg, she aimed a solid kick at the offending door. Pain shot through her foot. If she were capable of screaming, she would have. How had she failed to notice her shoes were gone?

Kira sat on the floor, hugging her bruised toes. They weren't only bruised from kicking the door but were covered with fresh scratches and small droplets of blood. She hoped her tetanus shot was current. No doubt the scratches were from brushing against the sharp pine needles that littered the floor. Daddy would be furious when he found—

How could she have been so stupid? Her father had nothing to do with the situation she found herself in. Just because her father was high-handed about protecting her, she shouldn't assume he was behind her abduction. The man who had strong-armed her into his van had implied he was following her father's orders, but her dad wouldn't condone anyone treating her this way. She'd been picked up and tossed in the back of the van like a bag of trash.

She remembered the drippy bottle of water. Falling asleep in the back of that van wasn't normal; she'd been drugged! The room she found herself in was dirty and lacked even common comforts such as a chair. Her purse, cell phone, and shoes were missing. Someone was obviously making certain she couldn't go anywhere if she did manage to escape.

Her head ached, most likely due to the drug she'd been given, though the blow she'd received when she'd struck the metal wall of the van likely played its part in causing the pain. She suspected she was still suffering the lingering effects of the drug, though it was wearing off. In spite of the pain in her head, she was beginning to think more clearly. She had to concentrate, find a way to escape. Her shoulders slumped. She had no idea where she was or if it was even still the same day.

She wasn't a quitter. Straightening, she vowed to find a way to escape her prison. Placing her hands against the rough log walls, she managed to regain her feet. She stood, trying to decide what to do. Trying to get someone's attention and demanding they unlock the door appeared to be a futile plan. She could return to the cot and hope she could sleep off the headache; however, she couldn't just do nothing and simply hope she'd be released.

Her eyes traveled to the small, narrow window. It didn't look like the kind of window that could be opened. Slats of some kind—shutters perhaps—blocked the outside of the window, letting in little light. Obviously she couldn't crawl through locked shutters even if she managed to get the window open, but perhaps she could gain some idea of where she was if she were close enough to look through the narrow cracks. There was a strong possibility she wouldn't be able to see anything, but she had to try.

She eyed the floor she'd have to cross to get to the window. She didn't relish walking on it barefoot. Several patches looked like some kind of liquid had been spilled and never cleaned up. In time dirt, pine needles, and other indefinable debris had formed a sticky mat. Leaves and dirt lay undisturbed in the corners of the room. From the door to the cot, large footprints were visible in the thick dust, and her own wobbly prints led from the cot to the door.

Picking her way across the room, she reached the window, where she peered through the bottom of the dirty, cracked glass. She felt a flutter of hope when she noticed a piece of one of the shutters was broken. Maneuvering onto her toes to look through the broken slat did little good. All she could see was a nearly solid wall of pine trees. She'd already assumed from the dried pine needles on the floor that she was in a forest but was disappointed to see no identifying features such as mountain peaks or ski trams.

The sound of a key in the lock behind her alerted her that someone was coming. Panic surged through her, and she hurried back toward the cot. Her previous assumption that her father was behind her abduction no longer gave her assurance that her kidnappers wouldn't actually harm her.

"You're awake." The man she felt pretty certain had been the driver of the van stepped into the room carrying a battered pizza box. She hadn't gotten a good look at the driver other than to note that he was thinner and not as tall as the man who'd grabbed her. His hair was thin, and he wore a ragged goatee. His sagging jeans were in need of a thorough washing. She eyed him warily from the opposite side of the cot as he moved toward her.

Noticing he'd left the door behind him open, she weighed her chances of making a run for it. She had no idea what lay beyond that door, and if she did make it all the way outside, there was no way to know which way to run. Still she couldn't do nothing. She gathered her courage and prepared to make a lunge for freedom.

"Don't try it!"

Somehow he'd guessed her intention. He reached across the cot to grab her arm. A hard yank forced her to a sitting position on the cot. "There ain't nowhere you can git I cain't find you. Nobody ever comes within ten miles o' this place, so there ain't nobody gonna help you escape or hear ya yellin'." He sat beside her. Instinctively she scooted as far away as she could.

"Daddy didn't send you."

The infuriating man laughed. "That Ed, he's a smart one. He thought up a good plan." He dumped the box he held on the cot. An unappetizing slab of overdone crust and congealed cheese slid halfway out of the box. "Eat up. It's all you're gonna git today."

She refused to even look at the unappetizing mess. He moved closer and suddenly reached out to grasp her chin. "Highfalutin chicks like you think you're too good for the likes of me. Stupid! I'll soon teach ya that iffin' you're good to me, I can make everthin' much better fer ya." He wrenched her face toward him and covered her mouth with his thick lips.

Gagging, she jerked back and struck him as forcefully as she could with her right hand. He raised his hand as though to strike her back when the sound of a slamming car door changed his mind. He stalked to the door, jerked it open, then slammed it behind him. She heard the key turn in the lock.

Kira collapsed on the cot, struggling to hold back tears. *How did I get in this mess? Better yet, how am I going to get out?* Crouching with her arms wrapped around her drawn-up knees, she thought of Ford. He'd know what to do; he'd be calm and brave. If she just had her phone, she could call him. He'd think of something. She could call Detective Daley or Daddy. She scrubbed at her eyes, refusing to let the tears fall. She didn't have her phone. She couldn't call anyone. For once in her life there was no one nearby, anxious to protect her. It was time to be the strong, independent adult she'd been trying to convince her family she'd become. She was on her own.

Well, not quite.

She looked at the dirty floor then opted to stay on the cot. Kneeling awkwardly, she prayed, pleading for the ability to think clearly and to discover a way to escape. She prayed, too, for protection from her abductors.

As she closed her prayer, she heard the sound of an engine. She cocked her head to the side and listened. The sound grew fainter and then faded away. Had one or both of the men left in the van? If she were alone, that might improve her chances of escaping, yet there was something chilling about the prospect of being abandoned in some remote place with no way to save herself if the cabin caught fire.

She waited for what she estimated was twenty minutes. Hearing nothing in that time, she rose to her feet to survey the room once more. There was nothing she could use as a weapon to defend herself or to break out. Even a club would be of little use against a man the size of her kidnapper. The creep who had brought her the stale pizza had referred to the other man as Ed. She couldn't help wondering if he was the same Ed who worked for her father's company. That would explain why he looked vaguely familiar.

She considered dragging the cot over to the window, but what would be the use? She couldn't use it as a battering ram. She could stand on it to see through more of the cracks between the slats. What purpose that would serve she didn't know, but at least it would be doing something.

If she could just get a better idea of where the men had taken her, perhaps she could devise a plan. She'd read several mysteries where the heroine figured out how to escape by asking to be allowed to go to the bathroom. She could try that; besides, she really did need a trip to a bathroom. It had been too long since she left the apartment. Gathering her courage she called as loudly as her dry throat would allow, "If someone can hear me, please let me go to the bathroom."

When there was no response, she rose from the cot and made her way to the door. She knew better than to kick it this time, but she knocked as hard as she could. This time she spoke more emphatically. "Help! I need to go to the bathroom!" There was no response.

Either she was alone, or the creep who had kidnapped her was ignoring her plea. Giving up trying to get a bathroom break, she wandered back to the cot. The stale pizza caught her attention. She was hungry but not that hungry. Besides it might be laced with some kind of drug. Not only did she not want to eat the nauseating mess, she didn't wish to risk being drugged again. What she really wanted was a drink. She thought longingly of the bottles of orange juice and lemonade she kept in her refrigerator. A sip of cold water would be welcomed by her dry, scratchy throat, but even if her captors brought her a drink, would she dare accept it? Somehow she must free herself.

CHAPTER TWENTY-TWO

FORD SANK INTO A CHAIR with his face in his hands. How could Kira just disappear? He felt confident she wouldn't leave without informing him of her plans. That left possibilities too terrible to consider. In little more than three months, she'd become the center of his world. He couldn't contemplate a life without her. At last he looked up to see Stan watching him.

"We'll find her. Daley has people reviewing the hospital surveillance tapes."

The words, meant to offer hope, lacked the conviction Ford needed.

"I think we can eliminate that punk kid we suspect of harassing her as having anything to do with her disappearance," Stan continued. "According to Daley, he's being watched pretty closely. Before he left to organize a search for those guys loitering in the park, Daley also said we have to consider the possibility she met up with a friend."

"She didn't meet someone," Ford insisted. "We didn't run together this morning because she wanted to go to the hospital to visit Mr. Andrews, and she thought I needed to sleep in since I've been up so many nights watching over her home. She told me she arranged to be late for work. She's too responsible to arrive even later, or not show up at all, without notifying her supervisor. I feel certain she would have let me know if she made different plans."

"I need to check in at my office." Stan spoke apologetically. "Garrett dismissed me, but Tracy is a friend. I consider Kira one too. I'm not leaving this in the hands of the police or that incompetent hack, Ed Ellsworth. After I have a little conference with my partner, I'll continue to search for Kira and look for answers to what's been going on. I suggest you return to her condo and continue to keep an eye on it."

Before Ford could agree or disagree to Stan's plan, the intercom buzzed, and he hurried to respond to it. Ford recognized Tracy's voice. With a sigh, Stan invited Kira's brother to come up. Assuming Garrett was with his son, Ford was surprised when Kaitlin instead of Garrett accompanied Tracy into the apartment.

She rushed to Ford's side. "I can't believe Kira has disappeared! I came to be with Tracy as soon as he told me. Why haven't the police arrested that hoodlum who has been terrorizing her?"

"The police don't believe he had anything to do with Kira's disappearance," Stan answered for Ford.

"You mean someone else took her?" Kaitlin's face revealed the same horror Ford had been struggling to keep in check. "She's been kidnapped? I thought just children . . . No, I'm not that naive. The news is full of stories . . ." She sank onto the sofa with tears running down her face. Tracy sat beside her and took her in his arms, patting her back as she sobbed.

Turning toward Tracy, she burrowed her head against his chest. "Your dad told me he worried someone might take one of you when you were little, especially Kira because she was so tiny. He said when she was about a year old, he sat in a dim room up at Primary Children's Medical Center, holding her while she struggled to breathe, and promised God that if she lived he'd do everything in his power to always keep her safe."

Ford choked back his own tears and felt a kinship with Garrett. How could anyone as small as Kira protect herself from someone who meant her harm?

"There hasn't been a ransom demand. Daley promised to let me know if one comes in." Stan shifted his weight from one foot to the other in a restless movement, indicating he was anxious to be on his way. His eyes met Ford's, and he seemed to be sending a silent message. Aloud he said, "Kaitlin, you and Tracy could help by staying at Kira's condo until this evening. I'll stay there tonight, and Ford can remain here in case she returns to his apartment."

Ford approved the plan. He suspected Stan was arranging to get Tracy and Kaitlin out of his way, leaving him free to investigate. It would also leave Ford free to check out a few things for himself. He wasn't sure why but his thoughts kept returning to something Stan had said at the hospital, and he'd like to talk to Mr. Andrews again. He pulled Kira's house key from his pocket.

"I won't need that," Tracy said. "I have a key to Kira's condo in case I might arrive sometime to pick up Jasper while she was at work."

"By the way, where is Jasper?" Ford looked around. He didn't recall ever seeing Tracy without the big dog in tow.

"He's in my car. I found a parking space in your covered parking area and left the windows down, but we better be on our way."

"Okay. Thanks. Oh, and don't let Jasper eat all of Kira's shoes." It was a dumb thing to say, but Ford knew how hard she tried to keep her shoes away from the dog, and since she wasn't around to protect them, it fell to him to do so.

* * *

Moving the cot to the other side of the room was more difficult than Kira expected. At first she tried to be quiet, but when the metal legs made a squealing noise and no one showed up to check, she stopped worrying about it. Several times she almost gave up, but fearing her only chance to escape might depend on moving the cot, she continued on. At one point she removed the thin cotton mattress from the cot and lugged it to a spot near the window. She crammed the stale pizza back in its box and dumped it beside the mattress.

Returning to the metal frame, she examined it more thoroughly. It consisted of two long rails and two short rails that formed a rectangle supporting dozens of rows of sagging metal springs. Both the head and foot of the cot consisted of one-piece arched pipes. By the time it was finally in place, Kira was tired, dirty, and desperate to relieve her bladder.

She wasn't sure why she felt she should move the cot next to the window. She might be able to see a little more, but there was little chance it would solve either of her immediate problems. It would neither provide a way to escape nor a bathroom.

Seating herself on the cot, she crossed one leg over the other. As she did, she eyed the spots on the floor with new suspicion and hoped they were the result of a leaky roof. As distasteful as she found the prospect, what choice did she have? She hurried to the far corner.

Feeling thoroughly humiliated, she returned to the cot with new determination. She had no intention of repeating that gross experience. Planting her feet firmly, she began tugging and twisting one of the sagging springs. It wouldn't be much of a weapon, but she hoped it would suffice to pry the shutters loose from the window.

Removing one of the springs proved easier than she'd expected. Each one was hooked to the wire frame, and because they were old and stretched, it required only ten minutes of determined twisting and pulling to free one of the curled pieces of metal.

Holding the metal coil in one hand, she climbed atop the cot. From her higher perch, she noticed at once that the wooden shutters were weathered and sported numerous cracks. For the first time, she felt a glimmer of hope. First she'd need to get the window out of the way; then she could work on the shutter. She raised the metal spring, ready to smash the glass when it occurred to her that when the window broke, bits of glass would fly everywhere. Even if she managed to create a space large enough to squeeze through, she could be cut so severely she might bleed to death before finding help.

She reached for the blanket, then spied the pizza box. She might need the blanket if she was in the mountains as she suspected. Even in the summer the temperatures dropped dramatically at higher altitudes, and already the light was growing dimmer, signaling the end of daylight. The blanket would be of no use to her if it was imbedded with glass.

With the blanket tucked under the mattress to protect it from flying glass and the pizza box close at hand, she struck the window. Nothing happened. If this was going to work, she had to use more force. Her second strike made her arm tingle, but she had the satisfaction of seeing the glass shatter into hundreds of tiny, flying pieces.

One by one she broke the panes of glass and, using a folded piece of the cardboard box to protect her hands, painstakingly picked out the bits of glass that clung to the frame. Satisfied she'd removed all she could, she pushed against the crossed pieces of wood that had separated the four small panes.

This was harder than breaking the glass, but after a discouragingly long time, the slender bits of wood snapped and she was able to wiggle them free. She paused to catch her breath. If just removing the window took close to an hour, how long would it take to remove the shutter? A close examination showed the shutter was nailed to the frame with bright new nails. Hoping she could use the cot spring to pry the nails loose, she attempted to work one end of the coiled wire under a nail head. Trying one nail after another, she met with failure. The nails had been pounded in so far there was no space to maneuver the wire.

Finally, Kira had to admit defeat. She couldn't budge the nails. *What now?* Half thinking and half praying, she leaned her head against the exposed shutter. Tears streamed down her face once more. In frustration she slammed a fist against the slats of wood that separated her from freedom. Pain shot through her arm, and a trickle of blood stained the wood.

But neither the pain nor the blood mattered. Her hand poked all the way through the rotten wood!

She stared at her arm, and hope surged through her body, lending new strength to her efforts. She pushed and pulled at the wooden slats, ignoring the inevitable splinters that jabbed her hands. Most of the thin slats gave way, but a few persistent ones clung to their frame, requiring repeated blows from the metal spring before they buckled and were pulled free.

* * *

Ford approached a young man pushing a mop back and forth near the beverage dispenser in the hospital cafeteria. Few customers lingered in the area. The lunch rush was over, and the dinner crowd hadn't yet begun to arrive.

"Excuse me." Ford had to repeat himself before the worker realized the words were directed at him. "Were you here early today?"

"I started at eleven." He sounded wary as though he expected to be accused of some infraction of the rules.

"Is anyone here who might have arrived earlier, say eight or nine o'clock?"

The young man straightened, giving Ford a long, measuring look. "Say, aren't you Mr. Kettering? I was in your drivers' ed class two years ago."

"I thought you looked familiar." Ford forced a smile. Ordinarily he was pleased to meet a former student, but today his thoughts were focused on Kira's disappearance. "Perhaps you can help me. I'm looking for someone who may have noticed a particular man stopping in here for breakfast this morning."

"That would be my boss. Mrs. Sedgewick practically lives here, and she doesn't miss a thing." He pointed across the room to an older woman with a hairnet over her gray hair.

"Thanks! I appreciate the help." Ford left his former student to hurry across the room to intercept the woman who was busy polishing a glass display case.

"Excuse me." He attempted to get the woman's attention. After a few more tries, she finally turned toward him. She merely raised her eyebrows as though asking a question.

"Could you tell me if a young man in his late teens with a shaved head and multiple tattoos was in here this morning?"

"I see kids like that all the time." She paused in her polishing to take a firm stance. "Their mothers should be ashamed, letting their boys run around looking like that, stealing everything they can get their hands on and spouting filth. Those hoodlums need to be cleaned up and put to work."

That was more than he asked for but no answer to his question. "Did anyone like that come in before nine o'clock this morning?"

She made a sound somewhere between a snort and a laugh. "That kind of lazy bum doesn't get up before noon. The only people we had in here that early were a couple of doctors, some nurses, an older couple whose daughter just delivered a baby—oh, there was a big guy, too, who came in for breakfast. He wasn't through eating when his friend came in all excited about something. He jumped up, then took time to wrap a couple of doughnuts in his napkin to take with him before rushing out."

* * *

Kira took care to spread pieces of the pizza box across the windowsill. The light had grown dim, and she viewed the shadowy trees that grew near the cabin with trepidation. As she had suspected, she was somewhere in the mountains, and judging by the direction the van had traveled from the hospital, the cabin was south of the Salt Lake valley. That left a lot of area.

When the cardboard was spread to her satisfaction, she said a quick prayer and attempted to hoist herself high enough to get her shoulders through the window. She would have to squeeze through head first since there was no way she could launch herself high enough to go feet first.

On her second attempt, she managed to grasp the firmly nailed shutter frame. Little by little, she pulled herself up. First the narrow window then the edges of the slats scraped her arms. She twisted to drag her shoulders through the narrow opening and continued to wiggle back and forth until she hung halfway in and halfway out.

Pausing to gulp air, she could only hope her lower body wouldn't get stuck and that she wouldn't be hurt when she dropped four feet or more to the ground. Placing her hands against the log wall as though attempting to hand walk down it, she straightened her body and twisted her hips to better accommodate the narrow passage. Suddenly she was falling! Her arms flailed as she made a desperate attempt to catch herself.

The fall was over as quickly as it began. Kira lay stunned. She didn't think anything was broken, but as if in slow motion, she wiggled her feet, then her fingers. Next she tried pulling herself to a sitting position. Finally, with her back against the log wall, she drew in a breath. That's when she heard the growl of an engine. It was coming closer, and she only had seconds to hide herself in the trees.

CHAPTER TWENTY-THREE

FORD STEPPED THROUGH THE AUTOMATIC doors and was surprised to see Stan leaning against a concrete planter box. Skipping a greeting, the security agent got right to the point. "I saw you speaking to some of the cafeteria employees and thought it best not to intrude. I hope you asked the same questions I meant to ask."

"I didn't learn much." Ford made a quick decision to share the little Mrs. Sedgewick had told him. He didn't care who found Kira; he just wanted her found, and the more everyone shared information, the better chance there was that someone would connect the dots that would lead to her. "One of the cafeteria workers said a big man had breakfast there. The way she described him, he sounds like the same guy you told me about who works security for Garrett. Another man came in to get him before he'd finished eating. I got the impression he was more interested in his breakfast than in watching Kira."

"That sounds like Ed." Stan scowled. "What about the other guy? Did you get a description of him?"

"Nothing helpful. She said he was average height and weight, middle aged, brown hair, shabby clothes, a goatee, and tattoos on his arms—though she couldn't describe the tattoos."

A voice came from behind Stan. "That's a pretty good match to the description we got from a couple of kids who hid out overnight in the park."

Startled, Stan and Ford turned to see Detectives Daley and Chetfield. "The only thing the kids added was that the pair showed up about four o'clock carrying a couple of pizza boxes. The big guy consumed slice after slice of pizza while the other guy watched the apartment building through binoculars," Chetfield told them.

Ford muttered under his breath.

"We didn't get anything useful from the surveillance camera either," Daley volunteered. "It merely shows her arriving a little after eight and approaching the doors on her way out less than an hour later."

"Have you had a chance to speak with Ed?" Stan asked. "Did he or his friend see anyone following Kira when she crossed the street and entered the hospital?"

Daley's phone rang before he could respond. He answered, listening more than he spoke, and his face grew more stern. When he returned the phone to his tool belt, he met Ford's eyes with a look of sympathy. "Garrett Paxton just notified the chief that he received a ransom demand approximately ten minutes ago. He and Ed were alone in his office when a secretary transferred the call. The caller demanded 2.5 million dollars for her release. The chief has already started a trace, but the phone was likely a cheap disposable one."

Ford felt like he'd been punched in the gut. How could this be happening? His head swam, and he tried to make sense of how the events of the past few months could possibly be related. Had the discovery of a murder victim set it all in motion?

"Perhaps you should go back to your apartment for a little while and get some rest." Stan placed a brotherly arm across his shoulders.

Resting wouldn't help Kira. He shrugged off the suggestion. But where should he go? What could he do to find her?

Daley took a couple steps before turning back to Ford. "You might like to know, we interviewed those kids you and Miss Paxton told me about. They said pretty much the same thing you did with the exception of admitting to shoplifting. We brought in the victim's boyfriend too. He verified everything the girls said and went further to say he heard her boast she could make you change her grade."

* * *

From her position behind the cabin, Kira heard the vehicle draw closer then the cessation of sound before a car door slammed. *Please don't come around to this side of the cabin.* Even if the men went directly inside, she was still in danger. A glance inside the room where she'd been locked would clearly show how she'd escaped. If anyone looked out the window, he would catch her huddled against the log wall. She had to reach the trees where she could hide as quickly as possible.

Waiting just long enough to give the men time to enter the house, she darted toward a large tree surrounded by a thicket of brush. Ignoring the aches and bruises from her fall, she prayed to reach safety unseen. Each step brought a stab of pain either to her tender bare feet or to the rest of her aching body.

Struggling to keep from sobbing aloud, she stumbled into the shrubs, which proved to be covered with thorns that snagged her clothes and scraped her arms. Forcing her way through the tangled growth, Kira collapsed against the white trunk of a quaking aspen. Her breath came in deep gulps until a voice inside her head reminded her she wasn't out of danger and she must avoid making any sound.

It took tremendous determination and self-control to still her breathing. When she felt she'd gained some control, Kira raised her head to peer back toward the cabin. Daylight was almost gone, but even in the semidarkness she could see the cabin wasn't large. The roof sagged, and there was a general air of neglect about it. As she watched, a figure rounded the corner and stood staring into the forest where she hid, almost as though he were looking directly at her. She recognized the smaller of the two men, the one she called the creep. He shouted something in a loud, angry voice. She couldn't make out the words, but she understood the threat and anger he spewed. She shivered and made herself as small as possible against the tree. Thank goodness she'd worn a white shirt that day, even if it was soiled now with dirt and blood. It blended perfectly with the white trunks of the trees surrounding her.

She was too close to the cabin. If that man walked into the trees looking for her, there was too much risk he'd find her. She needed to put as much distance as possible between them, but she feared moving would draw attention to her.

She'd almost decided to chance moving deeper into the trees when the man, who was little more than a dark shadow now, moved back toward the cabin and disappeared from sight. Resisting the urge to run, she crawled for several feet then, crouching low, began to work her way through the thick growth. Finding a path of sorts, she began to run.

A sharp pain shot through her foot, and she barely remembered not to scream. Limping toward a large tree trunk, she sank down beside it. It didn't take long to realize she'd left the aspens behind and was now surrounded by pine trees. Though it was now too dark to see, she suspected that a pine needle was the source of the pain.

Using her hands, she brushed the soles of her feet, wincing at several tender spots. Her hands came away wet and sticky.

A distant sound reminded her she hadn't traveled far enough. She had to keep moving, even if that meant stumbling around in the dark to put as much distance as possible between herself and the creep. She had no way of knowing whether he had come alone or if both men had returned and were now following her. She shuddered, thinking of the way the creep had looked at her and the familiar way he'd touched her. Of the two, he scared her the most.

Not having spent a lot of time in the mountains even though she'd grown up in Salt Lake, Kira tried to recall everything she'd ever heard or read about hiking, survival, and anything else remotely related to her situation. She might be lost, but staying in one place waiting to be found was out of the question. Avoiding trails and being quiet were the only practical pieces of advice that came to mind. She took a cautious step then another. She regretted veering off from the trail, but it made sense that the creep would assume she'd follow the trail.

The night was dark with no moon or stars, and she found herself bumping into rocks and running afoul of pine boughs. Strange sounds—which may or may not have been wild animals— sent shivers down her spine. Somewhere she'd heard or read that someone lost in the mountains should find a stream to follow or at least move downhill to eventually reach farms or towns. Most of the time she couldn't tell if she was traveling uphill or down.

Covering the face on her wristwatch with her hand, she pushed a button to illuminate the numbers. It was almost eleven. The sun had gone down around nine, so she'd been struggling through the dark forest for nearly two hours. If she just had some idea where she might be . . . She didn't know how long the drug she'd been given had kept her sedated, but her best guess was that she was no more than two or three hours south of the Salt Lake valley. There were many small towns and ranches in that radius, and it seemed she should have caught a glimpse of lights by now. She'd heard of lost people wandering in circles and hoped that wasn't what she'd been doing. She was tired and hungry. She almost regretted not eating the stale pizza the creep had given her.

Running had kept her in good physical condition, but she was exhausted, and it was becoming more difficult with each step to keep moving. Perhaps if she rested for a few minutes, she'd have the strength to go on. A rock didn't make a good pillow, but she settled down between two boulders that still retained some of the day's heat. Leaning her head against the hard surface of one that towered over her, she struggled to not give in to despair. She longed to curl up in her bed, feeling safe and secure. And warm! The day had been warm, but the night, especially when she wasn't moving, was cold. She wished she'd been able to hang onto the scruffy blanket she'd set aside at the cabin. Curling into a tight ball, she closed her eyes. She wouldn't sleep. She was too cold and scared for that.

* * *

Whether it was the vibration or the ringtone of his phone that awoke Ford, he couldn't say. He'd sat down to map out a strategy for finding Kira what seemed only minutes earlier, but he could see the sun had set and his apartment had grown dark. He picked up the phone.

"Stan, here," a voice spoke in his ear. "I thought you should know I've done a little snooping—though our friend Detective Daley would likely call it breaking and entering—and I discovered something interesting."

Ford was wide awake now.

Stan went on. "I sneaked into Ed Ellsworth's old van. It's pretty stripped down, with nothing but an old lounge pad in the back. The front is a cluttered mess of fast-food wrappers, dried french fries, and pizza crumbs." Ford was growing impatient and wished

Stan would get to the point. "I about gave up finding anything useful until I swept a hand under the passenger seat. I found Kira's phone."

"You what?" Ford was on his feet now. "That proves she was in his van! Have the police questioned him?"

"Not yet. They're on their way to pick him up."

"I'll meet you at the police station."

"No. Wait." Stan stopped him before he reached the door. "I've had some experience with Ed. He's a convincing liar, and even an experienced interrogator is going to need some time to get anything useful out of him. As a favor to Tracy, I investigated an inside theft job at Paxton Enterprises six months ago. I'm convinced Ed was in on it, but I couldn't prove anything. My investigation uncovered a couple of things that might lead us to Kira. Ed has a close friend who's served time and who lives with him off and on. The two are joint owners of a piece of remote property once owned by a sheep rancher in the Manti-La Sal Mountains. The other guy inherited it, and I'm not sure how Ed got to be a co-owner. Ed's van is covered in a thick layer of dust like it had recently been on dirt roads. I think we should check out that piece of property."

"That's a long way and will take us away from the investigation if you're wrong." Ford's heart was pounding, and he felt the first hope he'd had all day, but it wasn't in his nature to ignore the negative aspects of Stan's plan.

"I thought so too until I noticed what I think are fresh sheep droppings caught in the tread of the van's tires. There aren't any sheep on the roads around here, and that's sheep country there."

"Where shall we meet?"

"We'll pick you up in five minutes. And bring Kira's running shoes."

The call ended, and Ford wasted no time pulling on a flannel shirt and grabbing a warm coat. He poured hot tap water into a thermos, added a packet of chocolate mix, and stuffed his pockets with granola bars. He had no idea why Stan wanted Kira's shoes, but he dutifully stuffed them in his backpack. At the last minute, he pulled the throw from the back of his sofa and headed for the door, all the while wondering who Stan meant when he said *we*.

CHAPTER TWENTY-FOUR

FORD RECOGNIZED STAN IN THE passenger seat of the Jeep that slid to a stop in front of his apartment complex. At the wheel was Tracy. Before Ford had even finished fastening his seat belt, Tracy shot from the curb and careened down the street. A slobbery kiss covered his cheek, and he turned to see he shared the backseat with Jasper.

Stan talked while Tracy drove. He laid out everything he knew about Ed and his friend, Barry Skidmore, or Skid.

"What did he serve time for?" Tracy asked. When Stan didn't answer, Tracy became more insistent.

"He has a taste for young girls," Stan admitted with reluctance. "He was accused of molesting a twelve-year-old girl in a home robbery in Des Moines, but the charge was reduced to burglary. A second charge involving a teenager was dropped when the girl refused to testify."

The Jeep jolted forward at a faster pace, and Ford silently urged Tracy to push it as fast as it would go, praying they wouldn't be stopped by the highway patrol. He prayed, too, for protection for Kira, whose tiny frame made her appear younger than her true age.

It was well after midnight when Tracy slowed to make his way through a college town. A few minutes later, they left the pavement for a dirt road that wound around a mountain, skirting a small meadow. In the darkness, Ford couldn't see beyond the narrow ribbon highlighted by the Jeep's headlights, but there appeared to be a fork in the road ahead.

"Stop!" Stan called out, and Tracy slammed on the brakes. "Stay here," he ordered the other two men as he jumped from the vehicle carrying a flashlight. Ford watched him pick his way forward on the clumps of grass that bordered the road. After a few minutes of closely examining the place where the road split, he dashed back to the Jeep.

"Take the right fork." Tracy spun the wheel, and the Jeep shot toward the road on the right. Stan leaned forward, peering through the windshield. "The other trail didn't look like it had been used for a while, but this one has undisturbed tread marks in the dust. My guess is it's been used in the past twenty-four hours."

They traveled for what seemed a long time. Ford kept his eyes to the window beside him, eager to glimpse anything that might give them hope. The clouds had blown over, leaving glimpses of stars in the velvet blackness. The small slivers of light enabled him to pick out shapes and shadows. The trees were closer together, and rocky promontories towered over them like regal battlements. The road was growing steeper, necessitating shifting to a lower gear.

He remembered how frightened Kira had been when she'd found Marla's body; he hoped and prayed she wasn't scared into immobility as she had been then. He couldn't remember a time when he'd prayed harder for another person, nor been more frightened. *Please, please keep her safe!* repeated over and over in his mind. He rolled down his window to get a better view.

"Stop! Back up!" he shouted.

Tracy slammed on the brakes, and both men in the front seats turned toward him. "There's a road, maybe just a trail across that meadow," he explained, pointing out his side window. "I think there's a cabin on the ridge higher up. I saw something that looked more like a roofline than a rock outcropping."

"Back up slowly. When we get to the trail, I'll check it out." Stan once more gripped his flashlight. Ford wished he'd thought to bring a flashlight. He had a few matches in his pocket, but in his hurry to leave the apartment, he hadn't given a thought to needing light.

When Tracy stopped beside the trail, Stan jumped out. In a few minutes he returned. "I can't be sure, but it looks as though the trail has been used recently. We can't ignore any possibility, so let's follow it. If we run into a sheep camp, we'll just have to turn around."

In spite of a few jolts, it only took a few minutes to cross the small meadow and begin a steep climb. The rough road twisted around boulders and between towering trees to end in a grove of quaking aspens surrounding a derelict cabin. No lights shone through the two small windows on either side of the wooden door. The cabin looked abandoned except for a beat-up truck parked nearly on the doorstep.

Ford reached for the door handle as did Tracy.

"Wait!" Stan spoke in a low voice, though it didn't appear anyone was around to hear him. "If Skid's in there, he may have a gun. I'll approach the front door. You two skirt around the cabin from opposite sides. Keep quiet."

Ford thought keeping quiet mattered little at this point. Anyone in the cabin who hadn't heard them coming up that steep trail had to be an awfully sound sleeper, but he was willing to follow Stan's instructions. The security agent surely had more experience than he did. The worst Ford had ever faced was disarming two ninth graders with ink-filled squirt guns.

Tracy headed for the left side of the cabin, so Ford darted toward the right. There were no windows on the side of the cabin, so he passed quickly to the rear. It didn't take long to discover the single window on that side. Tracy joined him, and by the light of Tracy's flashlight they stood staring at shards of glass and splintered shutter slats scattered on the ground. Pieces of cardboard lay amidst the debris.

"Do you suppose someone broke that window and crawled through it?" Tracy eyed the window with a skeptical scowl.

"If anyone could make it through that window, it would be Kira, but I'm not sure even she could squeeze through such a small opening." He moved closer to the broken window. Tracy stuck his light in his shirt pocket and stepped forward, cupping his hands to give Ford a boost.

Cardboard had been placed over the lower portion of the window, obviously to protect someone from glass splinters. It was too dark to see much inside the room, and he was far too large to crawl through the window. He contemplated using his cell phone as a light, but feeling a nudge against his knee, he looked down to see Tracy nod toward his own small flashlight. Ford reached for it, then, resting his weight against the window ledge, used it to scan the room.

The room was empty except for a cot that had been pushed under the window. Someone as short as Kira would need to stand on something to reach the window, he mused. He slid back down and whispered his findings to Tracy. They were just ready to return to the front of the cabin when Stan poked his head through the window.

"There's no one here now, but someone was here a short time ago. There's a bag of fast food in what serves for a kitchen, and it looks like someone was held captive in this room but may have escaped through this window. My guess is Kira was here, and Skid is chasing her."

* * *

Kira hadn't meant to fall asleep, and she didn't know what awakened her. She only knew she was freezing. She awoke fully cognizant of her situation. A few stars now peeked through the dark clouds, and a chill wind swayed the trees silhouetted against the night sky. Strange sounds drifted toward her. She wasn't certain whether she was hearing the rustle of wings or if the cool breeze was causing pine boughs to scrape together. She felt certain she was imagining the faint tinkling of bells. Listening intently for footsteps or snapping twigs, she surveyed the small clearing before attempting to stretch her limbs.

Hesitant to move from her semi-sheltered position until she was certain it was reasonably safe to do so, she peered into the darkness, seeing only the outlines of trees and rocks. She stopped in shock. A short distance away, two eyes shone through the darkness. She choked back the scream that threatened to break free.

She'd read somewhere that if a hiker confronted a bear, he shouldn't run. What if the eyes belonged to a bear—or a mountain lion?

She didn't know, but she did know that cats pounce on anything that moves. She struggled to keep from fleeing in terror.

Suddenly the eyes were gone. That was almost more frightening. She had no way of knowing what had been watching her or where it had gone. She shivered imagining some wild beast circling around behind her.

The shiver wasn't only from fear. The mountain air was cold. If she didn't start moving again, she could begin to suffer from hypothermia. She struggled to her feet and took a painful step. Swallowing a groan, she took a second step. Every muscle in her body throbbed, and her feet were so tender and cold she felt like she was walking on glass. While casting periodic nervous glances behind her, she moved from the rocky ledge deeper into the trees.

Sound seemed to be amplified in the still mountain air, and she had difficulty separating real sounds from imagined ones. Twice she heard the snapping of brush, which sent her cowering behind trees. Once she thought she heard the distant barking of a dog. Was she near a farm or ranch? Was the creep tracking her with a dog? Should she look for a stream to wade through to avoid leaving a scent trail, or should she make her way toward the sound? She didn't even know if a coyote or wolf made sounds similar to that of a dog. Kira found herself praying for guidance to know which way to go as she stumbled on.

Suddenly a faint sound caused her to stop. Listening intently, she waited for the sound to repeat itself. Of course, there was the possibility she'd only imagined the sound, but some instinct warned danger was coming her way.

Taking meticulous care not to make any noise, she moved deeper into a labyrinth of boulders. Crouching down in a jumble of the large rocks, she waited with her senses on alert for any sound or movement.

Time dragged, and she'd almost decided she'd overreacted to a normal forest sound when a dark shape materialized where moments earlier there had only been shadows. She froze in place, scarcely daring to breathe. It disappeared as quickly and silently as it had appeared, leaving her wondering if the figure had merely been a figment of her imagination.

"I know you're here," a ghostly voice whispered.

Her heart slammed in her breast. Terrified she frantically searched the ominous shadows, unable to detect from which direction the voice had come. It took all the self-control she could muster to keep from jumping up and running. No doubt that was the creep's intention. He'd like nothing more than for her to reveal her hiding place by trying to run from him. Clenching her fists, she made herself as small as possible.

"It won't do any good to hide in the rocks," the mocking voice continued. "You can't get away."

Her head swam with fear. Forcing herself to think, she debated whether she should crawl behind a larger rock nearby. Would she be safer there or would movement expose her location?

"You thought you were so clever crawling out of that window, but now you'll pay for the trouble you've caused me. I warned you not to try to escape." The voice was closer now. Through a tiny crack in the pile of rocks she hid behind, she could see his dark shape moving toward her. Another ten or twelve steps, and he'd be close enough to touch her.

"I've been following that white shirt for a mile or more. You move right fast for a little bitty girl. You should have taken the shirt off. It doesn't matter now because I'll take it off before we go back to the cabin anyhow—if we go back." He laughed as though he'd said something terribly funny.

There was no hope she could stay hidden. Thought and reason fled. Panic ruled as she jumped to her feet and began to run. She was an experienced runner, and her only hope was to outrun him. Weaving her way through the boulders, she raced upward, ever conscious of pounding footsteps behind her. In moments she was past the rocky outcropping and into the trees again where she hoped she would be more difficult to follow.

Something flew past her head, and she heard a *thunk* as it struck a tree. She wished she'd had the presence of mind to smear her white shirt with dirt, but if she stopped now, the creep would catch up to her. Making a sharp turn, she ran on.

Spying the shadow of low shrubbery ahead, she ran toward it, hoping it would impede her pursuer. Perhaps it would provide her with a place where she could hide long enough to catch her breath.

She leaped, praying she wouldn't land in a patch of stinging nettle. Her foot didn't touch. Instead she spiraled downward into a black void.

CHAPTER TWENTY-FIVE

FORD WASN'T CERTAIN IF THEY should trust Jasper to follow Kira or not, but in the darkness, there were few options and Tracy expressed confidence in Jasper's ability to track her. Ford removed one of Kira's running shoes from his backpack and let Jasper sniff it. The black dog nosed under the window then shot across the clearing to a thick tangle of brambles with Tracy struggling to keep hold of his leash. The bushes had large red berries indicating they were wild roses, but what interested the three men most were the mangled, broken branches, a good indication someone had forced their way through the prickly shrubs. They followed. Ford was glad Stan's recent injury didn't slow him down too much.

For a short distance, the dog led them along a narrow "rabbit track" before angling off through the trees. Leaving the trail made following Jasper more difficult, but it relieved Ford's mind somewhat. If they were correct in assuming someone was following her, Kira would be better able to evade her pursuer away from a trail.

When Jasper doubled back, crisscrossing a point he'd already passed a couple of times, Ford's hopes plummeted. Either the dog lacked the ability to follow Kira or she was lost, which increased the risk she'd get caught.

They'd been following the dog's aimless wandering for a little more than two hours when he paused on a rocky outcropping overlooking a long, narrow valley. The long, drawn-out cry of a coyote floated in the air from a great distance. From the deep valley below came the restless tinkle of sheep bells. Jasper sniffed at the base of a couple of large boulders, tore at the dirt for a moment, then moved almost to the ledge before angling back toward the trees.

"Has he lost the trail?" Stan asked.

"No. I don't think so, but something is making him nervous." Tracy attempted to rein in Jasper, who seemed equally determined to move on.

Ford knelt where Jasper had pawed at the ground. Remembering the morning Jasper had found Marla's body, he hesitantly forced his hands into the soft dirt where the dog had been digging. Small clumps of the dirt were spongy and felt like mud between his fingers.

He flashed the light from his cell phone across the muddy substance, then at the base of the rock where Jasper had dug. A red smear showed near the bottom of several rocks. "Tracy! Stan! Come here." Both men raised their heads, but only Stan stepped over. Tracy struggled to maintain his hold on Jasper's leash. "This looks like blood. I think Kira has been injured." Rage almost blinded him. Whoever had caused Kira's injury was going to pay!

Stan's hand briefly touched his side, and Ford noted for the first time that the man wore a holster beneath his jacket. It should have occurred to him earlier that a security agent wouldn't undertake a search for a kidnap victim unarmed. Ford took several deep breaths, determined to calm himself. He'd be of no use to Kira when they found her if his focus was on revenge.

"Jasper!" Startled by the sudden shout, Ford turned in time to see Jasper disappear into the inky darkness. Tracy, holding the useless leash, ran after him. Though Kira had warned her brother the clasp on the leash was faulty, he obviously hadn't replaced it. Ford and Stan sprinted after Tracy. It didn't take long to outdistance Stan, whose injured knee was starting to slow him down. Tracy and the dog disappeared up ahead, leaving Ford uncertain which way to go.

* * *

Kira awoke to the sensation of being a little girl again. Her mother was scrubbing her face with a wet cloth, and she felt almost warm.

It took only the briefest moment to realize it wasn't her mother washing her face, but a large black animal licking her cheek. Before the image of a bear could fully form in her mind, she recognized Jasper. He lay sprawled against her side, and she welcomed the heat his body provided. It took a little longer for her hazy mind to deduce that if Jasper lay beside her, then Tracy must be near. Perhaps if she called his name . . . *But what if he didn't hear and the creep did?* She attempted to lift her head, and the narrow bit of sky above her tilted at a precarious angle. Pain shot through her skull, blinding her. She closed her eyes and prayed the pain would pass.

After a few minutes, she attempted to move her legs. The resulting pain convinced her at least one of her legs was fractured. Her entire body ached, and she was pretty sure she had gashes and bruises everywhere. She remembered running from the creep then falling. She had landed near the top of a pine tree then slid between branches as she'd frantically attempted to grab something to hold on to. Perhaps she was fortunate to not remember hitting the ground. She was lucky to be alive—as long as the creep didn't find her.

A tinkling sound came from close at hand. She'd heard of people hearing bells when they'd suffered a blow to the head, but she hadn't expected the bells to be so melodic. Hearing a sharp whistle, she struggled in spite of the pain to raise herself on one elbow until she could see her surroundings. Sheep! As far as she could see was a sea of white wool. If she could have laughed at her earlier supposition, she would have. Sinking back down, she tried to think what to do.

If she called out, the creep might hear her. She needed to move to a more secure hiding place, but judging by the pain in her leg, she couldn't walk or even crawl. A low growl sounded nearby, and it didn't come from Jasper. The dog's lip curled back, and he launched himself into the air. A scraping sound followed by the trickle of falling pine needles and small branches drew her attention back to the bluff behind her. The creep was descending hand over hand down the massive pine tree that had broken her fall. Strapped to his back was a rifle. She watched in horror as he paused and lifted the rifle to his shoulder.

* * *

After scraping his shoulder against the rough bark of a tree and nearly losing his footing on the edge of a steep drop-off, Ford slowed to better evaluate the situation. He could no longer see or hear the other two men or Jasper. He didn't dare call out for fear of endangering Kira if the kidnapper was nearby and armed. Moving away from the trees, he looked for a high point where he might be able to see better.

Stepping clear of the overhanging branches and the deep shadows they projected on the mountainside, Ford noticed the sky was showing the first faint hints of dawn. He stood on a steep precipice that ran in a shaggy line as far as he could see. Below him spread a valley. At first it appeared covered with snow, but as the blackness of night faded to early morning gray, he recognized the snow was actually a large flock of sheep beginning to rouse from slumber. A pair of black-and-white dogs patrolled the perimeter of the bedding ground, and in the distance a lantern descended from the herder's wagon.

A piercing whistle sounded, and Ford became aware of a third dog crouched low as it slunk along the bottom of the cliff where he stood. It appeared the animal was prepared to spring on whatever enemy had invaded his territory. A patch of white caught his attention, and he wondered if a sheep had strayed and lay injured at the foot of the cliff. Or could it be—?

A black shape erupted from the thick, shaggy grass beside the patch of white and launched itself forward.

Jasper?

Frantically Ford searched for a way down to the valley. A short distance away he spied a steep incline covered with grass and shrubs. At least it wasn't straight up and down. It would be difficult and dangerous but better than the sharp drop from the rocky rim he now stood on. He raced over and began a careful descent. Judging from the skid marks in the thin layer of soil and several small plants that had been wrenched from the cracks where they'd grown, he knew he wasn't the first to choose this spot to descend.

Spotting what looked like a paw print in the dirt, he found himself hoping Jasper was the only other one who had chosen that path.

A shot rang out, and Ford slipped almost ten feet before he managed to catch himself. Righting himself, he slid the rest of the way down to where he could stand. Forgetting his own precarious position, he ran toward the spot where he suspected Kira lay. With one part of his mind, he registered the frantic scattering of the sheep and the wild dash of two dogs to cut off the wanderers. The third dog was nowhere in sight.

"Ford! Get down!" He ignored Stan's shouted warning. His entire focus was on reaching the woman he could see lying motionless in the tall grass. Jasper stood over her with teeth bared and a low rumble emanating from deep in his throat.

A shot whooshed over his head just as he dropped to his knees beside the inert body. Ignoring his own danger, he held his breath and reached a shaking hand toward Kira's carotid artery. An erratic beat met his questing fingers. She was alive!

Barely aware of the sound of another shot, he took a shallow breath and began a frantic search to discover the extent of her injuries. Jasper ignored him and continued his guard stance. The angle of her right leg told its own story. Gashes and abrasions covered her arms and legs, and the condition of her feet explained the blood he'd discovered earlier. The sound of that gunshot continued to echo in the back of his mind as he searched her injuries. He breathed more easily when he failed to find a bullet wound.

After several minutes he became aware of someone standing over him. He glanced up into Tracy's anguished face. In a hoarse whisper, Ford informed Kira's brother, "She's alive but needs medical help. Get Air-Evac in here to pick her up."

"There's no cell service up here, or I would have already called." Tracy crouched down beside his sister and gently touched her face with the tips of his fingers.

"I heard a shot . . . two . . . ?" Ford's voice trailed off.

"You don't have to worry about the guy who was following her."

Ford pulled his first-aid kit from his backpack, applied antiseptic and ointment, and wrapped gauze around the worst cut on Kira's arm. He dampened a strip of gauze from his water bottle and gently daubed at the dirt and blood on her feet, wishing he could do more. It tore at his heart to see her unconscious and battered. He didn't dare even glance toward the body he'd just become aware lay a short distance away, knowing he wouldn't be able to live with himself if he allowed his anger toward the man responsible for Kira's injuries to take over.

"The sheepherder shot Skid. He was in that tree, drawing down on the dogs. I thought at first he'd shot Kira. He's not dead, but if Stan would let me near him, he'd wish he were." Tracy's thoughts ran along the same channel as Ford's.

When he felt in control of his emotions enough to do so, Ford turned his eyes toward where Stan and Jasper stood guard over a writhing body on the ground. Like Tracy, Ford would like to teach Skid a lesson with his fists, and he couldn't muster any sympathy for the man's pain, but Ford suspected he hadn't acted alone. Alive he could identify who else was involved. Turning him over to the police would bring greater satisfaction in the long run.

"We've got to get help for Kira. One of us should hike back to that cabin for the Jeep and follow the road around . . ."

"It's more than five miles to that broken-down old cabin." The sheepherder joined them beside Kira. He was a tall, lanky man, probably twenty years Ford's senior with a look of sadness in his eyes and a beard that reached to the first button of his red, plaid shirt. In one hand he carried a rifle. Standing next to him with teeth bared was the sheepdog Ford had first noticed. "These sheep belong to Thomas Swenson. He'll be by with supplies in an hour or so. Best you folks wait for him here, and he'll take you to the closest place where you can make your phone calls."

He gave a shrill whistle before turning away, adding, "The dogs and I'll be moving the sheep farther up the valley. Don't want them panicking if a helicopter comes. Sheriff Olsen knows where to find me if I need to make a statement." He ambled toward the restless flock that was bleating and making agitated movements as though set to run into the brush. All three dogs darted around their perimeter, easing the flock away from the chaos.

CHAPTER TWENTY-SIX

Kira drifted in and out of consciousness as they waited. Ford did all he could to staunch the loss of blood from her wounds and spoke soothing words to ease her fear. When he'd done all he could with his small first-aid kit and limited training, he handed the kit to Tracy and instructed him to make certain Skid didn't bleed to death before they could turn him over to law enforcement. Tracy grimaced but obediently did as Ford asked, though Ford suspected his ministrations weren't overly gentle.

They didn't have to wait as long as expected before a battered green pickup truck lurched its way toward them in a cloud of dust. It was followed by a newer truck with *Sanpete County Sheriff* emblazoned on the door.

When the two vehicles stopped, Ford paid little attention to the man who stepped from the first truck. His attention focused on a large-boned man with a shock of thick, blond hair, who stepped from the second truck wearing a star on his vest and jeans. He made his way to Kira, stooped to check her pulse, and returned to his truck for a bottle of water.

"Give her a few sips when she comes to," he advised then asked if Ford had ID. Stan joined them, handing the sheriff his ID. After that it didn't take but a few minutes for the sheriff to use his satellite phone to summon an air ambulance.

"Detective Daley up in Murray called this morning asking me to run up this way to check out a cabin where he thought a missing person might be. When I saw a couple vehicles parked in front of that old cabin, I figured something was up. I spotted Swenson's dust trail and thought I'd mosey over and see if he or his herder had seen anything."

The small town sheriff was justifiably proud of his role in the capture of a dangerous kidnapper. He checked on both Kira and Skid, assuring Ford and Tracy he'd had EMT training. Since Skid obviously wasn't in shape to run away, the sheriff wouldn't bother cuffing him.

While the sheriff checked on his prisoner, Kira opened her eyes to find Ford watching her. She attempted a smile to assure him she was all right. "Thank you for coming," she whispered. He held the water bottle to her lips. She swallowed a small sip. "I prayed you'd come." Her eyes drifted closed again. He longed to take her in his arms and tell her how hard he'd prayed for her safety and how he didn't want them to ever be parted again. As he wiped tears from his eyes, he heard the distant thrum of rotor blades.

The sound grew louder, and soon the sheriff was signaling the pilot to set down on a nearby grassy spot. Before the rotors had completely stopped, a paramedic and a flight nurse ducked beneath the blades and hurried toward the two forms lying on the ground. They lost no time taking charge. Soon Kira was moved to the helicopter with an IV attached to her arm for hydration.

Ford couldn't help but scowl when he saw Skid also being placed aboard the helicopter.

Whether it was his obvious concern for Kira or the sheriff showing caution for the possibility Skid might overpower the medical personnel, he instructed Ford to board the chopper as well. "Don't worry about your friends getting back to Salt Lake," the sheriff told Ford. "I'll take them back to their Jeep."

Ford needed no further encouragement to scramble aboard. Jasper protested being separated from Kira, and the flight nurse expressed concern for space on the helicopter, but with Ford in the copilot seat, they were soon airborne.

Ford wasn't surprised when Detective Daley and Garrett met the chopper at the hospital. Several uniformed officers were on hand as well and immediately flanked the gurney carrying Skid.

"Kira! Sweetheart, I've been so worried." Garrett's voice trembled as he rushed to his daughter's side.

"I'm okay, Daddy," she mumbled, making a weak attempt to smile.

"Sir, we need to ask you to move back." Medical personnel swarmed around Kira, and in moments they whisked her out of sight.

Ford stood, feeling lost and alone as Kira disappeared. Knowing Kira needed a doctor's help more than his, he still found it difficult to step aside and turn her care over to someone else. He felt a hand on his shoulder and was surprised to see the look of sympathy on Garrett's face.

"Son, this is where we retreat to the closest waiting room to pace the floor." Perhaps there was hope for his relationship with Kira's father after all.

* * *

She awoke slowly, conscious first of being warm and lying on a comfortable bed instead of the hard, cold ground. Her head was at a slight angle, giving her a view of the room, which looked much like the one where she'd visited Mr. Andrews. Beside her, Ford sat slouched in a chair asleep. Beyond him, she could see her father sprawled across a short divan. He too was asleep. Sunlight streamed in from a window. Never again would she underestimate warmth, safety, and being loved.

She was alive. She couldn't count the number of times she'd doubted she'd survive the previous night—or was it two nights ago? She'd completely lost track of time.

"You're awake. How do you feel?" Ford's eyes were open, and he was watching her. She gave him a wobbly smile.

"I'm not sure how I feel other than grateful to be alive. How did you find me?"

Ford picked up her hand and held it between both of his as he recounted the events of the past couple of days. While he talked, her eyes closed again, and she drifted back to sleep.

Each time she awoke she exchanged bits of information with her father or Ford about her ordeal, but staying awake was impossible. From a nurse, she learned her leg was broken. The cuts and bruises

that covered her from head to toe would eventually heal, but a couple
of the larger gashes had been stitched and would likely leave scars.
She also learned that the doctor had ordered strong painkillers, which
accounted for her sleepiness.

At last she awoke fully to find Detective Daley occupying the
chair beside her bed with Detective Chetfield sitting on the small
sofa a few feet away drumming his fingers against his knee.

Detective Daley smiled and greeted her. After a few comments
concerning her health, he asked if she felt up to answering a few
questions.

"I can't promise to stay awake." She attempted to make light of
her situation.

"That's all right. How about recounting everything you can
remember after you left Mr. Andrews's room the morning you
visited him." He smiled encouragingly.

"Ma'am, we need your permission to record your statement."
Detective Chetfield set a small recorder on the bedside table before
retreating to his previous seat. Daley lifted his eyebrows, and she
interpreted his questioning expression as a signal he was waiting for
her response.

"Okay. You can record what I say." She took a moment to
elevate the head of her bed a small amount to make conversation
easier. She wasn't anxious to revisit the ordeal. She recognized that
fussing with the bed was only stalling, so she closed her eyes for a
brief moment then began. "Daddy was adamant I should return to
his house instead of staying at Ford's apartment. At first I thought
the big man worked for him and he was taking me to Dad's house,
even though I didn't want to go, but when we passed the freeway
exit, I became suspicious. He gave me a bottle of water. I'm sure
it contained a sedative." The further she got with her account, the
more difficult it became to speak as the memories of waking up in
that locked room, the things the creep insinuated, and her desperate
attempt to flee were relived.

"Did you jump or were you pushed from the cliff overlooking the sheep camp?" Daley handed her the box of tissues from
her nightstand. She wasn't sure when the tears had started flowing
down her cheeks.

She mopped her face and struggled to speak coherently. "The creep was chasing me, but he didn't actually push me. I fell. I thought for sure I would die, but I landed in a big pine tree. I tried to grab a branch, but I couldn't hold on. I kept sliding from one branch to another until I hit the ground. The pine needles probably kept me from breaking more than my leg, but they kept jabbing into me. I remember trying to crawl away from the tree, but I didn't get far before I passed out."

The detective leaned forward. "Did you know the men who took you to that cabin, and did you go with them willingly?" His question surprised her.

"Of course not." Her mind clicked on her first impression of the big man who dragged her from the hospital to the van. "At first I thought the big one was a man who works for my father, but none of Daddy's employees would treat me the way he did."

"Do you think you could identify either of the men who kidnapped you?"

"Yes." She shuddered. "I'll never forget either of them."

"I have some pictures here." He reached for a folder the other detective held. From it he withdrew a stack of photos and spread them across the hospital table before drawing the table across her bed so she could see them better.

Her eyes went at once to a photo of the creep. She pointed but found she couldn't speak. Just seeing his face made her feel sick to her stomach.

"Is this the man who was with you in the cabin?"

She nodded her head.

"I need a verbal answer," the detective's voice gently reminded her. "Are you identifying 4A as one of the men who was with you at the cabin?"

"Yes. That's him." She reached for the box of tissues then dabbed at her eyes and blew her nose. "Sorry," she mumbled.

"It's all right. You've been through a lot," the officer sympathized before returning to his questions. "Do you see the other man's picture?"

She searched for several minutes. Her eyes kept returning to one picture, but she didn't feel certain enough to select it. She hadn't had a clear look at the big man's face. She was too busy trying to free herself when he pushed her into the van, and he'd worn a hat that partially hid his face. "This one kind of looks like the man who grabbed me and shoved me into the van." She pointed to the picture that had caught her attention. "He implied he worked for my father, and he fit the description my brother gave of a man called Ed who works in security at Dad's office. I only saw Ed once from the back and at a considerable distance. The one man addressed the other kidnapper as Ed."

"Ed Ellsworth was in your father's office when he received the ransom call, but he hasn't been seen since. We're looking for him."

"Do you think he . . . ?"

"Let's just say we want to talk to him."

* * *

Long before nine o'clock Kira was ready for everyone to go home and allow her to go back to sleep. She couldn't remember ever before being as tired as she was now. Her nurse had mentioned adding something to the IV for pain. Kira suspected that something was a sedative. Even though she'd missed a night's sleep, she had slept most of the afternoon until a swarm of visitors arrived, leaving her exhausted. A sedative probably wasn't necessary to guarantee sleep. She welcomed the nurse's announcement that visitors should leave, allowing her to rest. Her thoughts began to drift away.

"Honey," Ford's voice pulled her mind back to her hospital room. She faintly registered that he looked as tired as she felt. Over his shoulder she caught a glimpse of her father, who also looked exhausted. "I have to leave now, but I'll be back early in the morning. The call button, if you need help, is clipped to your pillow, and there's an officer stationed outside your door. The doctor said you're doing great but need rest." He leaned forward to press a light kiss on her lips. A vague awareness that her father left a kiss on her cheek as well preceded the oblivion of sleep.

One moment she was asleep, the next she was awake and back in the cabin. Again she lay still, pretending to be asleep while she took stock of her surroundings. Her heart pounded with fear.

Something was amiss. She gave the air a cautious sniff. It was the strong smell of antiseptic that brought remembrance of her exit from the cabin and reminded her she was in a hospital room. However, she wasn't alone.

Standing near the pole that held her IV was a large man dressed in scrubs. She swallowed a scream, somehow sensing she should remain quiet. She didn't find it unusual for a nurse to enter her room to check on her medications while she slept, but with his back to her, he bore an uncanny resemblance to the large man who had abducted her. As her eyes adjusted to the semidarkness, he came into better focus. He didn't look like any of the nurses who had come and gone earlier, but there had likely been a shift change while she slept. His scrubs were stretched so tightly across his back she wouldn't be surprised if a seam gave way.

Between the dim light filtering through the open blinds and the small night lights placed strategically around the hospital room, she watched the man make stroking motions along the tube leading from the machine to her arm. Was he hurrying something through the narrow tube, or could he be wiping up a spill? Removing fingerprints? The scent that had awakened her grew stronger.

A sense of urgency overpowered her. If he was a nurse making certain her IV worked properly, she'd make a fool of herself by screaming. But if he turned out to be the kidnapper, he could be attempting to silence the only person who might identify him. What if he'd added something lethal to her IV? Her hand snaked toward the call button.

It was gone!

Sensing her movement the man turned and reached for her. Twisting and screaming, she attempted to evade him. Items flew from the bedside table, including a water pitcher that landed with a resounding thud on the floor and sent water and ice cascading across the room. A loud grunt told her a kick from her good leg had landed hard in the man's midsection. Her hand tangled in the plastic tubing, and she gave a fierce jerk. Her scream of pain and fear was stifled as a pillow covered her face, held in place by two strong arms that also pinned her to the bed.

Her flailing leg bumped the controls that raised and lowered the bed, elevating her feet and sending her attacker staggering to maintain his stance. His hands lost their grip long enough for her to draw in a deep breath. Before she could scream, though, he covered her face once more; a knee pinned her lower body to the bed. Pain from her broken leg and from her arm where the IV had been ripped out swirled in her head in dizzying black circles magnified by her need for air. Blackness turned to oblivion.

Awareness returned with a surge of pain in her extended arm. When she attempted to draw the arm back, she found it was securely held in the grip of a woman dressed in green scrubs. Her opposite hand was held in a tight grip as well. Panic stricken, she turned her head from side to side seeking escape until several points began to register in her dazed mind. She could breathe, the lights were on, a nurse was bandaging her left arm where she'd ripped out the IV, and Ford was kneeling at her bedside with her right hand in his.

"You're safe now." Ford's voice soothed away the last of the cloudiness hovering in her mind.

"A man was here. I think he was the same man . . ." She tried to explain her fear and confusion.

"It's all right. The police got him."

"But how did they know—"

"All done," the nurse's voice interrupted. "Your doctor planned to remove the IV in a couple of hours anyway, so he said not to restart it. Would you like me to change your sheets now? Some blood and water spilled on them."

"Could you come back a little later?" Holding onto Ford was the only thing she wanted at the moment—that and finding out what had just happened.

"I'll give you ten minutes." The nurse gave her a knowing smile and left the room.

Moving to sit on the edge of her bed, Ford continued as though there had been no interruption. "When the police guard outside your door didn't check in as scheduled, his supervisor contacted hospital security. One of their officers found the guard wasn't at his post, called for reinforcements, and barged into your room. He was getting the worst of a wrestling match with Ed Ellsworth when Stan and a half dozen police officers arrived. While the officers hauled Ed off to jail, Stan called me."

The doctor arrived, insisting on a thorough checkup and a session with a physical therapist before releasing Kira from the hospital. Ford lingered near her door until the nurse assured him she wouldn't be left alone and handed him a pain prescription to be filled at the pharmacy.

He returned to find Kira sitting in a wheelchair, waiting for him. When they got outside, he fussed over her, making certain she was comfortable in the passenger seat of his truck before beginning the drive to her condo.

"I can walk!"

Ford ignored her words, scooping her up in his arms to carry her to the front door of her condo. He unlocked the door and didn't stop until he reached her sofa.

"I'm okay. You can put me down." She really could get around on crutches, and the physical therapist at the hospital had prepared her to take care of herself.

"Maybe I don't want to put you down." Ford grinned and moved his lips in a series of kisses down the side of her neck. "I kind of like having you in my arms."

Silently she agreed that she liked it too. She savored the feeling for several minutes before asking, "How long do you think it will be before Daddy learns I've been released from the hospital and comes barreling out here to try again to convince me to go to his house?"

Ford sighed. Garrett and Tracy could show up any minute. With great care he transferred Kira to the sofa and made certain her leg in its heavy cast was supported before returning to his truck for her bag.

Seating himself on the love seat opposite the sofa, he broached the subject he'd been avoiding. "I'm not sure you should stay here alone. I know how you feel about your dad treating you like a baby and controlling your life, but you need to consider your safety. Until you get that cast off your leg, the stairs up to my apartment would be difficult for you to manage. Ed and Skid are both in jail, but I don't think they're the ones who broke into your house or shot at you."

Kira kept her head down. She'd like to think she was safe now with the men who kidnapped her in jail. Still, the points Ford mentioned niggled at her mind. Was she being foolish to insist she needed to be in her own space? She couldn't stop thinking out loud. "I wonder if anyone else had considered that being kidnapped likely had nothing to do with those earlier attacks."

"We saw some of the people who tagged your house and were harassing you," Ford reminded her. "They looked like teenagers, not men in their thirties or forties like Ed and Skid. It appears the kidnapping was a crime of opportunity."

"But why? I don't know anyone who's involved with a gang. As far as I know, I've never done anything to hurt someone else. I don't even recall cutting off another driver! The worst I can think of is I've angered a few people who I denied loans at the credit union. The whole thing has to be related somehow to discovering Marla Hayden's body."

"It's been almost four months, and the police haven't made an arrest. They haven't found the gun or any link to Luis Vincent. I'm not sure they'll ever solve who murdered her." Ford knew his voice revealed his frustration. "Daley told me the police haven't found any link between Luis Vincent and Ed Ellsworth either. You need protection, but I have no idea who you need protection from."

* * *

The doorbell rang before they could discuss the matter further. Ford opened the door to find Garrett, Tracy, Kaitlin, and Jasper on the doorstep. While they filed in, Stan strolled up the walk behind them. Before Ford could close the door behind the newcomers, Mrs. Gleason called over from her front door to ask about Kira.

"She's doing fine. I'm just trying to convince her to rest for a while." He added the rest as a hint for her family not to stay too long.

"Tell her I asked about her," the elderly woman said. "Tell her not to worry about a thing. My grandsons are coming to stay with me while they go to school at the university. I'll feel much safer with them here. I'll bring them over to meet her a little later."

He closed the door and was surprised to hear Kira giggling. Jasper had taken up a position at her side. She buried her face in his fur then looked up and laughed harder seeing the puzzled faces around her. "I heard Mrs. Gleason. She talks about her grandsons a lot. She's very proud of them. They're twins and, according to her, look a lot like Hoss from her favorite old television program, *Bonanza*. One has a wrestling scholarship and the other a football scholarship to the U. Evidently they've been drafted for guard duty."

"Actually that makes me feel better." Ford couldn't see that it would hurt any to have a couple of able-bodied young men added to those already looking out for Kira.

"I'm looking forward to meeting them." Stan grinned. "If they're as promising as they sound, I just might hire them."

"I'm not going to try to dissuade you from staying here," Garrett said, speaking to Kira. "But you will have to accept around-the-clock security from Stan and his people and—"

Kaitlin cut him off. "Also, Kira, if you don't mind, I'll stay here with you—at least for the first few days. With all of these men worrying about your safety, I thought you might like another woman around to help you with cleaning up after all of your knights in shining armor."

It seemed Garrett and Stan had made up, and Stan was once more in charge of Kira's security. It was also quite obvious to Ford that he and Kira wouldn't be finding much privacy in the immediate future.

CHAPTER TWENTY-SEVEN

HAVING NEVER LIVED WITH A woman before, Kira found sharing her condo with Kaitlin a different experience. She'd often wished her mother had been alive during her teen years. She'd longed for a sister and later a roommate. She soon discovered that she and Kaitlin had different ideas concerning the proper way to fold towels or load the dishwasher but that they shared similar tastes in music and movies. For the first time in her life, Kira enjoyed discussing characters from her favorite books or comparing the pluses and minuses of various clothing styles and cosmetics. She began to understand what she'd missed in her male-dominated life.

"I need to go shopping." Kaitlin returned the brush and tightened the lid on a bottle of pale-pink nail polish. She straightened her leg and wiggled her toes, which were separated by thick wads of cotton.

Kira stifled a giggle. She knew many women polished their toenails, but she'd never witnessed the procedure, let alone attempted it herself. It was one of many "girl things" she'd missed out on. "For nail polish?"

"No." Kaitlin laughed. "For food. Tracy promised he'd make certain your cupboards and refrigerator were stocked before you came home, but either you have odd food preferences or he's just a typical man."

"What do you mean?"

"You haven't been doing the cooking the last few days. Don't get me wrong; I'm not complaining. I know it's difficult for you to do much in the kitchen with a cast on your leg and bandages on your feet and arms. But here's the problem. Tracy loaded your refrigerator and cupboard with Italian sausage, thick-crust frozen pizza, soda, pepper jack and mozzarella cheeses, hot dogs, baked beans, six kinds of chips, twenty cans of dog food, and hamburger buns."

"Oh my!"

"I saw Stan a few minutes ago. I'll just let him know I'm leaving." Kaitlin removed the wads of cotton from between her toes and reached for her flip-flops. She slipped outside and up the trail that had been worn through the trees leading to the nearby canal. She was back in minutes to pick up her purse.

The house felt strangely quiet once Kaitlin closed the door behind her. It was the first time Kira had been completely alone since she'd left the hospital. A glance through the window assured her she wasn't really alone. Stan was now on the back patio talking to Mrs. Gleason's grandsons. Her description of the twins was pretty accurate. They were huge. Stan was six feet tall, but they surpassed him—in both directions.

As she watched, a fourth man joined the gathering on her patio, and she smiled to see Ford. She was a little disappointed he hadn't come inside to say hello to her first. Their time together was rapidly diminishing, with school set to start the following week. His contract required him to spend part of each day this week at the high school, preparing for the new year.

Moments later Ford and Stan tapped on the door and, without waiting for a response, entered her condo. The twins remained behind sprawled in patio chairs.

Ford made his way to where she reclined on the sofa. "Hi, honey." He leaned over to lightly brush her lips with his. "There's something Stan needs to tell you."

She looked expectantly at the security guard she'd come to think of more as a friend than someone her father had hired to watch over her. As he walked toward her, she was glad to see he no longer limped and his arm had healed from his encounter with the vandals.

He didn't waste time on pleasantries. "It looks like our taggers showed up again. When they spotted our people and knew they couldn't get close to your house, they left messages on tree trunks and sprayed their graffiti on the bridge a block away."

"I guess that proves Ed and Skid are off the hook for the harassment I've been receiving." Her shoulders sagged. She knew it was unlikely the men who kidnapped her had been involved in the earlier trouble, but she'd hoped the turmoil that had surrounded her since discovering Marla's body last spring was at an end. "I don't suppose there's a chance this graffiti is just part of the unsightly garbage vandals spray on any convenient surface? Bridges seem to be a favorite target of taggers."

"No, I'm sorry. Some of it we think is explicitly directed toward you." Stan shook his head, and though the words hurt, she was grateful he respected her enough to be truthful. Protecting her from physical harm was one thing, but assuming she was too delicate to know what was going on was something she wouldn't tolerate. "Some of the graffiti has been crossed out and painted over with another gang's markings. I'm not certain whether this will escalate the problem for you or not. I understand from the gang unit that the gang Luis Vincent belongs to and another gang are feuding. They might keep each other busy and forget about you, but I'll instruct my people to watch for any possibility of your being caught in the middle of their dispute."

Kira made no response. She was so tired of the whole thing. If she hadn't moved into her condo right after it was built, she'd suspect gang members had her confused with a previous occupant—and if Marla Hayden's cousin wasn't a member of the gang tormenting her.

"Kira," Ford knelt beside the sofa, where she sat with her cast propped in front of her, "Stan called Detective Daley. He'll be here shortly. Stan and I talked and agree you should know the graffiti is more serious than what we found before. It carries a definite threat of violence."

"He threatened to shoot me?" She could barely force the words out as her mind flashed back to the incident at the mall and the threatening phone call she'd received. She wasn't sure she could cope with one more frightening incident. All her life she'd obeyed her parents, obeyed doctors, done all that was asked of her. She'd worked hard, and it hadn't been easy to scrape out a small measure of independence. Now with a broken leg and her body being so sore it was difficult even to move. What was she to do? It wasn't fair! In the back of her mind ran a reminder that life isn't always fair and that to complain about a lack of fairness was a little childish. She needed to get her thoughts together, to figure out why this was happening and find a way to protect herself.

"We're not sure if the threat involves guns, but there's a strong indication that your life is in danger." He squeezed her fingers, and she didn't even recall when he'd picked up her hand. Ford went on in a quiet voice, "The threat wasn't actually made by Luis or his gang. It's in the colors of the rival gang."

That made no sense. Nothing made sense.

Raised voices penetrated her shock and confusion. She turned her head toward the window, where she caught sight of Mrs. Gleason, who appeared to be crying. Both of her hulking grandsons stood with their arms awkwardly around her shoulders as they attempted to comfort her.

"It was that dog!" Mrs. Gleason's voice carried through the door Stan and Ford had left open. Jasper lay his head against Kira's arm and watched her with mournful eyes. Kira immediately glanced around for mangled shoes.

"No, Grandma. It wasn't the dog. Those guys who've been bothering Miss Paxton found your cat when she got out last night. As soon as that detective sees her and takes some pictures, we'll bury her nice and proper for you."

Bile rose in Kira's throat. Surely they weren't talking about Mrs. Gleason's cat. She turned dazed eyes toward Ford.

As if he could read her mind, he nodded. "They strangled her and left her stuck to a tree with a knife. Stan found the cat pinned to a tree as part of the threatening message."

"Who could do such an awful thing?" Her question went unanswered. "Poor Mrs. Gleason. She loved that cat and will be so lonely without her. And to think of the cat dying like that . . ." Tears ran down Kira's face. She couldn't comprehend anyone so sick and cruel they could kill a defenseless pet. Jasper had barked at the cat a few times and even chased her from one side of the yard to the other, but Kira had always suspected that in a real confrontation the big tabby could hold its own.

The front door rattled and burst open. Ford turned to see Kaitlin stagger into the room carrying two large grocery bags. She dropped them on the counter before turning to take in the solemn faces. "What's going on?" she demanded. When all were slow to answer she went on, "Someone better come up with an answer. In the meantime I need help bringing in the rest of the groceries." She glared at Stan and Ford. "There are so many cars in the driveway, I had to park on the street."

Before either man could move, a firm knock sounded on the open front door. Ford hurried to invite Daley and Chetfield to join them. The detectives were accompanied by two other officers, one of whom carried a camera and a black satchel. After letting them in, Ford continued out to Kaitlin's car to gather the rest of her purchases.

He knew Stan would lose no time describing the grisly discovery and lead the officers outside to take pictures. He chose to stay close to Kira.

Kaitlin let out a little squeak and dropped onto the love seat just as Ford struggled to let himself back in with four bags of groceries in his arms. "We can't stay here," she gasped. "We should go to my apartment."

Ford attempted to reassure the women and lighten their mood. "You'll be fine. Stan has round-the-clock guards watching the house, and you've got enough food here to hold off an army." He set the heavy bags beside the ones Kaitlin had already deposited on the counter and rejoined the two young women in the living room.

"You can leave if you want to," Kira told Kaitlin. "But I'm staying here. No way I'll let anyone scare me away from my home."

"If you won't go, I won't either." Kaitlin folded her arms and glared as though daring anyone to try changing her mind.

* * *

Idly picking at the cereal remaining in the bottom of her bowl, Kira stared out the window, not really seeing the early-morning sprinklers shut off or the dusty dry appearance of the trees and wild grass beyond her small patch of lawn. Summer was winding down, and the air held the ominous warning of a storm soon to break.

Three days had passed without any further trouble, and Kira hoped the danger was past. Kaitlin needed to return to work in a couple of days, and the school where Ford taught would begin classes on Monday as well. It'd been fun having Kaitlin around, and they'd grown close, but she knew her future sister-in-law was anxious to return to her own life, including spending a weekend in St. George making wedding plans with her mother. She'd enjoyed Ford and even Tracy spending every possible minute with her and Kaitlin.

Kira also needed to think about returning to work. Her boss had been sympathetic and understanding, but she was getting around well on crutches now and felt a need to be doing something useful. Most of her work involved sitting at a desk anyway, so she could see no real reason for staying at home any longer.

The doorbell interrupted her thoughts. "I'll get it!" Kaitlin called. Hearing the door open then her brother's voice, Kira stayed in her chair, allowing Tracy and Kaitlin a few moments of privacy. She was surprised when they both entered the kitchen seconds later.

"Hi, Kira!" Tracy kissed her cheek. She ducked before Jasper could do the same. "I've been thinking. Now that you're feeling better and summer is almost over, we need to have a cookout. Kaitlin and I will go get everything, and I'll let Stan know to invite all the guys who have been doing guard duty. They can bring their wives or girlfriends. We might even get Mrs. Gleason to come. Several of your neighbors have stopped me to ask about you and say you've been missed at church. We could invite anyone you got to know at Ford's apartment and your friends from work. What time is Ford coming over?"

"School starts Monday, so he has to be at the school all day today. Sometime after four will be the earliest he can come."

"No problem. I'll get the twins to set up tables and borrow chairs from your ward."

"You better check with Stan." She wasn't sure about an impromptu party. Perhaps she was just hesitant because she couldn't get around well enough to be part of the preparations, but she didn't have a good feeling about it. To be honest, she'd had a restless, uneasy feeling ever since she'd awakened that morning.

CHAPTER TWENTY-EIGHT

BETWEEN TRACY AND FORD, WHO split the grilling duties, everyone's plate was kept filled. Kira found herself propped on the chaise lounge with Jasper at her feet and Mrs. Gleason's grandsons determined to wait on her. She noticed they had a lot of help from some of the girls from her ward. As she looked around at the group, she felt a touch of guilt for her reluctance to hold the party. Her neighbors and friends had been compassionate and helpful through the summer. A party was the least she could do to thank them. Everyone was apparently enjoying themselves, and it was good to see them. With so little notice, it was surprising so many people accepted the invitation. Many had even brought dishes to add to the food table. She hoped Mrs. Gleason didn't mind that the large group spilled over onto her side of their backyard.

As if her thoughts conjured the neighbor up, Mrs. Gleason left her house and crossed her backyard, coming straight toward Kira. Kira held her breath, hoping the older woman wouldn't cause a scene or complain about the noise. Mrs. Gleason gave Jasper a wide berth and settled in a chair on the opposite side of Kira.

"I hope you're feeling better, dear."

Breathing a sigh of relief that her neighbor didn't sound upset, Kira assured the older woman she was doing better. She wondered if she should express sympathy for the loss of the woman's pet. Perhaps this wasn't the best time to bring up the painful subject, she reasoned.

"I wanted to apologize," Mrs. Gleason began.

Kira wasn't sure what Mrs. Gleason could possibly be apologizing for.

"I assumed before I had all of the facts that your dog was responsible for my dear Charlotte's demise." She swiped at her eyes with a corner of the handkerchief she held clutched in one hand.

Kira ached with sympathy. She reached out to take the woman's hand in a comforting gesture. "I'm so sorry. I don't understand how anyone could do such a thing." Jasper loved to bark at the cat, but Kira was convinced he'd have never hurt her. She glanced down to where the dog had stationed himself since his arrival and was surprised to see he was gone. She hoped her closet door was closed. His absence made her uneasy. All she needed was for him to suddenly jump in the canal or run into the monsters who killed Mrs. Gleason's Charlotte.

One of the twins—she couldn't tell if he was Trevor or Tyrone—appeared with a plate heaped high with a bit of every salad Kaitlin had ordered from the deli along with a stack of barbecued ribs. He handed the plate to his grandmother. His brother followed with a glass of root beer. A cluster of young women trailed behind them with napkins and utensils. Kira appreciated their looking after her neighbor.

A few couples were dancing barefoot on the grass, but most stood around in small groups talking or sat at tables enjoying their dinner. Ford and Tracy stood near the grill. Tracy slapped Ford on the back, and they both burst into laughter. Their laughter was suddenly cut short. She watched both men drop their long handled spatulas and break into a run along the path worn over the past months from the back of her lawn into the trees.

Kira turned her head, fearing what she might see. Jasper galloped out of the trees and made a beeline straight toward her. Behind him was Stan attempting to catch up. Just as she feared, the dog was dripping wet. A wet, soggy clump dangled from Jasper's mouth, but it wasn't a shoe. She held her breath, fearing the worst. As the dog got closer, it became obvious he was carrying some sort of animal. It looked like a rat!

"Jasper! Put it down," Tracy yelled as he made a futile lunge for the dog's collar, but he slipped on the grass and went down.

Pandemonium broke out as Jasper wove through the crowd, dodging attempts to stop him. Several people screamed.

"No, Jasper!" Kira recoiled from the dog's approach then watched in shock as Jasper passed right by her to deposit the object in Mrs. Gleason's lap. The woman gasped and looked as though she might jump up and run away in horror. The small animal struggled to free itself and made squeaking sounds. Whatever it was, it was alive! The twins collided as they rushed to their grandmother's aid. Simultaneously they reached for the soggy, squirming creature.

"Wait a minute," Mrs. Gleason sputtered before they could snatch up the wet ball of fur. She held up a hand to ward off her would-be rescuers. "I think it's . . . It's a kitten! Quick! Somebody get a towel." She began daubing at the creature with a napkin. One of the twins raced toward her back door, presumably to find a towel, while the other remained beside his grandmother eying the kitten with a great deal of skepticism. He poked it with a large finger, and Kira heard the distinctive mew of a kitten. She couldn't hold back the giggle that escaped.

"I'm sorry. I tried to stop him," Stan sputtered as he slid to a stop before Kira's neighbor, panting and clearly out of breath.

"Jasper, what's gotten into you?" Tracy scolded his dog at almost the same time.

"It doesn't seem to be hurt." Mrs. Gleason continued patting the kitten with napkins donated to the cause by everyone who had gathered around. "I wonder who he belongs to and how he got so wet?" She looked up at Stan as though she expected an answer from him.

"I've no idea who he belongs to," Stan admitted. "But I can tell you where Jasper found him. He was floating in the canal. Maybe floating isn't the right word. He was yowling like crazy and frantically paddling, trying to reach the bank. Jasper leaped in, lifted him out of the water, and took off in a beeline for you."

"Oh, the poor thing," one of the young women sympathized as she wormed her way to Mrs. Gleason's side just as one of the twins arrived with a thick towel. "Thanks, Tyrone," the girl said with a flirtatious smile. She took the towel from him and bent to wrap the kitten in it.

Mrs. Gleason took over, wrapping the towel around the animal and snuggling it against her cheek. "Aren't you the bravest thing?" she cooed. It was the happiest Kira had seen her neighbor in a week. Mrs. Gleason reached over to pat Jasper. "And you knew just who would help this poor baby."

"Well, I'll be," Ford whispered in Kira's ear. "That dog's smarter than I thought. I don't think you'll get any more complaints about him."

"Miss Paxton." Startled, Kira looked up to see Detective Daley walking toward her. For just a moment she wondered why, after all this time, he was still so formal. She'd mentioned to him several times that he should call her Kira.

"Might I speak with you for a moment?"

"We could go inside." She indicated the door leading into the house. Ford helped her to her feet and handed her the crutches she'd left under the lounge chair. She could have managed on her own but was glad Ford stayed at her side as she made her way into the house. Having the detective seek her out on a weekend evening raised all kinds of alarms in her mind. The detective signaled to Stan to join them. Tracy, with a firm grip on Jasper, looked torn between remaining with their guests or following, but he finally opted to stay with their guests.

Kira invited the detective to be seated, but he remained standing. He appeared ill at ease which raised her own anxiety level. She wished he'd just say why he'd come. As if he'd heard her thoughts he spoke in a rush to get the words out.

"I'm sorry to barge in on your party. I thought it best that I tell you, not leave it for you to hear on the news. Luis Vincent was shot in a gang fight tonight. He was pronounced dead at 7:42 p.m. at the University Medical Center."

She didn't know how to react. She couldn't be happy over the loss of any life, particularly of someone so young, yet she had a sense of a burden being lifted from her shoulders. She hoped this meant an end to the harassment she'd endured all summer.

"The rival gang member who shot him has been arrested," Daley added. "The shooting was out of my jurisdiction, so I really can't add any details yet."

"Have you determined whether either gang was responsible for that young woman's death last spring?" Stan questioned. "My investigation hasn't turned up anything definitive."

"No, nothing definite, but the case isn't closed. There's strong evidence suggesting Vincent had nothing to do with his cousin's death. I really can't say more, other than to tell you there are a few matters I'm not at liberty to talk about. We do have pretty conclusive evidence he was responsible for the damage to Miss Paxton's home and property, however."

"But why? That's what I want to know. I can understand his grief over losing someone he cared about, but why punish me? I only found the body. And what about poor Mr. Andrews? He certainly didn't deserve to be beaten." Kira leaned heavily on Ford. She was relieved the worry and fear she'd lived with so long was at an end, but she'd like to know what had prompted Luis to target her.

The detective looked uncomfortable. "I've been thinking about something. I spoke with some of Marla's neighbors a few weeks after her body was found. Several of them told me there was a story going around that you and Mr. Andrews were overheard talking about her. They said you called her a tramp and a dog that needed to be stopped. Her mother said you deserved everything that happened to you because of the cruel things you said about her daughter. We suspect she embellished the story and passed it on to her nephew."

"What?" She would have fallen if Ford hadn't kept a firm hold on her. "I didn't even know her. Mr. Andrews told me about some of the earlier trouble she was involved in, but neither he nor I called her names." Suddenly it clicked. "We talked about my brother's dog, who trampled the flowers I set out last year because I was buying big pots to put my flowers in to keep them safe—the pots that were smashed by Luis and his friends."

"I'm just guessing, mind you, but it's possible Luis believed that story and was upset you were saying bad things about someone he was close to."

"You think he shot at me, made threatening calls, and did hundreds of dollars worth of damage to my home because of gossip? Someone took a few words out of context and made up stories—lies—and that's the reason I've been stalked and threatened all summer?" Kira had never been so angry before in her life.

"We can't be sure," Daley attempted to soothe her. "We'll do a ballistics test to see if the gun found on him—or any of the others that were confiscated tonight—could have fired the shot at the mall."

"My investigation uncovered much the same information." Stan looked thoughtful. "I kept looking for something more because many of the people I talked to said they had doubts about the story. They claimed both Marla and her mother had reputations for making up stories and causing trouble."

Sensing how shaky she felt, Ford helped Kira to the love seat and sat beside her. He put an arm around her shoulders. "That's pretty much what that injured veteran told us," he reminded her. "He said Marla and her mother were both liars. When we talked to her closest friends, they accused her of blackmailing them into backing up her lies. I know personally that she had no regard for honesty."

Exhaustion settled in waves over her, and she couldn't explain why tears were running down her cheeks. Could lies and gossip really cause so much trouble?

"I need to be on my way." Detective Daley edged toward the door as they all said good-bye.

After the door closed behind the detective, Stan sat down across from Kira. He reached out to touch her hand. "The police may consider the case closed, but I'll continue to investigate."

"I'm so tired, and I need space to think." Kira leaned her head against Ford's chest. "Do you think anyone will mind if I don't go back outside?"

He kissed her forehead. "Go ahead; crawl in bed and get some rest. I'll corral Tracy and Kaitlin into helping me clean up."

"I'll keep someone watching your house for a few days, but I suspect you'll soon have us out of your hair." Stan stood and moved toward the door. "Or maybe not. Your dad will be back tomorrow."

* * *

Resuming her usual activities proved more difficult than she'd expected. She missed Kaitlin, yet it felt good to regain a measure of independence. With her right leg in a cast, Kira hadn't been sure how she would get to and from work until Trevor and Tyrone volunteered to drive her to work each morning since they didn't have any early classes. Ford said he would be there to take her home when the credit union closed at five. With her transportation problems resolved, Monday morning found her at her desk at the credit union.

Everyone at work showed consideration for her limitations, but by the end of the week, she was exhausted and her head ached. She suspected her fatigue was as much emotional as physical. The past few months had been difficult, and dragging even a lightweight cast around sapped her energy. Concentrating on the client speaking to her on the phone only seemed to make her head throb harder. Reaching into her desk drawer, she located her purse and fished out a bottle. She shook two ibuprofen tablets into her hand and swallowed them with a sip of water from the bottle she kept on her desk.

By the time Ford arrived to take her home, she was happy to let him pick her up and place her in the passenger seat of his truck before going around to the driver's side.

"I think you better drop me off and let me sleep for a couple of hours," she told him when he suggested going out for dinner.

"Are you sure? We could go somewhere quiet and be back to your place early." He sounded disappointed.

"I'm sure." She didn't want to forego an evening with Ford, but she didn't want to fall asleep with her face in her plate either.

"Okay. Get comfortable, and I'll be back in half an hour with something to eat. If you're going to sleep through the night, you'd better do it on a full stomach." He pulled into her driveway and walked her to her door, making certain she was inside and the door locked before returning to his truck.

Grateful Ford was being so understanding, she changed into a comfortable sweat suit that Kaitlin had altered to accommodate the cast. Kira made her way from her bedroom back to her living room, where she noticed a faint thumping noise coming from the backyard. She froze then chided herself for still being jumpy. The threat was over. Detective Daley had assured her several of Luis's gang members had admitted to the harassment she'd faced all summer. A ballistics test proved his gun had fired the shot at the mall but not the one that killed his cousin. With his death there was little likelihood his gang would bother her again.

Making her way to the window, she peeked through the blinds and smiled. Trevor and Tyrone were tossing a football back and forth. Mrs. Gleason sat on her back patio with the rescued kitten in her lap. She knew Mrs. Gleason had been frightened by the gang's activities, especially after her cat was killed. But after adopting the kitten, the older woman appeared more relaxed, and Kira was thankful for that.

The doorbell sounded. Even though she was expecting Ford she jumped, almost losing her balance. How long would it take before she stopped expecting the worst? Each swing of her crutches as she made her way to the door seemed to remind her a murderer was still out there somewhere. Luis's friends readily admitted to the graffiti and harassment, but no one had claimed responsibility for the murder of Marla Hayden.

CHAPTER TWENTY-NINE

KIRA WAS SURPRISED TO SEE her father instead of Ford on her doorstep. He gave her a careful hug. "Are you all right?" he questioned as she led the way to the sofa and gingerly seated herself.

"I'm fine," she attempted to assure him. "I'm tired and glad it's Friday." She smiled in an attempt to prove he had nothing to worry about. She gestured toward the love seat, indicating he should sit.

"You're sure you didn't return to work too soon?"

"Daddy, I'm fine. I won't pretend the things that happened were no big deal, but I really am okay and getting stronger. I appreciate all you've done to ensure my safety. I love you, and it's good to know you've got my back when times are tough."

Garrett sank down across from her, leaning forward with his hands clasped between his knees. It was one of the few times she'd seen her father appear unsure of himself. "You might as well know I've been worried about you, but I've been trying not to annoy you by breathing down your neck. I did check with Tracy and sometimes Stan every day I was away. Stan warned me I stood a good chance of losing you if I didn't back off and give you room to breathe."

"Dad—"

"No, let me finish. I was angry at first, but while I was in New York, I did a lot of thinking about what he said. I never meant to make you uncomfortable or lead you to think I didn't believe in you. I came so close to losing you so many times when you were little, I guess I never got over feeling protective. Then I lost your mother. I always blamed myself because I didn't notice she wasn't well and insist she see a doctor sooner. Somehow that all translated into trying to wrap you in cotton. I'm sorry, and you have my word I'll try to do better, but I hope you'll understand old habits are hard to break."

"Daddy, I've been so afraid of missing out on the real world, I've behaved childishly at times." She reached across the narrow space between them to rest her hands on his. "I know you love me, and I love you. I've learned being protected isn't a bad thing. I've also learned I'm stronger than I thought, and I no longer have to prove myself to anyone but me." Her voice grew husky, and she searched in her pocket for a tissue.

The rattle of a key in the lock sounded, and Ford walked in, bringing with him the aroma of burgers and fries. "Hello, Mr. Paxton." He set everything on the coffee table and extended his hand. Garrett took it but didn't look happy. "Would you care to eat with us? I brought plenty of food."

Kira noticed the scowl on her father's face directed at the key that now sat beside the fast food bags. It was clear he didn't approve of Ford having a key to her home. She'd given the key to Ford when they'd switched apartments. He'd offered the key back when she returned to her own apartment, but she'd told him to keep it until it was less difficult for her to answer the door.

"No, thanks," Garrett declined the invitation. "I just got back in town and only came out here to assure myself that my daughter is doing well. I'll be on my way now." He got as far as the door before pausing to turn back. "I saw that detective when I stopped at my office. He was there to tie up a few loose ends concerning Ed. He said he thought you'd be interested to know the young man who shot Luis Vincent admitted to killing a cat he thought belonged to you. From what the shooter said, it appears his gang didn't start watching your condo until after you returned from staying with your father. They weren't aware of the damage to your home and got involved in harassing you because they had someone follow Vincent and the only reasons they could see for him spending so much time around you was either you were his girlfriend or you were dealing his gang guns or drugs. He threatened you to discourage you and your friends from supplying Vincent's gang."

Once her dad was gone, Ford handed Kira a hamburger and set a carton of fries in front of her. "Either that doesn't make sense or proves a little misinformation goes a long way."

"Nothing has made a lot of sense to me since Jasper and I went running that morning last April." She shoved a straw into the chocolate shake Ford had set in front of her and swallowed two more ibuprofen.

Eating seemed to take more strength than she could muster. Dutifully she took a bite of her hamburger and swizzled a couple of french fries in dip before nibbling on them. Her eyes kept closing in spite of her efforts to stay awake.

"Either I'm boring you or you really are too tired to eat," she heard Ford chuckle as if from a great distance away. Her head throbbed from the effort to stay awake, and after a long day, her injured leg ached as well. She just wanted to put her head down and close her eyes. His arm came around her. "Okay, off to bed with you. I'll put your dinner in the fridge and lock up." He handed her crutches to her and kissed her good night. "I'll see you tomorrow," he whispered.

Slowly she made her way down the hall, pausing in the bathroom to swallow a couple more ibuprofen tablets. Placing her crutches beside the bed, she used both hands to lift her cast onto the bed then slid between the sheets. She only had time to register the soft pillow beneath her head before sleep claimed her.

* * *

Pesky fly! Kira brushed at her face, but the irritating buzzing continued. Her hand flailed uselessly, searching for her bedside clock. *It can't be morning already.* She tried to sit up but collapsed back against her pillow. The sound continued. At last her foggy brain connected the buzzing with her doorbell. "It can't be morning already." Surely she'd only been asleep a few minutes.

"Ford must have forgotten his key," she mumbled aloud.

Light poured through her window, causing more confusion until she recognized it wasn't sunlight. Her patio light shone through the window where she hadn't pulled the blinds before collapsing on her bed. It took several minutes of groping before her hand connected with her crutches and she managed to pull herself out of bed. Balancing herself was more difficult than usual and the hall seemed extra long. She shook her head in a vain attempt to clear her muddled thinking as she made her slow way toward her living room. From habit her hand slid along the living room wall searching for the light switch. At the flip of the switch, a knocking sound was added to the buzz of the doorbell. It was probably only seconds, but it seemed to take ages to make her way to the door, where she fumbled with the dead bolt.

Pulling the door open, she stared in confusion. She'd expected to see Ford. Instead an attractive, neatly dressed teenager stood on her front step. She felt certain she'd never seen him before, and she had no idea who he might be. A swirl of thoughts ran through her head, adding to the dizziness and confusion that had plagued her since awakening. *Who is he? Why did he ring my doorbell in the middle of the night? Is it the middle of the night? Why didn't I check who was ringing the doorbell before opening the door?*

Unable to speak coherently, she stood in front of the open door saying nothing. The boy stood still, watching her intently. He didn't speak either. Frustrated by her inability to think clearly and the sensation that her good leg had turned to rubber, Kira swayed against the door. The boy put out his hand as though to prevent her from falling.

She shook her head, wishing to convey the message she was all right.

"Miss Paxton? Kira Paxton?" the boy spoke in a soft voice.

She stared in dismay at tears running down his face. "Are you okay?" she managed to choke out.

He nodded his head, took a deep breath, then whispered, "I'm sorry. All those awful things were my fault."

Why was he apologizing? "I don't understand."

"I did it. I shot Marla."

She stared at him blankly. He couldn't mean what she thought she heard him say.

His shoulders shook, and he wiped at the tears streaking down his face with the back of his sleeve. "I loved her. I did everything she wanted me to do. She said she'd never marry me because I was too weak to get a gun. I took my uncle's gun, but she laughed at me. She said I'd never be man enough to use it. Then she slapped me and said I didn't have the guts to pull the trigger. I didn't mean to hurt anyone."

She felt an irrational urge to comfort him. At the same time, sickness roiled in her stomach, and she felt herself sway.

"I should have shot Luis, not Marla." There was a touch of bitterness or perhaps sorrow behind his words.

Waves of blackness pulsed around her. She was losing her mind. She couldn't be standing in her doorway carrying on a conversation with the person who murdered . . . She felt herself sliding toward the floor. A flicker of awareness warned that falling on an already broken femur could result in serious injury, but then the blackness became complete.

* * *

She awoke to familiar surroundings but with no idea how she'd gotten there. She was back in the hospital. Looking around, she caught sight of Ford and her father, both asleep in chairs positioned near her bed. She watched them for several minutes with an odd sense of déjà vu. Deciding not to wake them, she let her mind dwell on the strange dream she'd had. Or was it a dream?

"Ahh, you're awake." Ford had awakened and was watching her.

"You're the one who was sleeping," she teased, happy to see him.

"You were asleep or unconscious when the Gleason twins found you."

"Found me? Was I lost?" She wrinkled her nose and looked askance at Ford. He didn't seem to be making sense, but being back in the hospital didn't make sense either.

Seeing her confusion, he explained, "They'd been out and were coming home close to midnight. Your front door was standing open. After all that's happened, they decided to check on you. You were lying on the floor just inside the door. When they couldn't wake you up, they called for an ambulance and notified Stan."

"I don't understand. What happened? Why was I on the floor?" Pieces of the frightening dream flashed through her mind.

"We don't know for sure." Garrett was awake now too and joined the conversation. "The doctor said tests indicated a larger than normal amount of painkillers in your system. It appeared the pills were taken on an empty stomach, making your reaction worse than it might have otherwise been."

"You were exhausted when I took you home last night," Ford added. "You were too tired to eat. Instead you went to bed while I cleaned up and let myself out."

"I remember that. I had a headache, so I took two ibuprofen before going to bed."

"Are you sure the pills you swallowed were ibuprofen?" Garrett reached for her hand. Ford already held the other one.

She looked from one concerned face to the other, wondering what they were accusing her of.

"Honey," Ford said in a soft voice, "Stan found your purse in your bedroom. In it, he found the pain prescription I picked up for you when you were released from the hospital. Only six pills were missing. He also said there was an almost empty ibuprofen bottle. He said the bottles are similar."

Kira stared at him in horror. She'd forgotten about the prescription and had never even opened the bottle. Instead she'd taken ibuprofen or Tylenol for pain. "I took two ibuprofen an hour before I left work, then two more . . ." She remembered reaching into the drawer where she kept her purse at work, finding the bottle, and removing the pills while talking to a client on the phone. As soon as she ended the call, she'd popped the pills into her mouth and swallowed them with a gulp of water. "Perhaps that explains the weird dream I had." She recounted the fragmented bits she could recall of the previous night.

"Are you sure it was a dream?" Ford asked when she finished. "Mrs. Gleason told the twins she heard your doorbell ringing repeatedly around eleven."

She hadn't mentioned the persistent ringing of her doorbell. An uneasy feeling crept over her. "It seemed real, but I don't recall ever seeing the boy before. If it was real, why did he come to me to apologize?"

"What did he look like?" There was more than curiosity behind Ford's question. She tried to recall his features. He'd been polite, almost shy, and there had been something childlike in his deeply fringed dark eyes. As she spoke, Ford's mouth drew into a tight line.

"I don't know, but I think we should play it safe by calling Detective Daley. Stan notified him when you were brought in, but this may be more serious than an accidental overdose." He was already punching numbers into his phone.

Both Ford and her father were sporting morning stubble and looked like they'd dressed hastily then slept in their clothes. Neither showed any inclination to leave to shave and shower. A nurse took pity on them, bringing them cartons of orange juice and packages of graham crackers when her breakfast tray was delivered. They refused to consider checking her out of the hospital until she talked to the detective.

"Really, I'm fine," she attempted to reassure them.

"After the detective comes." Garrett was adamant.

"At least go to the cafeteria and get a real breakfast." Neither man bothered to answer.

A second tray, lunch this time, was brought to her room, and she was wondering if she could convince either of her persistent visitors to visit the gift shop to get her a book when the detective finally arrived. She noticed his shoes were splotched with mud, and he looked as though he carried the weight of the world on his back. Ford stood, and Daley settled into the chair he'd vacated.

Skipping polite chat, Daley greeted her with what sounded much like his interrogation into her discovery of Marla's body. "Tell me about your late-night caller."

"I'm not sure if what I remember was real or a dream." Nervously she plucked at the sheet that covered the lower half of her body.

"Just tell me what you think happened."

"I was awakened by the constant ringing of the doorbell. I was groggy and disoriented. It seems I took too many pain pills I mistakenly thought were ibuprofen. When I got to the door, a teenager a little younger than Mrs. Gleason's grandsons was standing there. He said 'I'm sorry,' then he said he killed Marla Hayden. I must have fainted because I don't remember anything after that."

The detective asked several other questions, and Kira found herself remembering more details. The more questions she answered, the more certain she became that the event had been real.

"Did he hurt you? Or threaten you in any way?"

"No." She paused, realizing she'd stood face to face with a murderer and hadn't been frightened. "I think I fainted from shock, not fear."

"I don't think he meant to hurt you. Most people considered him a good kid." The detective stood, making it clear the interview was over and he was ready to leave.

Her eyes sought Ford. He looked sad or disappointed.

"Who . . . ?" Perhaps she shouldn't ask. She suspected he was one of Ford's students—one he knew and liked, one she'd heard a great deal about but never met. A sick feeling began to grow in her stomach.

"We're pretty certain he was Aaron Maughan."

The boy's words made sense now.

"We may never know for sure," the detective went on. "Aaron's body was recovered from the Jordan River around ten this morning with a .45 caliber bullet hole in his temple, not far from where we think Marla was shot and dumped in the river."

CHAPTER THIRTY

A CHILL WIND SWEPT THROUGH the park, signaling winter wasn't far away. Kira turned up the collar on her jacket and smiled up at Ford. He drew her closer, partially sheltering her from the wind. At least her hand felt warm, clasped in his. They moved slowly, enjoying their first walk since the removal of the walking cast from her leg. She wasn't ready to run yet, but she had every intention of working her way back up to a daily 5K. They'd decided on the smoother trail at the park rather than the Parkway trail for her first outing. Emotionally she wasn't sure she was ready to handle the Parkway trail yet anyway. It was difficult to disassociate one of her favorite places to run with the tragic loss of two young people and the nightmare that accompanied their deaths.

Jasper tugged at his leash, wanting to go faster. "Whoa, Jasper. No running today." Ford gripped one end of the leash and grinned at Kira. "Why is it that on the first day you're able to take a stroll, you invited Jasper along?"

Kira laughed. "Tracy called me this morning from the hotel where he and Kaitlin spent their wedding night to tell me Dad was called out of town and that if I didn't take Jasper, he'd have to take Jasper with them on their honeymoon. What could I say? Dad brought him over on his way to catch his flight."

"Let's stop and rest a few minutes. I don't want you to tire yourself." He wrapped an arm around her shoulders, leading her off the path into a sheltered alcove beside the small stream. Only a thin trickle of water wound its way between the rocks of the creek bed. He gestured for her to sit on a large boulder; then he sat beside her.

"We'll rest a few minutes then start back. I wouldn't have suggested walking this morning if I'd listened to the weather report and known the temperature was dropping."

"I'm fine. Please don't turn into a worrier like my dad. Anyway, I'm glad the weather waited to change until after Tracy and Kaitlin's wedding. It was all so beautiful. Everything from the temple ceremony to the reception in the capitol rotunda was like a fairy tale come true." She was glad her doctor had released her from her walking boot in time for her to be one of Kaitlin's bridesmaids.

"You have no idea how many pictures I managed to sneak of you dressed like a Southern belle in all those flounces and ruffles." He leaned close, dropping his voice to a whisper as if telling her a great secret.

Flinging the back of one hand to her forehead, she drawled, "Mercy, kind sir, ah do hope none of those pictures reveal ah was the only bridesmaid wearing flat shoes instead of those dahling platforms the other bridesmaids staggered around on. It was truly a disappointment to miss my chance to be tall." They laughed together, then Ford turned serious.

"I'm glad you enjoyed your brother's wedding. You've faced a lot of challenges in the past few months. It was good, too, for you to be part of a truly beautiful event after so much ugliness."

"You've had plenty to deal with too," she reminded him. "I know how much you care about your students, and losing two troubled teens hasn't been easy for you."

"I thought I was handling Marla's death pretty well. At the time she was found I was angry over her lies and obnoxious behavior and didn't really mourn her, but after Aaron's suicide, I realized Marla was as troubled as he. Perhaps that's what drew them to each other, a recognition of how messed up both their lives and values were."

Kira stared at the water, lost in thought, as she tried to put her feelings into words. "For a long time, I resented my dad's fussing over me and his insistence on determining what I could or couldn't do. After seeing the unhappiness related to no rules and a lack of discipline, along with an attitude that lying to cover up for bad behavior is acceptable, I'm willing to cut my dad some slack. Parents need to set rules and be involved until their children are ready to make mature decisions. I've always felt handicapped because of my father's reluctance to let me grow up, and though my rebellion has taken a milder form than what those two kids chose, I see now that I took risks which could have been as serious as theirs." She shivered in the cold air.

Ford was silent for several minutes before pulling his arm out of one side of his fleece jacket and extending the jacket around Kira, pulling her closer to him. She snuggled against his side, enjoying the shared warmth as he talked.

"Since Aaron's death I've thought a lot about how his upbringing differed from mine," Ford spoke at last. "As a child I was taught that each person has a right to grow and determine the course to take in this life. We hear a lot about agency at church, and I think most people think it makes sense—until someone we love makes a choice we don't agree with or is just plain dangerous. That's when our belief is challenged. I've watched you struggle against a too-controlling parent and compared your experience to that of Luis and Marla, who had *no* parental controls. I hope that when my turn comes to be a father I'll know where to draw the line between too much and too little control over my family." He paused. "Maybe *control* is the wrong word. I suspect raising children involves more love, prayer, and patience than control."

"I think you're right. I know single parenting is hard, but it can be done, and Dad certainly tried. I'll probably never convince him completely that I'm ready to take charge of my own life, but at least I know he loves me."

"Love matters most, but he isn't the only one who loves you. I do too." He took both of her hands in his. "This isn't the romantic setting I planned, but it feels right. I want you and me to be partners who discuss and share our lives, make decisions together, and respect each other's individuality through all eternity. I want us to always be there for each other. Will you marry me? Will you be my forever bride?"

"Yes! I want that more than anything." She turned more fully against him. His hands cupped her face as he lowered his head and his lips met hers. The sharp breeze was forgotten, replaced by a soaring heat that spread peace and joy throughout her body. His hands slid from her face to her shoulders, then to her waist.

"M-mm." He lifted his head to look into her eyes. "I could definitely get used to this."

Feelings between a desire to shout her happiness as loud as she could and a curious longing to hold the moment sacred deep within her heart overcame her, bringing a hint of moisture to her eyes. It was a strange experience to feel light and free and at the same time pampered and cared for.

"Jasper!" Suddenly she remembered the black lab. "Where's Jasper?"

Ford looked startled then looked around in confusion as if expecting the leash to still be in his hand. Their absorption with each other had caused him to forget the dog. "I'll find him," he promised. He scrambled up the small incline from the creek. She followed.

"Jasper!"

"Jasper!" They took turns calling the dog's name.

"I think I see him." Ford pointed to a black speck rushing across the dry grass. After a shortcut through a grove of bare trees, it became clear Jasper was running all out toward them. He ran as though on a desperate mission. Kira hoped he hadn't gotten into some kind of mischief.

As the dog raced closer, Kira's heart began to beat faster. Something bulged from his mouth. Jasper skidded to a stop in front of her, where he dropped an almost-new but soggy tennis shoe at her feet.

At least it wasn't another kitten! She didn't want to think about the previous spring when Jasper had found a different wet shoe. She lifted her eyes to Ford's. He silently pointed up the hill where a line of little boys raced toward them. As the boys drew closer, she could see their shorts and shoes were wet from playing in the creek—all except one. He seemed to be missing a shoe.

"Give it back!" Ford commanded the dog.

Looking dejected, Jasper picked up the shoe and dropped it beside its mate. The boy giggled as he snatched it up and jammed it on his foot.

"Good dog!" He gave Jasper a hug. Soon all of the boys were romping and playing with the big black lab. Laughter and happy barking filled the air.

Ford's arm circled Kira's waist, and she leaned against him as they watched the dog play with the children. She couldn't help smiling. With Ford around to help keep them in line, she hoped her future held a lot of children's laughter and playful dogs.

ABOUT THE AUTHOR

 JENNIE HANSEN MOVED A GREAT deal while growing up. She remembers living in twenty-two different houses and attending eight schools. The two colleges where she earned degrees, Ricks and Westminster, make ten. She worked as a model, secretary, newspaper reporter and editor, legislative page, teacher, and librarian. She was first published at the tender age of seven and has since published twenty-five novels, numerous short stories, and many magazine and newspaper articles. For the past fourteen years, she has written reviews of LDS fiction for *Meridian Magazine*.

She and her husband have five great children, four wonderful sons-in-law, a fantastic daughter-in-law, and thirteen grandchildren. After serving in numerous ward and stake callings, she now teaches Relief Society and serves at the Oquirrh Mountain Temple.

You can learn more about Jennie Hansen by visiting her blog at http://notesfromjenniesdesk.blogspot.com or by contacting her publisher at Covenant Communications, PO Box 416, American Fork, Utah 84003-0416.